"Chiavaroli delights with this homage to Louisa May Alcott's *Little Women*, featuring a time-slip narrative of two women connected across centuries."

PUBLISHERS WEEKLY on *The Orchard House*

"Beautifully written, this God honoring and compelling story is Heidi Chiavaroli's best yet."

CATHY GOHLKE, Bestselling, Christy Hall of Fame and Carol Award-winning author on *Hope Beyond the Waves*

"*Hope Beyond the Waves* tugged at my heart from page one, and I was totally immersed in the seemingly insurmountable challenges of both the past and present day characters. Kudos to Heidi Chiavaroli for pouring out this beautifully raw and moving story about finding love and hope in the most unexpected of places."

MELANIE DOBSON, Carol Award-winning author of *Catching the Wind*

"*The Hidden Side* is a beautiful tale that captures the timeless struggles of the human heart."

JULIE CANTRELL, *New York Times* Bestselling author of *Perennials*

"First novelist Chiavaroli's historical tapestry will provide a satisfying summer read for fans of Kristy Cambron and Lisa Wingate."

LIBRARY JOURNAL on *Freedom's Ring*

"*The Edge of Mercy* is most definitely one for the keeper shelf. "

LINDSAY HARREL, author of *The Secrets of Paper and Ink*

WHERE PROMISES REMAIN

HEIDI CHIAVAROLI

Visit Heidi Chiavaroli at heidichiavaroli.com

Hope Creek Publishers LLC

Cover Design by Evelyne Labelle at Carpe Librum Book Design

Edited by Melissa Jagears

Scripture quotations are taken from the New International Version.

Where Promises Remain is a work of fiction. Where real people, events, establishments, organizations, or locales appear, they are used fictitiously. All other elements of the novel are drawn from the author's imagination.

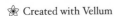 Created with Vellum

ALSO BY HEIDI CHIAVAROLI

The Orchard House

The Tea Chest

The Hidden Side

Freedom's Ring

The Edge of Mercy

Hope Beyond the Waves

The Orchard House Bed and Breakfast Series

Where Grace Appears

Where Hope Begins

Where Love Grows

Where Memories Await

Where Dreams Reside

Where Faith Belongs

Where Promises Remain

To Aunt Jodi,
Thank you for your loving support and excitement for each of my books.
(And for loving Hope Beyond the Waves as much as I do!)

There was nothing like a new project to distract from self-pitying thoughts, and the email I received this morning might be just the ticket to accomplish the task.

I got up from my seat at the kitchen bar and walked with hurried steps through the butler's pantry into the guest living quarters where my oldest daughter Maggie worked at the bed and breakfast's front desk. What would she think of the email?

"Maggie, did you see—" I stopped short. A burly man with a close-cropped beard and hair graying at the temples stood with his finger hovering over the bell on the desk. He wore a button-down flannel shirt with the sleeves rolled up, revealing forearms covered in tattoos. I glimpsed the intricate ink of a compass and a rope.

I tore my gaze off him to scan the room but my daughter wasn't behind the desk, or anywhere in sight, for that matter. "I'm sorry. I thought my daughter was here. Welcome to Orchard House. Can I help you?"

He smiled, and it was a nice smile. A little worn and rugged around the edges, but warm and genuine, spreading all the way up to his eyes which crinkled at the corners. He held his hand out to me. "Hello. My name's Kevin. Kevin Williams. I just moved in next door."

"Oh!" I placed my hand in his, the large warm fingers enveloping mine. "I'm Hannah. It's nice to meet you." The Perry home had sold only a few weeks ago. If I'd known our new neighbors were moving in so quickly, I would have planned to reach out —at least bring over a coffee cake. Then again, with Amie and August's wedding fast approaching and my increase in volunteer hours at Amos's mission, I'd been a bit out of sorts. Not at the top of my planning game.

He squeezed my hand and a flush worked over my body. Huh. Now *that* was new. Unless it was simply a hot flash. Those certainly were becoming more and more commonplace.

I released his hand. "How are you enjoying Camden?"

"Great town. I'm looking forward to the fishing."

"Be sure to try Penobscot River. It's famous for its landlocked salmon. The best I've ever had."

His eyebrows raised. "You a fisherwoman?"

I laughed. "Good grief, no. But I try to know a little bit about everything to help our guests find their adventures."

He nodded, stroking his beard thoughtfully. "A woman who knows a little bit about everything. I'll keep that in mind."

His gaze didn't leave me, and although I'd received my fair share of admiring glances from the opposite sex in my fifty-two years, this one served to rattle me in an altogether different way. Not an entirely unpleasant way.

I blinked, breaking the connection, and walked behind the desk. I shuffled papers in an attempt to hide my blush—ahem, hot flash. I glanced at his left hand. No ring. What was I doing? Why did it matter if he was married or not?

Must be my hormones or the fact that the last of my children was about to fly the nest.

I'd never been alone—not in my entire life. For goodness

sakes, even Aunt Pris had up and left Orchard House—the only home she'd ever known—last year when she'd married her long-time love, Ed Colton.

And I was happy. Happy for Aunt Pris and for Amie. Happy that Maggie and Josie had built families with the men they loved. Happy Lizzie had found Asher and was trying to have a baby. Happy that my only son, Bronson, had also married the love of his life this past New Year's Eve.

Yes, my children were all finding their way. In love, in their careers, and in faith. Nothing could bring me more joy. Why then, did this impending dread fill me when I woke each morning at the thought of being on my own?

I cleared my throat. "It's wonderful to meet you, Kevin. If you ever need anything—a cup of sugar, restaurant recommendations, a book to borrow, please don't hesitate to call on us."

There. I was being neighborly, but I was also signaling the end to any possible flirtation—because I didn't need more crazy emotions stirring up the hormones I was already battling.

"Actually, I was hoping to talk to you about a shed I'm building."

"Okay . . ."

"I'm considering cutting down a tree to make room for it. An old elm. It shows signs of rot, but still has plenty of foliage. I wanted to ask your thoughts on it."

"My thoughts?" Was he concerned I'd think the shed ugly? A distasteful addition to the neighborhood?

"Well, I'm a tree-guy myself. Can't live without my trees. I tend to get attached to them, particularly if they've been around for a while. I didn't want to cut it down without your approval."

I squinted at him. "Is the tree on my property?" If so, why were we even having this conversation—the tree was not his to cut down. Then again, why would he plan to build a shed on our property?

"No, ma'am."

I shook my head, bristling at the "ma'am." "Hannah."

He nodded, smiled. His eyes were the color of pine trees in midwinter. "Hannah."

"I'm sorry, Kevin, but if the tree is on your property, I don't see as to how I have a say in the matter."

"Well, like I said, trees are a big deal in my estimation, and you can see this tree from your back patio, maybe even get a little shade from it in late summer. If you're attached to it . . ."

Oh. Well, that was considerate. I moved to place my hand on his arm, but stopped myself. "That is extremely thoughtful, but it's your tree. If you want to cut it down, you should. I promise not to take any offense whatsoever."

He shifted from one foot to the other. "I might sleep better tonight knowing you took a look at it with me."

This burly, tattoo-covered man would lose sleep over what a near stranger thought about him cutting down a tree on his own property? If I let him know I was more concerned about the aesthetics of his shed ruining my backyard view—he might never slumber again.

I smiled and started toward the door. "Far be it from me to mess with a good night's sleep."

He chuckled, scooting ahead to hold the door open for me. Side-by-side, we walked around the back of the Victorian toward the bookshop and the back patio. Kevin gestured to the orchards. "Beautiful property."

"I never get sick of it. It was my late husband's great-aunt's. We renovated the home and moved in four years ago." Aunt Pris had gifted the home and property to me for Christmas last year. I still found myself choking up at the gesture. Yes, I knew she intended to hand it over to me in her will, but the fact she would do so while she was still alive meant even more to me.

"Ed's home is my home now," Aunt Pris had told me. "The Orchard House is thriving under your touch, Hannah. I want you to have it in every sense of the word."

Kevin's voice broke into my remembrances. "And you run the orchard and the bed and breakfast?"

"My son, Bronson, is in charge of the orchards. He and his wife run a summer camp here. They've done a wonderful job."

"Busy place, then."

"It is, but we try not to bother the neighbors." I gave him a sidelong glance.

"No bother on my end. I love kids."

We strode past my herb gardens, the faint scent of basil reaching my nostrils. That reminded me, I needed to make pesto for the pasta tonight. Bronson wouldn't eat pasta without . . .

I sucked in a small, short breath. Bronson wouldn't be coming to dinner. Neither would any of my other children. Even Amie, who still lived at Orchard House, would likely be off with August planning last-minute wedding details.

It was fine, of course. More than fine. The entire crew came over every Saturday night for dinner, and I was grateful for that blessing.

I shook my head, focusing on the man beside me. "Do you have any? Kids?"

He raked a hand through his hair. "No children, unfortunately. My wife had some medical issues in her teens that prevented her from having children. It was the one thing she regretted not being able to give me, but if I could do everything all over again, I wouldn't change a thing."

We stopped in front of the ancient stone wall that divided our property. I mulled over Kevin's comment. *I wouldn't change a thing.* "You lost your wife?"

He nodded. "Six years back, to cancer."

I couldn't deny the sudden kinship I felt to this near stranger. I'd never gone to a grief support group, but perhaps I could have benefited from one. "I'm sorry."

"I'm sorry about your husband."

"Thank you." I still missed Amos, the way his passion for life kept him immersed in new projects, the way he would come out of his study with an open book to discuss a new theory or thought, the tender way he treated each of our children on those rare occasions when he was fully present—teaching them to love deeply, to think wisely, to be curious about everything under the sun.

Strange how five years had, in some ways, flown by without him. Though I'd give anything for one more day with my husband, time had eased the sting of his absence. And while I still sometimes shed tears at night when I found the other side of the bed cold and empty, I also could honestly say Amos would be pleased with how I'd led our family these last five years.

Kevin pointed to the tree growing up from his side of the property about three feet from the stone wall. Tall and stately, it reached long arms over the wall and into Orchard House property, sending shade into a generous portion of our yard.

"It is beautiful," I said. "But Bronson complains every autumn about the leaves he has to rake up. You said there's signs of rot?"

He pointed to a hanging branch about halfway up. "Lots of missing leaves. Also, the bark is gray in spots instead of brown and it's splitting from the main part of the tree." He pointed again. "See there?"

I nodded. "If it falls, it could do some damage."

"Normally, I'm not one for cutting down trees at the first sign of a little rot, but you're right—it could hit your patio and your house the way it's leaning. Not to mention, this seems to be the best place for my woodshed."

I turned to him. "I heartily agree. I hope you can sleep better knowing we've discussed this."

He grinned, his green eyes sparkling. "Thanks, Hannah. It was nice to meet you."

"You too. And if you need a tree guy, I can ask my son-in-law for a recommendation. He's in the construction business and knows some good people."

"That's mighty thoughtful, but there's no need. I'm the tree guy."

"Oh. Well then, be careful." I shook my head. "Sorry, mother of five speaking—it's a reflex. I'm sure you're always careful."

"I am."

I smiled. "See you around, then."

"I might be low on sugar soon. Could come knocking."

I waved and turned before another hot flash could be seen on my face. It had been a while, but was he *flirting*? More so, how did I feel about that? While I'd grown used to rebuffing the advances of Stuart Stanley, the unsavory owner of Stanley Construction who made a habit to race up to me when I passed his home on my walks, I wasn't used to welcoming a flirtation.

If that's what this even was. Had Amos and I ever flirted? He'd been so sincere and direct with his affection that I couldn't remember if we ever had. Huh. Too bad. Maybe we'd missed out.

As I ducked back into the Orchard House, this time through our rear living quarters, I decided a call to my best friend Charlotte was in order. She'd likely be cleaning guest rooms in her own inn at this time, so I'd wait until later this evening. Now, I returned to the email I'd received.

An email that had the potential to bring new life—and profits —to The Orchard House Bed and Breakfast. The attempt would at least keep me busy—so busy I wouldn't have time to dwell on the fact that very soon, I would be completely and utterly on my own.

❦ 2 ❦

K evin watched his new neighbor walk toward the big Victorian home, half kicking himself for flirting so easily with her. He didn't want her to think less of him. Truth be told, he didn't make a habit of flirting with women, or even dating, since his Katherine died.

He sighed, looking down the hill through a small grove of pines and maples toward Camden Harbor. His wife would have loved this place. They'd talked about retiring here one day. After he'd sold the logging business, after she'd retired from teaching.

But God's plans had been different. Plans Kevin couldn't quite get on board with, even after six long years.

He peered up at the elm, looking forward to getting back in a tree. It'd been too long. But now was the time to do things again. Climb all the trees he wanted, take some hikes, fish, check out that little church down the hill, maybe do some camping . . . who knows, maybe he *would* end up borrowing some sugar from his pretty new neighbor.

His phone rang and he dug it out of his pocket, his heart speeding up at the sight of the Portland number. "Hello?"

"Mr. Williams? This is Rita Bridges."

8

He swallowed around the grapevine-sized knot in his throat. The social worker had only conducted the home inspection yesterday.

"Ms. Bridges. I didn't expect to hear from you so soon."

She cleared her throat and he imagined the stout middle-aged woman adjusting her thick glasses with the gesture. "We've already conducted the home study and the background check. We only needed the inspection to complete your application."

One of the reasons he'd made a quick job of unpacking. He'd tidied the dickens out of his new home—a simple cape. He'd made up the guest bedroom to be as welcoming as possible. Considering he never had any kids, much less a teenager, he wasn't sure he had passed the social worker's sharp eye.

"I've just signed off on the last of the paperwork, Mr. Williams. I'd love to bring Owen by this afternoon if that works for you."

His chest felt like it had been struck by the force of a falling oak. "This afternoon?"

Ms. Bridges tone softened. "Owen's been here in our office. There's nowhere for him to go, as is often the case with teenagers. We've rushed your application, Mr. Williams. As I stated before, our hope is to reunite Owen with your sister. This is a temporary placement."

His sister. Deidra. His insides twisted. How had his little sister fallen so deep into drugs and prostitution? And how had he allowed their separation to go on for this long—so long that he hadn't even known a sixteen-year-old nephew existed until Ms. Bridges had tracked him down two months ago?

He released a long sigh. "Of course. I'll be home this afternoon. What time did you say you'd be by?"

"Three o'clock okay?"

"Yes, see you then." He hung up, shoving his phone deep in the pocket of his loose-fitting jeans. He glanced up at the elm and imagined the woodshed he'd build in the future. But not today.

Today, he needed to go to the market and stock up on food fitting for a growing teenage boy. Not that he knew what that was—none of the many kinship or foster care books he'd read covered what to feed a sixteen-year-old boy. But he'd been one himself forty years ago. He'd figure it out.

He glanced over to the bed and breakfast, but his neighbor was nowhere in sight. He thought he'd have some time to settle in before Owen's arrival. Cut down his tree, start his shed, do some fishing . . . but he hadn't even had time to run out of sugar.

Everything would have to wait. As soon as he'd submitted the kinship care application, he'd vowed to make Owen a priority. In some ways, he credited God with the timing of it all. He'd just sold his business and, for the first time in his life, had spare time on his hands. Not that he'd planned to spend it taking care of his sister's son, but he couldn't live with himself if he'd turned the boy away.

No matter how far Deidra had fallen, she was family. Somewhere in her troubled spirit was the little girl he'd given piggyback rides to, the girl who grinned as wide as the heavens when he'd plunked extra marshmallows into her hot chocolate during Christmas.

Maybe Owen was the key to finding his way back into her life.

Kevin opened the door to his new home and grabbed his car keys and wallet off the counter. Tonight he'd grill hamburgers. What kid didn't like hamburgers? He'd grab some chips and pickles and maybe some of those sugar cookies from the bakery. They'd eat outside on the picnic bench. Maybe they'd talk fishing. Or maybe Owen would want to help him plan his shed.

As he drove to the market, Kevin's spirits lifted. Surely, this wouldn't be so bad. Yes, some people had a hard time with foster and kinship care, but his sister's kid would probably be grateful to be out of the DCYF office and in a real home with his uncle. What else did a teenage boy need besides good food, a warm bed, and some honest work to keep him occupied and out of trouble?

❦

"Hey, Mom." Amie breezed in the back door of the Orchard House.

I looked up from where I loaded the last of the breakfast dishes into the dishwasher from this morning's meal service. Fruit, coffee cake, avocado toast with cashew cream, yogurt with my homemade granola, and our guests' choice of Snicker-doodle Crepes or Lobster Eggs Benedict with Lemon-Herb Butter—my personal favorite—both served with crispy bacon. Though I wasn't one to boast, I took special pride in preparing the five-course breakfasts. The quaint location and the old Victorian, complete with author-themed guest rooms that included Louisa May Alcott, Henry David Thoreau, Emily Dickinson, Ralph Waldo Emerson, Nathaniel Hawthorne, and Robert Frost drew the first-timers, but my breakfast was what brought them back. Not to mention the regular referrals we enjoyed. I couldn't imagine a more fulfilling job. Sure, it was sometimes exhausting, but that was a small price to pay for doing satisfying work.

"Hey, honey. You're home early."

Amie opened the fridge. A splatter of yellow paint marred her otherwise flawless cheek. She scrunched her nose. That's right—I'd bought the sparkling waters in the plastic again instead of the glass bottles. She hated that.

She grabbed an orange. "Half day today. We have a class coming in for a field trip tomorrow, so I might have to stay later."

Amie worked at a nonprofit art camp with a mission to provide community for those with autism and their families. She thoroughly enjoyed the work and had started painting again on the side, selling several on consignment at the shops downtown. Josie, my second oldest daughter, had even mentioned we'd sold one of Amie's paintings in the gift shop yesterday.

She sat at the kitchen bar and peeled the orange over a

napkin. "Just caught the new neighbor pulling into his driveway. He's kind of cute."

My head snapped up, seemingly of its own volition. "Is he now?"

She narrowed her eyes at me, the yellow paint on her cheek crinkling. "You've noticed!"

To my horror, my face heated again. Pretty sure this one wasn't a hot flash. Quickly, I averted my eyes to squirt dishwashing liquid into the soap compartment. Good grief. Was I a schoolgirl?

"He actually stopped by earlier today." My tone was breezy. Definitely breezy.

Amie wiggled in her seat. "And?"

"And nothing. He wanted to ask me about a tree that's close to our property line. He seems very nice."

"Married?"

I gave her the same look I used to give her when she'd ask me to buy more sculpting clay after buying her some the day before. "Are you in the market for a new groom?"

She slapped her hand on the counter. "Ew, gross, Mom. He's, like . . . *old*. For me, anyway. I'm talking about for you."

I sighed, closing the dishwasher and pressing the *start* button. "Amie, if you think I'm chasing after our new neighbor—"

"Not chasing. More like, open to possibilities."

I crossed my arms at my waist and leaned against the counter. "Even if I were open to possibilities, I simply don't have time to date." I walked to the adjoining breakfast nook where my laptop sat and opened the email I'd read earlier. I brought the computer back to my youngest daughter. "Look at this. You think Orchard House would stand a chance?"

Amie bent to read the email. She flung her blonde hair over one shoulder, her ocean-blue eyes lighting up. "Camden's Hospitality Grant?" She kept reading. "Twenty thousand dollars? Mom, that would be great, and no one deserves it more than you, but how would you use it?"

I bit my lip. "A few things. I need to update our booking engine. We should really be cloud-based. I'd also love to create some sort of loyalty program for our returning guests. I need new linens—which I plan to order regardless of the grant. I could also use more help—with you moving out, Lizzie not feeling well with the IVF treatments, not to mention Bronson's trouble keeping up with the yardwork—I could benefit from hiring someone from the outside. Maybe even from Dad's mission."

Amos's mission was his legacy. I did what I could to support the men and women trying to get back on their feet, paying them for odd jobs and yardwork as I was able, but perhaps it was time to offer more permanent positions.

"That all sounds great."

"And . . ." I hiked in a big breath, as I hadn't yet voiced my newest idea. "I want to add more guest rooms."

Amie's mouth fell open. "What? Where?"

"In the back of the barn. Bronson only uses part of it for the camp and we have more than enough room for our events. I'd like to create a carriage suite, something a bit bigger than we have upstairs. Perhaps transform the apartment above the bookshop into another suite as well. Guests who want a more private experience might really enjoy it, and two more rooms—suites—would create an incredible potential for profit."

"And a lot more work for you. More cleaning, more laundry, more breakfasts." She narrowed her eyes at the running dishwasher. "More dishes."

"Hence hiring the outside help."

Amie tapped her perfectly polished nails on the table. "I don't know, it all sounds great, and you know me, I'm all for women-owned businesses and you're doing a kick-butt job, but don't you think you might want to slow down a little?"

I shut my laptop. "Golly, sweet daughter, you make it sound

like I have one foot in the grave. The Lord is not anywhere near done with me and I refuse to sit back and twiddle my thumbs just because all my kids are—are . . ." My bottom lip trembled. *Leaving*, is what I intended to say, but I couldn't push out the words.

Amie stood and wrapped her arms around me. "None of us are going far. And you know me—I can't cook for anything. You'll probably be so sick of me and August begging you for a decent dinner, you'll be wishing for some alone time."

I blinked away impending tears and forced a smile as she released me. "Don't you dare be planning to stop by out of pity. I'll be perfectly fine. And if I get this grant, I'll be busier than ever."

"That's just it. There's more to life than work. You and Dad are the ones who taught us that. All I'm saying is you could be open to certain"—she jerked her head in the direction of our neighbor's property—"possibilities."

"I'm open to possibilities, dear. I'm just not chasing them down."

She tapped her chin. "So, you're open to them, huh?"

"Amie Martin, don't you dare start meddling in our neighbor's affairs."

She shrugged. "No worries. You know me, I'm always on my best behavior." She winked and flounced up the stairs to her bedroom.

I groaned. My youngest daughter had matured by leaps and bounds the last few years. Surely, she wouldn't be so bold as to approach our neighbor on my behalf. *That* would be downright humiliating.

I blew my hair out of my face and opened my laptop, intending to begin the application for the grant. But as I downloaded the form and began filling out the lines, my thoughts kept snagging on the handsome face of a certain new neighbor and wondering how soon it might be before he ran out of sugar.

"What's a guy gotta do to get some chips around here?" My son Bronson craned his neck over the picnic table, where his sisters chatted with paper plates filled with hamburgers, hotdogs, and potato salad.

One of my favorite nights of the week was Saturday, when all of my kids and their families—including my biggest loves, the grandkids—came over for dinner. This being the first warm night of the year, we'd taken our get-together outside, my growing family spilling over from the back patio into the yard. Aunt Pris and Ed sat in lawn chairs wrapped in thick sweaters. Maggie and Josh's nine-year-old twins Davey and Isaac conducted a swordfight with sticks while Josie's three-year-old, Amos, looked on with wide eyes.

"Hold your horses, haven't you ever heard of ladies first?" Amie dumped a generous portion of potato chips onto her plate.

Bronson scoffed. "Ladies, huh?"

His wife Morgan elbowed him playfully. "Be nice, Bronson, or Amie might change her mind about you walking her down the aisle."

August, Amie's fiancé, shoved in, dumping a few chips onto

his own plate. "No risk of that happening, Bronson. She needs you." He thrust the chips at Bronson. "Take 'em while you can."

Bronson made a show of putting the chips under his arm like a football and squeezing through the press of bodies to his chair on the corner of the patio. Josie's husband, Tripp, caught the action. "That reminds me. We need to start playing some flag football around here. It's been too long."

Josie bounced eleven-month-old Eddie in her arms. "Only if we take turns handing off this one so I can play."

"I'll watch the grands after dinner so you can all get in on the fun." I lowered myself to a seat beside Aunt Pris and her husband Ed.

Amie shook her head. "Count me out. I refuse to walk up the aisle with broken bones."

"I'll help Mom watch the kids." Lizzie moved her potato salad around with her fork and Asher squeezed her arm, mouthing, "Are you okay?" She nodded and gave him a small smile.

My stomach lurched as I tried not to worry about my sweet, quiet daughter. She'd conquered thyroid cancer as a teen and had overcome a lot of anxiety as she matured, including conquering her stage fright. She and her husband Asher wrote and recorded songs, many that hit national top forty lists. But her latest struggle—trying to get pregnant—may be her toughest challenge yet. With Asher being paralyzed from the waist down, they knew they'd likely need help conceiving. But the hormones had been tough on Lizzie, as well as a failed attempt at one round. She seemed more fragile these days, and every morning and night I prayed that God would grant her a child of her own. That He would strengthen her body and her spirit.

We ate with the usual loud, boisterous tumult that ruled our family gatherings. Josh and Tripp broke off into a serious conversation about the Red Sox's chance at the World Series that year, Amie and Maggie debated the necessity of a wedding guestbook, and the rest of us laughed at Josie admonishing Amos not to put cheese curls up his nose.

As dinner wound down, I began clearing the table. I'd just come out of the house a second time to grab the condiments when I spotted my youngest child jogging lightly toward our property line. Amie waved her hand and shouted a greeting into . . . a tree?

Wait. The elm tree. I craned my neck, squinting at . . . yes, a man up in the tree, attached with some sort of harness.

"Hello, neighbor!" Amie was shouting. My family quieted at her greeting, even the kids.

Amie Martin, do not embarrass me, I scolded her in my head as I remembered her words to me a few days ago. Was this her way of "opening me up to possibilities?"

"Hello," Kevin called back. Was he *grinning*?

"I'm Amie. I think you met my mother the other day?"

He answered more quietly this time, and I pretended disinterest as I continued to clear the table. By the time I had gone in the house and back outside again, however, Amie was approaching the patio with a smug grin on her face. "Turns out he loves football." She shrugged.

I hid a smile and shook my head. I couldn't get onto her for being neighborly.

A few minutes later Kevin came over, a teenage boy with hunched shoulders at his side. Amie took the lead in introducing them to everyone, assuring Kevin there wouldn't be a quiz on names later. When she got to me, she paused. "My beautiful and available mother, Hannah, but you've already met her, haven't you?"

"Amie," Maggie hissed.

I wanted to crawl under the table. But no. I was a mature, grown woman. I refused to allow my daughter to embarrass me. "Hello, Kevin. Wonderful to see you again. And who's this?" I looked at the boy, long dark hair falling in front of one eye, pale skin, and large circular holes in each of his ears.

Kevin put a hand on the boy's shoulder. I didn't miss how the teenager pulled away at the touch, nor how Kevin's mouth turned downward. "This is my nephew, Owen. He's staying with me for a bit."

"How lovely. Do you like football, Owen?"

He shook his head.

"Well, no pressure to play. I was just about to take out ice cream sandwiches if you'd like one."

The poor kid looked ten kinds of out of place. But he nodded. The group split into teams and I ducked inside to get the ice cream treats for the grandkids. Aunt Pris and Ed bid their good-byes. Amie, Lizzie, Owen, and I watched the group toss the football. To my surprise, Kevin kept up with Tripp and Josh, throwing an expert pass to Asher, who caught the ball near the makeshift endzone, dropped it in his lap, and wheeled his chair backward to score a goal. A flutter of something foreign moved in my chest as I watched my neighbor reach out with muscled, tattooed arms to punt the ball.

"Single, huh?" Lizzie asked.

"Yup." Amie hadn't lost her smug look.

I rolled my eyes just as a beat-up Honda pulled into the drive-way, parking in a spot we usually reserved for guests. Huh. All our visitors had already checked in for the night and none drove a Honda according to their check-in surveys. I always kept an eye on the parking lot so I knew when it was the best time to clean a lodger's room.

A skinny young woman in tight jeans and a midriff top spilled out of the car. She closed the door and straightened, smiling at us. The football crowd had just called a break and was swigging waters and digging into ice cream sandwiches. Little Eddie whined in my arms and I stood, bouncing him as I started toward the young woman—a girl, really.

Something about her looked familiar, but I couldn't place her. Had she stayed here before? Or maybe she was a friend of one of my children? But none of them were running up to greet her.

"Hello. Welcome to Orchard House." I smiled.

She pushed dark hair behind one ear. "Hello. I—I'm not sure I have the right place."

"This is the Orchard House Bed and Breakfast. Were you looking for another inn? There's quite a few in this town."

"I'm not looking for an inn. I'm actually looking for a person."

"Perhaps I can help. It's a small town." Eddie whined again and I readjusted the pacifier in his mouth and bounced him a bit more.

"I'm looking for a man named Amos Martin."

I stilled, my mouth suddenly dry. Was this woman a former student, then? Or perhaps someone my late husband had counseled? I hated to be the one to tell her the news.

I bit my lip before answering. "I'm sorry, but Amos passed. Five years ago, actually."

The woman's mouth fell open. She blinked, shook her head. "No . . . no, he couldn't have . . ."

I led the woman to a nearby chair and Lizzie handed her a bottled water.

"I'm so sorry." I placed a hand on her thin shoulder. "He touched many lives. Were you a student of his?"

She looked up at me and piercing brown eyes stared back. All at once, I knew why they were so familiar. But no . . . that was impossible, of course. Amos didn't have a younger sister, especially not this young. Perhaps she was a relative I'd never met? I bounced Eddie, and Josie came to my side, sliding him from my arms.

"How did you know Amos?" I lowered myself to the chair closest to the young woman.

"I didn't know him, actually, although I was hoping to. You see, Amos Martin is—was—my father."

❦ 4 ❦

K evin hadn't missed Hannah's shocked expression nor the way her pretty mouth fell open after hearing the young woman say that Amos was her father. Hadn't Hannah said her late husband's name was Amos?

Kevin looked to Josie, who wore a countenance almost identical to Hannah's. Quickly, it turned to one of anger as she shifted her son onto the hip farthest from the new stranger and straightened her spine. The girl had been aggressive when playing football—she'd already scored two goals for their team. Clearly, she wasn't a wallflower off the field either.

"What are you talking about? That's impossible. What do you want from us?" Josie glared at the newcomer.

The woman's eyes widened. She shook her head. "N-nothing. I wanted to meet m-my father, is all."

"Stop saying that," Josie snapped. "He's not your—"

Hannah's oldest daughter—Maggie, if he remembered correctly—placed a hand on Josie's arm. "Perhaps this is just a terrible misunderstanding." Maggie forced a smile. "Let's talk. Can we get you something to eat?"

The woman gave a tentative smile to Maggie. "No, I'm okay."

Kevin elbowed Owen and gestured toward their house. They didn't have any business hanging around any longer. There surely would be no more football.

He didn't have to hint to Owen more than once. With what appeared to be obvious relief, the boy turned toward his property.

"Nice family, huh?" Kevin stepped over the stone wall that marked the property line.

Owen shrugged. "Sure."

The kid hadn't been what Kevin expected—not that he had any right to expect anything from a nephew he'd never met. While not defiant, Owen showed a sincere disinterest in Kevin, his home, and all conversation.

Their first night, he'd asked Owen if he liked fishing.

"Nope."

"What do you like?" Kevin asked.

He'd raised hooded eyes. "To be left alone."

Huh.

Kevin hadn't pushed. Surely, the boy needed time. Though he'd likely never join him fishing or chopping down trees. Paler than chalk, Owen's hair hung in front of his eyes, as if he wanted to hide from the world. Maybe he was into video games. Kevin had been a pretty hard-core Pac-Man addict himself, back in the day. Maybe they'd eventually find common ground over a PlayStation. Eventually.

For now, he'd take it slow. Let the kid know he was safe. A warm bed, good food . . . eventually he'd open up, wouldn't he? Even talk about his mother?

"Kevin!"

He turned at the sound of the feminine voice behind them. Hannah's youngest daughter, Amie. Definitely the most brazen of the bunch.

"I'm sorry." She jogged up to them, a bit breathless, her many necklaces jangling together. "I don't know what's going on, but I can assure you it's all a terrible mistake."

Mistake or not, he was the last one to judge. "No need to apologize. But I thought it best we slip out quietly, so you could handle your private matter without worrying about us."

"Thanks for joining in. I think my mom likes you." She grinned, her blue eyes sparkling.

He tried not to take the bait . . . but the jump in his chest proved he'd bite. "She seems like a great lady. I'm looking forward to getting to know her better in the future."

Amie's smile didn't fade. Her gaze flicked to Owen's. "Thanks for coming over, Owen."

The boy's face reddened. He waved a hand through the air before turning back toward the house.

"Maybe you guys could join us for dinner tomorrow night? If you don't have plans, that is."

Yep, no subtlety with this one. He shifted from one leg to the other. "Seems like your mom has her hands full. Maybe when things settle down, she'll invite me herself."

"Oh, I'm sure she will." The young woman took a step back. "Nice meeting you, Kevin."

"Next time you all play football, holler if I'm here."

"Definitely!" She waved and jogged back toward the house. He searched out Hannah, still sitting in the chair beside the young woman, her fingers massaging her temples.

A heaviness weighed on his chest. It was clear Hannah was a strong lady to have started what appeared to be a thriving and successful business after her husband died, to be the one who had raised all those kids. But it seemed this new young lady had thrown her for a loop.

Which of course it would. What if that young woman had showed up on his doorstep instead, claiming to be Katherine's daughter. How would he handle it?

He didn't know.

Sighing, he turned from the Orchard House and headed into his own home. It lay quiet. He trudged upstairs and knocked on Owen's closed door. No answer. He knocked again.

"Yeah."

Kevin opened the door to see his nephew sprawled out on his bed, earbuds in, phone in hand.

"I was thinking of taking a walk downtown, maybe checking out the library or the boats down in the harbor. You want to come?"

"I have homework."

"On a Saturday night?"

The boy shrugged. "I don't like saving it for last minute."

"Okay," Kevin ground out, half-tempted to order the boy away from his phone and out into the world. Surely, taking a walk on a beautiful night would be better for his mental health than squinting at a tiny screen for hours at a time. And did kids do homework on their phones these days?

He knew nothing about teenagers. He'd been fooling himself, thinking he knew what to do with a kid, especially in today's world.

"Guess I'll see you later, then."

"Yeah."

Kevin closed the door, partly relieved at being out of the boy's presence. He hated to admit it, but it was actually easier when Owen stayed holed up in his room. But was that what a good foster parent—role model, uncle, whatever he was supposed to be —would think?

He sighed, heading back down the stairs. Maybe he should have taken Ms. Bridges up on the offer of a support group. Not that it was too late, but support groups really weren't his thing. What he needed was to talk to someone who knew a thing or two about raising young people.

His mind turned to Hannah. Maybe, in time, she'd be open to giving him some advice. Some pointers on guiding and raising teenaged humans into functional, well-adjusted adults.

As he shut the door behind him, he cast off the idea. She didn't need a muddled man nosing around for advice. No. He'd not inconvenience Hannah and her family right now for the world. But maybe he could do something small to help.

Amos Martin is—was—my father.

Somewhere in the distance, I heard Josie and Maggie talking. Josie, upset. Of course, Josie was upset. My dear girl, despite her tough exterior, wore her heart on her sleeve.

Amos Martin is—was—my father.

I moved my tongue around in my mouth, searching for words. Searching for sense amid the horrifying knowing that built in my gut. In my muddled state, I grasped onto the solidity of numbers, doing the math in my head. Counting years, calculating possible ages against that of Amie.

When the numbers slid into place, a cold sweat broke out over my skin.

I'd never thought my children would have to find out about Amos's transgression, but then again, I never thought that one night had produced a child.

A daughter.

"Excuse me." Somehow, I found strength in my legs—enough to push myself out of the chair and propel my body into the house. I heard voices behind me, someone at my heels, but I ducked into Orchard House, its warm folds welcoming me like a mother hen does its chicks. Here, I was safe. Here, I'd built a life after my husband's death. Here, my faith had deepened.

Hadn't it?

"Mom, are you okay? Mom?"

I blinked, leaned on the kitchen counter, nodded in response to Josie's words.

"I have half a mind to call the cops. Who does she think she is?" Josie's hand clamped around my arm. "I wonder if she's one of Lizzie's fans? Or even mine? Should I call the police? There's some wackadoodles out there and they'd do anything to—"

My gaze met my second-oldest daughter's probing one. "Josie."

She waited for me to continue. But I couldn't. I didn't have the heart to diminish Amos in Josie's eyes. Especially now, when he wasn't alive to even try to redeem himself.

Maggie, Lizzie, and Amie—my other daughters—would handle the news better than Josie, who refused to see any fault in my late husband. Amos and Josie had shared a special bond of books and philosophy; a union of knowing what it was to be misunderstood, of possessing a deep-thinking, probing, overly curious mind.

No, Josie would not take the news well, and right now, I couldn't bear to share the truth with her, even if that did make me a coward.

"Don't call the police. I'll talk to her in a moment. Can I just —can you give me a minute?"

Her dark brows furrowed. For the first time since entering the house, I realized she still held Eddie. I reached out a finger and he curled his tiny fist around my own. My heart lurched. God help me, if Amos was still alive, I'd have half a mind to strangle him for putting us through this mess and leaving us alone to wade through it all.

"Sure, Mom. Okay. A few minutes?"

I nodded and she straightened her shoulders before going back outside. As soon as the door shut, I rounded the corner to the stairs that led to our bedrooms. Once inside my room, I closed the door, leaned against its sturdiness, and closed my eyes.

In truth, I had feared a scenario such as this one ever since that horrible night Amos had confessed his adultery. The man had been beside himself with grief. No one held himself to a higher standard than my husband.

And he'd failed. He'd failed me. He'd failed our children.

Not that I had been blameless in our deteriorating marriage. But I wasn't the one who had slipped into another's bed.

My throat cinched tight. I thought I'd forgiven long ago, but this new revelation threw a twist in things.

I crossed our room and sat on the bed, staring at the framed picture of my husband on my nightstand. He'd been ridiculously young in that picture—early or mid-twenties. He was sanding a changing table we'd found on the side of the road and had glanced up at me and smiled for the camera. I'd been pregnant with Maggie. We'd been young and in love and completely naïve to the many joys and struggles that awaited us.

Struggles like the one I encountered today, alone.

I scooped up the picture and searched my husband's dark eyes. A surge of anger, surprising in its intensity, pummeled me, and I squeezed the framed picture until my knuckles turned white. More surprising was the anger I felt on behalf of the young woman downstairs. A young woman who had never—and would never—know her father. Shouldn't Amos have known if his one-night affair had produced a baby? Though I'd feared it, I never asked him, not wanting to ponder the possibility.

And now, the possibility was a reality on my back patio.

I breathed deeply, whispering a prayer for wisdom—not only in how to handle the entire situation, but how to approach my grown children with their father's past, a past I'd planned to hide until my dying day.

I released a breath, long and slow, facing the fact that I couldn't hide up in my room all night. Right now, my children were entertaining this young lady alone—I didn't even know her name. Josie wanted to call the cops.

I stood and placed Amos's picture carefully on my nightstand, throwing back my shoulders much as Josie had done in the kitchen. I inhaled the deepest breath I could manage, then opened my bedroom door, unsure what frightened me more—facing a daughter my husband shared with another woman, or admitting to my children that the marriage I shared with their father hadn't been quite as idyllic as I'd led them to believe.

WHEN I REACHED THE BACK PATIO, STREAKS OF PINK, ORANGE, and purple cast light across the sky. A chill hung in the air. Bronson was conversing amicably with our guest, Josie glaring at them, while Amie, Maggie, Lizzie, and my sons-in-law rallied the kids for a game of hide-and-seek.

I approached the young lady where she sat, chatting with Bronson. She was a pretty girl. Pale and willowy, I hated to admit that I saw a strong resemblance to my husband. Not only those haunting eyes, but the sharpness of her nose, the high arch of her forehead. Even if Amos hadn't confessed his transgression to me all those years ago, I wondered if I'd be able to deny the evidence before me now.

The young woman stood. "Mrs. Martin, I'm sorry to have barged in here. I can see now that I should have called first."

"It's all right. How about we start with our names. I'm Hannah."

The girl's posture relaxed. "I'm Luna."

Luna . . . a creative name, for sure. Nothing like the more traditional names of Amos's other children. "How about you and I go inside to talk? I can make some tea if you'd like, or coffee."

Luna looked from me to Bronson. "Okay. Nice to meet you, Bronson."

"Nice to meet you." Before I could turn to follow her, Bronson reached for my arm. "Mom, are you sure this is a good idea?"

I placed a hand on his. "I'm sorry to end our evening so abruptly, but I have a feeling this isn't something I should brush aside."

"You can't save the world, Mom. She really thinks Dad is her father."

"I know."

While Bronson and I didn't always see eye-to-eye on the ways I attempted to help the needy in our community, he'd long ago accepted that reaching out to the stranger was a part of who I was. It had been a part of who Amos was—something we had worked on together.

"It's okay, Bronson. I'll text you later?"

His mouth pressed into a thin line. "All right. Is it okay if the kids finish their game of hide-and-seek?"

"Of course." I hugged him, holding him close a little longer than necessary. Finally, I pulled away. "Good night, honey."

"Night, Mom."

I slid into the back door of Orchard House, smiling tentatively at Luna standing with her arms crossed in between the breakfast nook and the kitchen bar. One side of her mouth lifted in an anxious smile.

My own smile must have mirrored hers. Well, at least we were anxious together.

I strode into the kitchen. Surely, I'd find comfort in my favorite room in the house. "Coffee or tea?"

"Do you have decaf coffee? I prefer it black."

Oh my, she *was* Amos's daughter.

I spun around the kitchen, grabbing mugs and saucers.

"This is a beautiful place." Luna looked around at the cathedral ceilings and wooden beams of the kitchen.

"We're blessed to have it." I scooped coffee grounds into the filter. "Amos's aunt grew up here. We opened the bed and breakfast a year after he died."

"Is she not alive either?" The girl's bottom lip trembled.

I brought the coffee cups to the breakfast nook and pulled out a chair, gesturing for Luna to sit. "No, she's alive and kicking. She married last year and moved out of Orchard House. Perhaps I'll introduce you sometime."

The young woman raised her eyes to me. "You—you believe me, then?"

I swallowed around the lump in my throat. "I do."

She released a visible breath. The act drew attention to the prominent cleavage her tight shirt put on display. "I'm so glad."

I tapped my fingers on the table. "I was aware Amos had a . . . liaison with another woman some time back."

"I'm twenty-one," she said, almost proudly.

"And when did you . . .?" Lord help me, I couldn't voice my question. I'd never asked Amos about the woman he'd been unfaithful with. I assumed she was a student of his, but I never questioned and he never volunteered. Better to have her a muddle in my mind rather than a vivid, life-breathing, authentic person. But now . . . well, Luna would tell me, wouldn't she?

"My mother never spoke of my father. Not until . . ." She pressed her lips together and her shoulders began to shake.

I reached out a hand to her, waiting.

"She was in a car accident on her way home from work this past Christmas Eve. By the time I made it to the hospital, they knew she wasn't going to make it. She was conscious and she told me—told me the name of my father."

My mouth fell open. "Oh my goodness. Honey, I'm so sorry."

"We didn't have anyone else. Just each other. I guess she figured if she was going to leave me she should at least tell me where I could find my father. But, he's gone too?"

I nodded. "Amos died of a heart attack five years ago. I'm sorry, Luna."

Her jaw grew firm and she straightened, the act reminding me of Josie. "It's okay. I've been on my own this long. I'll survive."

I admired her tenacity. Clearly, she hadn't had it easy growing up.

Her eyes flickered. "I'm sorry, Mrs. Martin. I didn't mean to come here and disrupt your life. Your children don't like me much, and I can't blame them. But please believe me that if I had anyone else—anyone at all—I wouldn't have disturbed you."

I nodded, the fact that this girl was one of the very people my late husband tried to help through his mission not lost on me. "How did you find us?"

"My mother told me the town where my—where Amos lived. I googled him but didn't see an obituary. I only saw the history of this bed and breakfast."

That's right. When Maggie had built the Orchard House website, she'd included a page of its history. She must have mentioned Amos's relation to Aunt Pris.

I sipped my coffee, allowing the hot liquid to scald my throat. Part of me wanted to wish this girl the best and send her on her way. Another part of me burst with compassion. The circumstances surrounding her conception were not her fault. And there'd been sixteen years of her life where her father *had* been alive.

"Amos didn't know you existed, Luna. If he had, he would have wanted to be a part of your life."

The girl's eyes shone with moisture. "He would have?"

I nodded. "Absolutely. Like all men, my husband owned his share of faults, but he would have never ignored his own . . . child." I swallowed, the word harder to push out than I thought possible.

"Mom never talked about him. I don't think she wanted to screw up his life."

I pressed my lips together. This news *did* mess up someone's life, but not Amos's. Mine. Our children's. And yet, what a horrible way to live—to feel as if your very existence was a threat to the man who'd been responsible for your birth.

"I'm sorry she felt that way. But I can say with absolute certainty that Amos wouldn't have viewed you as messing up his life." I thought of his mission, of the many ways my husband sought to help people. Luna should know a little bit of his legacy. "What are your plans?"

Her gaze shot across the kitchen. "I—I don't know. I thought if Amos was here, I'd want to spend some time getting to know him, if he wanted to know me."

Oh, poor girl. How could I even think to send her away?

Swallowing down a large gulp of hesitancy, I opened my mouth before I could think too much about what I was about to say. "Amos is not here, that's true. But you have five . . . siblings who you have a right to know. We have plenty of room here, if you'd like to stay for a bit—"

Her dark eyes sparkled even as her chin trembled. She reached for my hand. "Really? Do you mean it? I promise I won't be an ounce of trouble, Mrs. Martin. I could help with whatever you need."

Something about her spoke of a childlike innocence that both calmed and unnerved me. She seemed incredibly young for her age, and I gathered she hadn't the slightest clue what having her here would cost me.

And yet, did any of that matter? She was an orphan. I possessed the means—maybe even an obligation on Amos's behalf—to help. At least make sure she knew her half-sisters and brother. As hard as it might be, it would be all the more difficult to let her go.

"I mean it. Do you have any bags? I could show you where you'll be staying. And perhaps, I could have a few minutes alone with my children. It looks like they're still poking around."

I glimpsed Asher wheeling toward his truck, Josie packing up Eddie's diaper bag. If I could catch them tonight, all the better.

"Yes, of course. I can sit here if you'd like?"

"No. Let's get you settled first." I led her outside. Josie's hawk-eyes studied Luna as she dug in the back seat of her car for a duffel bag. I scurried over to Amie and Lizzie, who stood closest to me, putting the covers on the outdoor furniture. The air smelled like rain.

"What's going on, Mom?" Amie's gaze darted to Luna, who slid back into the house.

"I know you all have your families with you, but I wonder if I could talk to the five of you in the bookshop after I get Luna settled?"

Lizzie's eyes widened, but she nodded. "Sure. We'll work it out."

I forced a smile and walked back inside, leading Luna upstairs to Lizzie's old bedroom. I hadn't changed it since she'd married Asher, keeping her flowered bedspread and the desk she'd had since childhood by the window. Luna set her bag on the ground and glanced around. "This is beautiful."

I looked at the room again, trying to see it through her eyes. To me, it was plain and serviceable enough, but rather spacious, I supposed. "Wait until you see our guest rooms." I smiled.

She grasped my hands, and although my gut reaction was to pull away, I didn't.

"Thank you again, Mrs. Martin. And I meant what I said about helping. I plan to earn my keep while I'm here."

I nodded. "I'd appreciate the help, actually. With Lizzie and Bronson out of the house and Amie getting married in a few weeks, I've been shorthanded."

"Maybe this is perfect timing, then." Her eyebrows raised, those dark orbs sparkling. And while I wasn't certain there was ever a perfect time to find out your late husband's unfaithfulness had given you a fully-grown, orphaned daughter, I didn't have the heart to disagree.

I withdrew my hands from hers, signaling my leave. "Have a good night. The bathroom is right across the hall, towels in the closet. Make yourself at home."

"Thank you. You don't know what this means to me."

I didn't, though I had an inkling I would soon find out what it all meant to me.

❦ 6 ❦

"**M**om, what's going on?" Josie crossed her arms and tapped her foot against the bookshop floor.

"Yeah, who is that girl?" Amie flopped onto a cushioned chair nearest the gas fireplace. The small flames lent a cozy atmosphere to the shop—a coziness that usually calmed. Not this night.

The dim recessed lights offered an air of privacy to the empty gift shop. Normally Josie's domain when open to customers, the bookshop also served as an occasional space for us to have get-togethers and private conversations away from guests. If my plan to put in a carriage suite went through, it may not feel quite as private.

Maggie sat beside me on the couch and inched out her hand. I couldn't help but compare the pale warmth of her tiny fingers to Luna's long ones.

Lord, grant me wisdom.

I dragged in a deep breath. There were no perfect words for this moment. Delaying wouldn't provide any amount of relief. "Your father loved you guys with all his heart. I think we should keep that at the forefront of our minds as we enter into this conversation."

Lizzie's face scrunched. "Mom?"

I swallowed. "Your father and I had a good marriage. But we hit a rough patch when you all were young." I remembered the desperation of that time. How Amos worked hard to make tenure at the university and start the mission, how I'd felt neglected and alone with five young children. Amie had been colicky, awake all hours of the night. I missed my work as a librarian. I loved being a mom—loved it more than anything in the world. But I missed my husband. I missed feeling like a team instead of a one-man band, juggling school events and diaper changes and pureed baby food and naps and homework and sleepovers with friends. I was exhausted, and when Amos was home, I'd nagged and complained. We'd argued.

Not that any of that gave him the right to run into another woman's arms, even on a drunken whim, but I wasn't sure I could cast the full blame on Amos, therefore, I needed to choose my words now with care.

I licked my lips. "The last thing I want to do is tarnish your father in your sight. He loved you guys beyond reason." I closed my eyes to save myself the hurt of seeing their faces. "Luna is Dad's daughter. I—I didn't realize what happened all those years ago produced a baby. But after seeing her, after knowing what your father confessed to me . . . there's no denying it. I'm so, so sorry, kids."

Slowly, I opened my eyes. Five stares gaped back at me, as if not comprehending my words.

"No." Bronson was the first to speak. He shook his head, hard. "Dad wouldn't have done that. This is a mistake."

Bronson, my only son. He'd always held his father in such high regard. I thought that had been a beautiful thing. A healthy thing. Had we made a mistake hiding Amos's transgression even as our children reached adulthood? Would the truth cause more damage now?

"I'm so sorry, Bronson. I wish it were," I whispered.

Josie's face turned red, the corners of her eyes wet. "Dad wouldn't. But even if he did, that woman has no proof. She shouldn't be in our house, Mom. How do you know she isn't an axe murderer or a thief?"

I gathered myself, chose not to point out that we had strangers sleeping under our roof nearly every night. "I know because the math is right. What's more, I see your father in her."

I allowed my gaze to roam over each of my children, trying to put myself in their shoes. My mom had died when the kids were small and my father had made a new life in Florida, not keeping in touch all too often. I wondered how I would feel if someone told me my dad had fathered a daughter I never knew about. I'd be surprised, of course. But as an only child, I might have welcomed a sibling.

Something my kids obviously didn't plan on doing.

Maggie leaned back on the couch, her hand on her forehead. "This is just . . . this is . . . *big*."

Amie held up a hand. "Wait a minute, let's back this truck up. You *knew* Dad cheated and yet you stayed with him?"

One corner of my mouth lifted in a sad smile. "I did. He didn't have to tell me about it—I'm not even sure I would have ever found out—"

"Until now," Amie growled.

"That's right. Until now. And I for one am glad we were able to seek forgiveness and healing while your father still walked this earth."

Lizzie sniffed. "But—but now he's not here to help us through this mess."

Josie nodded. "He's not here for us to yell at him either. Why didn't you tell us sooner?"

I raised an eyebrow at her. "Guys, your father loved you and he loved me. But he made a mistake—a grievous mistake. I didn't want that to ever ruin your view of him."

"Kind of late now." Bronson muttered the words, taking a chair and swinging it around to sit on it backward, legs splayed.

"Of course, we didn't know he had another daughter. If we'd known, it would have changed everything. We would have had to tell you. I'm certain we would have welcomed Luna into our lives, however hard that may have been."

"And now you want us to do the same." Maggie stared straight into the warm flames of the fireplace.

"Yes. I think that's what your father—"

Amie waved her hands, cutting me off. "But why did you stay? I mean, I don't think I could take it if August ever slept with another woman. Isn't adultery like, the one thing the Bible gives you a pass on as reason for divorce?"

"Honey, I have no regrets about staying married to your father. I hate what he did, yes. But sometimes love finds a way to forgive the unforgiveable."

Josie's expression glazed over, and I wondered if my words reminded her of her own past, how her husband Tripp had a lot to forgive before they could move forward in their own relationship. She licked her lips. "It won't be easy. I—I don't know her and already I'm not a fan."

"She's just a girl." Lizzie stroked the throw pillow on her lap. "She's never known her father. Unless, did she grow up with a dad?"

I shook my head. "From the sounds of it, it was just her and her mom. Her mom died in a car accident last Christmas Eve. She told her about Amos on her death bed."

Lizzie's bottom lip trembled. "Oh my goodness. That's terrible."

"And just like a Nicholas Sparks' novel. How do we know any of this is true? Shouldn't we at least have a blood test or something?" Josie said.

So much for my second-oldest rethinking things.

I straightened my spine. "I refuse to demand any such thing."

"Mom, it's not completely out of line." Bronson drummed his fingers against the back of his chair. "Most people don't show up unannounced, claiming to have a birthright."

Amie rolled her eyes. "A birthright? Are we in colonial times or something? She's not demanding our inheritance or anything." Her eyes widened. "Wait. Is she?"

"Amie!" Lizzie threw a pillow in her younger sister's direction.

I laughed, and it felt good. "Hate to break it to you kids, but Orchard House is about the only inheritance I have for you." They knew that. It wasn't a secret how their father's many interests and start-up charities ran us in the red over the years. Only with the help of Ed Colton and the sale of our house had we been able to renovate Aunt Pris's Victorian home and make it into a charming bed and breakfast.

"Did you know her?" Maggie's gaze met mine. "Luna's mother."

I dragged in a deep breath. "I—I don't know. I don't think so. I never asked who she was. I didn't want to know. I suppose, with Luna here, I may end up finding out."

Lizzie slipped her hand into mine. "I'm sorry you have to go through this, Mom."

I squeezed her hand. "I'm sorry for the shock. But now that we know what we're facing, we need to decide how to proceed. Luna is an orphan. She wants to get to know you all. I want that for her. It won't be easy, but we've never done things the easy way in this family, now have we?" I forced a bright smile around the circle of humans I loved more than anything in this world.

Lizzie was nodding. Maggie followed.

Amie bit her lip, then raised ocean-blue eyes to me. "I'm not the youngest anymore."

The back of my eyelids burned and I got up to wrap my arms

around her, her soft blonde hair tickling my nose. "Honey, you will always be my youngest."

She swiped at her eyes. "I'll be nice to Luna. It looks like she could use a tan, maybe we can go to the beach together sometime or something."

Josie glared at Amie. "A tan? Like that's what we need from her. I still say we ask for a blood test."

"I second that," Bronson said.

I sighed. "I'm not doing that. Sorry, kids. I've already asked her to stay and that's that. Next time you talk to her, look into her eyes. No blood test will convince you better."

A moment passed before Josie gave a huffy sigh. "Fine."

"All right." Bronson agreed. "It's your decision."

"Thank you." I smiled. "We're going to get through this. Can I pray for all of us?"

They nodded and I bowed my head, begging God to help us through this trial. I prayed for each of my children, and then I prayed for the daughter that wasn't mine. The daughter that I would try like the dickens to *not* think of as a symbol of my husband's unfaithfulness.

7

*D*inner's ready.

Kevin sent the text to his nephew, then turned back to the stove to stir the chili. After four days of trudging upstairs to knock on Owen's door for a solid minute in order to communicate with him, he learned Owen's response time was a lot quicker if he communicated through text.

Yes, Kevin thought it insane to text someone ten yards away from him, but he was also man enough to admit when he'd been beat.

He placed the wooden spoon on a small plate by the stove. He only wanted to help his nephew, but how long would it take before the teenager would let him in? If he ever let him in.

K.

Owen's text came back in ten seconds—a significant improvement from the sixty-second door knocking. Maybe Kevin was getting somewhere after all.

He grabbed a bowl of salad from the refrigerator and placed it on the circular wooden table in the dining room. Protein, check. Vegetables, check. Oops. He grabbed the milk from the fridge and poured it into the glass by Owen's plate. Calcium for growing bones, check.

He was doing okay, wasn't he? Why then, did he feel like any progress he made was slower than tapping sap from a maple tree?

The stairs creaked as Owen came down.

"Hey." Kevin tried for a nonchalant tone as he grabbed water for himself from the tap.

"Hey." The boy flopped down in his chair and started slurping the chili in his bowl.

Kevin cleared his throat as he sat down. "Mind if I pray?"

The teenager shrugged, but stopped eating the chili.

Kevin said a simple blessing over the meal and then started dishing out salad from the large bowl onto Owen's side plate. "How was school today?"

"Fine."

"Have any tests?"

"Nope."

"What'd you have for lunch?" Owen received his lunches for free from the school. Kevin was grateful for that—one less thing he needed to worry about.

He raised hooded eyes to Kevin. "Chili."

The school served chili? "Huh. Well, you'll have to tell me if my chili's better than the school's." It was, he was sure of it.

"It's all right," Owen said.

All right? All right! His mother's award-winning chili recipe had won multiple contests at state fairs. Kevin had added a secret ingredient of cinnamon and his mother had assured him it beat out the original recipe by far.

"What kind of subjects you taking?" He continued the questioning, determined to get more than two-word answers out of the boy.

Owen attended a vocational school just out of town where he was enrolled in a machine shop. Apparently, the kid was pretty smart.

"I'm in shop this week."

"Oh, nice. What'd you do in there?"

"Worked on a CNC machine."

"What do you make on that?"

"Metal stuff."

Kevin gritted his teeth. If he wasn't careful, he was liable to blow up at the kid one day soon.

They ate in silence. When Owen finished his chili, he sat back. "Can I be excused?"

The politest thing he'd heard all week. "What about your salad? Kids need green veggies and all of that."

"What do you know about kids?"

"Not much, but I know the importance of vegetables."

"I'm sixteen and I'm not a kid anymore. Besides, Mom never made me eat stuff I didn't like."

It was the first time Owen had mentioned Kevin's sister. He shifted in his chair, grasping for a question that could segue into more about his estranged sister. "What kind of meals did your mom feed you?"

"You going to report her if it doesn't include green stuff?" He stood. "I have homework. Thanks for the chili."

And then he was gone. No offer to help clear the table or do dishes. And though he thought about calling Owen back down to pitch in, the blessed silence that followed Owen's slamming door was too precious to forfeit.

A pain started at the base of his chest as he thought of Deidra. She hadn't shown up at her first scheduled visit with her son yesterday. That likely wasn't sitting well with the boy.

He released a defeated sigh and began clearing dirtied bowls and utensils from the table. He ran the hot water and squirted dish soap into the sink. The dishwasher had been acting up since he moved in. Though he fiddled with it every night and considered himself a handyman, he suspected the old model had finally given up the ghost. He'd head to the local appliance store tomorrow.

He glanced out the window into the backyard of the bed and breakfast. Except for seeing a few of the Martins at church on Sunday morning, he hadn't interacted with the family since Saturday night. He wondered how Hannah fared with the young woman that had shown up.

Hopefully better than he was doing with Owen.

The sun slid behind the trees as he finished the dishes. He glimpsed Hannah make her way onto the back patio and fiddle with the outdoor fireplace. After a bit, soft flames illuminated the patio pavers and small sitting area.

Kevin dried his hands. Perfect timing. He had a stack of wood, split into small, serviceable pieces from a felled tree in the back of his woods. Surely, Hannah would appreciate a neighborly firewood drop-off.

He grabbed his spring jacket from the hook by the door, killed the lights in the kitchen, and walked to where the elm tree had been by the stone wall. He snatched an armful of wood and stepped onto the Orchard House property, raising a hand.

"Hello!"

Hannah startled, but smiled at the sight of him. "Hello, Kevin. How's the new house treating you?" She yelled to cover the distance.

He started walking over. "Good. Can you use some firewood?"

"Oh! From the elm tree?"

"Afraid that won't be seasoned until next year. This is from another tree. It's dry stuff, should work great for this fireplace." He gestured toward the stone structure.

"That's thoughtful. Thank you." She stood, helping him stack the logs neatly on the side of the patio.

"There's more where that came from. Whatever you need." He straightened and shoved his hands in his pockets, vacillating between bidding goodbye or attempting conversation.

She answered his dilemma by gesturing to the wicker chair beside hers. "Would you like to sit?"

"I don't want to intrude on your quiet time." Was that a lie? Because while he didn't want to bother her, he really did hope she'd allow him to intrude.

"No intrusion at all. I'd love the company, actually." Her white teeth shone in the firelight. She really was a beautiful woman. Her shoulder-length hair framed her high cheekbones and full lips.

He lowered himself in the chair, relishing the pull of his tight leg muscles from climbing the last few days. An outdoor rug spread before them, and then the fireplace, pouring heat.

"You got this going like a champ."

She chuckled. "I'll tell you my secret if you don't tell my kids."

He cocked his head.

"A blowtorch. No matter how much dry kindling I use, I can't make a fire with just a match no matter how hard I try."

He laughed. "Hey, if it works, it works."

She leaned her head back and closed her eyes, a soft smile on her face. A comfortable silence filled the air. "I love this time of year. Coming out here to think and pray gives me a better perspective."

"I really didn't mean to interrupt—"

"Kevin." She opened her eyes, looked straight at him. "I'm many things, but I am not a woman who says one thing and means another. I told you I'd enjoy your company, and I meant it."

Good thing for the dim lighting. He'd hate for her to see the red on his face. It'd been some time since a woman had made him blush. He cleared his throat. "Well, then. That's good to know."

"Thinking and praying is good, but sometimes talking to someone is good, too."

He stuck his tongue in the side of his cheek. "I'm actually a pretty good listener."

If this woman would trust him with her secrets, maybe she'd trust him with even more.

He shook his head at himself. He'd known her for what? A minute?

But he definitely knew he'd rather talk to her right now than a door. That was it—he was just craving adult company with someone who'd actually look him in the eye.

And if her eyes were the clear blue color of a robin's egg, then all the better.

8

I blew out a gentle breath. What was with me? I usually vented to God or Charlotte, in that order. "There's nothing wrong exactly. Well, you were here Saturday night when Luna showed up. I'm not sure how much you heard."

"I wasn't eavesdropping, mind you, but I did hear her say she was your husband's daughter. That must have been quite a shock."

I appreciated his direct manner. I nodded. "It was. My husband told me he'd been unfaithful a long time ago, but he never knew there'd been a baby."

"I'm sorry."

I shook my head, smiled. "Aren't you glad you sat down so I could unload my garbage on you?"

"Nah, we all have garbage. At least you're being open about it. How'd your kids take the news?"

"Some better than others." I thought of Josie and Bronson's denial. A fierce love for them overtook me. "It was hard for them to believe. Their father had high morals. Most of the time."

"We're all susceptible to the human condition, I suppose. Not that I'm making excuses—"

"I know you aren't. But Luna has Amos's eyes. I saw the

resemblance before she even told me the news. She's staying here for now. She doesn't have anyone else."

"Wow, that's good of you."

A soft smile curved my lips. "I couldn't turn her away, even if I'd wanted to. As far as I can tell, she's a good kid, but . . ." I clamped my mouth shut. I didn't want to complain at all, and to a virtual stranger no less.

"But she's a reminder of a past you'd rather not think about?"

My head snapped up. "That's exactly it."

He shifted in his seat. "I can only imagine how all this might feel for you."

I stared into the flames, folded my hands in my lap. "Did—did you and your wife ever—" I bit my lip. Hard. "I'm sorry. Just because I've chosen to heap all my hidden secrets on you doesn't mean—"

"Hidden secrets, huh?" He wiggled his eyebrows. "You're making it sound juicy."

I laughed. "Juicy, all right. Like a soap opera."

He smiled, and I studied his face by the fire. Such a ruggedly handsome man. Open, it seemed. Comfortable in his own skin. I thought of the tattoos his jacket covered, and then, to my horror, I wondered what it'd feel like if he leaned over and kissed me. I looked away.

His smile dimmed. "Like most couples who've been married for any length of time, my wife and I had our share of problems. Infidelity was never one of them."

"Oh." I wondered what his marriage had been like, what problems he and his wife *did* have.

"The only hidden—or maybe not so hidden—secret I have is my nephew. Owen. I'm watching out for him because my sister, who I haven't seen in twenty years, isn't able to do it. Owen's in state custody. My custody now, I suppose."

"That must come with its challenges."

"More than I was expecting. Never had kids before, let alone a teenager. But I'm failing Owen, so I feel like I'm failing my sister all over again. That's what I meant about being reminded of the past."

Without thinking, I reached out a hand and placed it on his arm. "You are not failing that young man. You are doing a beautiful thing for him." I drew my hand back to my lap. "Raising teenagers is tough enough, never mind a teenager you didn't already have for sixteen years."

He raised an eyebrow at me. "I'm open to pointers."

I smiled, leaning back in my chair and thinking back to my own children's teenage years. Back then, Amos was still alive. Alive, but not fully present, with his many charitable and teaching endeavors. There'd been challenges, for sure—Josie punching a boy who'd called her an unseemly name, Maggie getting caught making out under the bleachers, Amie staging a walk-out because the school refused to prove that the chicken served in the cafeteria were humanely-raised, Lizzie's anxiety-producing cancer diagnosis, Bronson having a full-blown panic attack before taking his SATs.

"I remember praying a lot," I offered.

He chuckled. "Already covered there. Morning, noon, and night. Most of the time, more."

A praying man. Maggie had told me she'd spotted Kevin in church on Sunday, but I hadn't given it much thought until now. The fact that he prayed for his nephew made him ten times more alluring.

I blinked, trying to rein myself in. "Where there's rebellion, there's pain." I stood to grab another log and threw it in the fire, the flames brightening with the extra wood. "Amie wasn't a teenager, but just last year she left home without saying goodbye. I didn't learn until later that she felt like she didn't belong. We can't heal all their hurts, but we can listen. We can stand by their side when no one else will."

Kevin studied the fire. "I'm afraid Owen's more interested in staying cooped up in his room on his phone than venting his hurts."

"He's gone through a lot."

"So I should leave well enough alone?"

"I'm no authority on children. My own baffled me at times, but spending time with them is the only way to build a relationship."

"I think the last thing he wants to do is spend time with me."

"You could give him a reason."

"He doesn't want to do any outdoor work, any meal prep. I don't even think he'd be open to playing video games with me."

My mouth twitched. "Can I tell you another secret?"

"Sure."

"Most kids don't want to do chores. But chores are good for them, gives them purpose."

"That's what I thought before he came along, but I'm worried about being too hard on him too soon, about pushing him farther away."

"Start slow. Hey, I'm actually looking for someone to power wash the house. It's a paying job. You think Owen would be interested?"

"I wouldn't want you to pay him. We could do it as a neighborly favor."

I shook my head. "Absolutely not. If you refuse, I'll have to find someone else." There were plenty of men at the mission who would be up for it.

He rubbed the back of his neck. "You drive a hard bargain. I'm sure Owen will appreciate some extra cash. Although I'm not sure this qualifies as a chore if he's getting paid."

My mouth twitched. "Might be a good way to ease him in, though."

He stared into the fire, nodded. "We could manage Saturday if that works for you?"

"Perfect. Thanks so much."

"Thank you." Kevin's booted foot tapped on the pavers. "So, I feel like you helped me with my problem, but I didn't help you with yours."

Luna. The girl had kept her end of the bargain and pitched in plenty around the bed and breakfast. Though her tasks were not always completed to my high expectations, I tried not to make too much of it. It wasn't a great matter to rewash a bathroom sink or straighten a comforter. If only re-tidying was my biggest problem.

"Luna is a sweet girl. She's just . . . always there." I whispered the words, almost ashamed of admitting my feelings. Here I'd been, anxious about being alone. Now, I wasn't sure being alone would have been so bad.

"I see."

"She's helpless in many ways. Has no one. She's reaching out for meaning, for family. My kids haven't exactly embraced her— not because they don't want to, although that may be true for Bronson and Josie—but because they're all busy with their own lives."

"She doesn't know anyone in town?"

"Not yet. I'm sure once she gets more comfortable or finds a job . . ." Yet, pushing Luna to find a job felt so *permanent*. And if I hired someone to take her place at Orchard House, she'd feel horrible. I hadn't thought the girl would stay long-term, but the more she spoke about her future, the more it seemed she viewed my invitation to stay at Orchard House as open-ended.

"The church announced some sort of picnic on Sunday afternoon. Maybe she'd meet some friends there?"

I slapped my thigh. "The picnic! I completely forgot. That would be a wonderful opportunity. I'll mention it to her tomorrow."

Kevin stretched his arms behind his head and propped his right ankle onto his left knee. "Glad to help. Guess we're even now."

I laughed. "I suppose so."

"Well then, suppose I should head back before I overstay my welcome."

I let his words hang in the air between us a moment before answering. "I'm not sure you could overstay your welcome."

He smiled at me, and I turned to stare at the flickering flames.

Had I just *flirted?*

Spring peepers boisterously serenaded the starry night, and I allowed them to take the show. No use me opening my mouth and getting myself into trouble.

But then, if I had to add more trouble to my life, maybe this kind wouldn't be so bad.

9

Kevin, I'm not sure you could overstay your welcome.

My words from the night before replayed in my head over and over as I bustled around the kitchen preparing breakfast. Heat prickled my skin. Had Kevin seen that as innocent flirting—or very forward? What had I been thinking?

But I hadn't. It had been a long time since I'd spent time with a man, especially one I was attracted to. Kevin had stayed for a half hour after my comment, and he'd talked easily about his logging business as well as a few vacations he'd taken with his wife. We'd spoken of the grief of losing a spouse and an unseen bond had begun to form between us. For the first time in five years, I imagined what it'd be like to become involved with a man again. Though I'd always thought the trouble of dating wasn't worth it, talking with Kevin wasn't trouble at all. Far from it.

"Good morning!" Luna trotted into the kitchen, dressed in tight jeans and a tank top that showed her midriff. If Amie came down to serve breakfast in such an outfit, I'd have her march straight back upstairs to change.

But Amie was my daughter. Luna was not.

"Good morning." I smiled at her and grabbed an apron from a drawer, handing it to her. "You up for serving again?"

She took the apron from me and tied it around her waist, covering the front portion of her middle. Much better.

"Absolutely."

I turned back to the counter, where I scooped out the flesh of a tomato to pack it with pesto and goat cheese. "I have to say, Luna, I appreciate your enthusiasm." The girl couldn't be accused of laziness, that's for sure. And what did it matter if I didn't know how long she'd stay with us? She needed our family right now. Like it or not, she needed *me* right now.

"I'm having so much fun. This place is like a new adventure every day. I feel like I live in a mansion!"

"We're blessed to have it." I turned to the oven, where the bacon crisped. "Hey, there's a church barbecue on Sunday afternoon. Are you interested?"

She ran her tongue over her lips. "Will anybody else be there?"

From the hesitant look on her face, she didn't mean the other parishioners. She meant my kids. Her half-sisters and brother.

"Oh, well I haven't talked to the kids yet, but I'll be there. You're welcome to attend if you want, but no pressure. I'm going to make my hummingbird cake—it's always a big hit."

She smiled and it made her look quite pretty. "Okay. I guess that sounds fun."

Amie lumbered into the kitchen, yawning. She wore a t-shirt and jean jacket, her hair pulled up with dangly, beaded earrings decorating her lobes. "Morning."

"Morning!" Luna called as she grabbed the kettle and placed it on the stove. "Do you want the same tea you drank yesterday?" She rummaged in the basket of teas.

I exchanged a look with Amie, silently begging her to put the girl at ease.

My youngest child shook her head. "I can get it, really. Save all your energy for the guests."

"Oh, but I don't mind. It was the peppermint tea, wasn't it?" She held up a tea bag with a green peppermint leaf.

Amie nodded. "That's the one. Thank you." She sat at the bar and cleared her throat. "So, how are you liking Camden, Luna?"

"Oh, it's great." Luna reached in the cabinet for a cup and saucer. "I mean, what I've seen so far is great."

Amie shifted in her seat, looked down at her polished nails, then glanced up at me. "I'm going to yoga class later if you'd like to come. I could walk you through downtown after, maybe we could grab some ice cream?"

My insides flooded with warmth. *Thank you, dear child.*

Luna's pale complexion glowed for the first time since she arrived. "I would *love* that."

"Great. Class is at seven, and if you need any yoga clothes, I have tons. You're a little taller than me, but I think they'd fit."

"Yes, I've never done yoga before."

Amie waved a hand through the air. "No worries. The class is adapted for all levels. My friend Lacy teaches it—she's a rockstar at making everyone feel comfortable."

Luna beamed. "Okay. I can't wait!" The kettle boiled and Luna poured water into Amie's cup, sloshing a little over the side. With careful steps, she brought it to the bar. After Amie thanked her, Luna grabbed up the notepad magnetized to the refrigerator that I kept for guests' drink orders. Though we served specialty coffees at the bar, we offered different juices straight from the kitchen. "I'll go see who's awake." She bounded out of the kitchen, the door to the butler's pantry swinging behind her.

"It's too bad she's finding being here such a drag." The corners of Amie's mouth twitched.

I smiled. "Thank you for spending time with her. It's going to take some effort to make her feel comfortable, I think." I spooned pesto into the hollowed-out tomato bottoms.

"How about you?"

My gaze flicked to my youngest daughter.

"I mean, how are you handling her being here? I give you a lot of credit, Mom. Like, I knew you were a saint but this takes you to a whole new level."

"I am far from saintly." If she knew some of the unholy thoughts I wrestled with regarding her dead father, she would know that. "I'm trying to be decent. She has no one. If I don't dwell too much on how she's here so much as the fact that God placed her here for a reason, then I find it easier."

"I'm sorry Dad . . . you know."

My mouth turned downward, and I stopped mid pesto scoop. "Me, too."

"Did you guys get better after it all? Did you work out your problems?"

"We went to counseling. We talked more. Your father tried to work less. I tried to trust that he was at work when he said he was."

Amie lifted the tea bag out of her cup and placed it on the saucer. "Was it because of us? Is that why you stayed with him?"

Were our kids the reason I stayed with Amos after he'd been unfaithful? I bit the inside of my cheek. "If you guys were the reason, I couldn't think of a better one. Despite your father's faults, I loved him. I wanted us to work."

Luna swung through the door. "Three orange juices, two cranberry, and six apple." She opened the corner glass cabinet where I kept the wine glasses, obviously remembering that I liked to serve the morning juice in the fancy glasses.

I turned back to the tomatoes and forced Amie's questions from my mind. Yes, I regretted what Amos had done, but I hadn't regretted our marriage. Our marriage had been made up of good and bad, like much of life. I couldn't quantify our relationship with one terrible mistake. And right now, I refused to quantify my relationship with Luna by holding it up to the light of Amos's mistakes, either.

"Wow." Maggie curled one strand of dark hair around her ear from her seat at the front desk.

I drummed my fingers on the raised portion of wood beside the bell. "What do you think?"

"It's thorough, Mom. Completely professional. If it were up to me, I'd give you the grant in a heartbeat."

"Do I sense a 'but' in there somewhere?"

She smiled. "Not exactly a 'but.' More like a 'wowza, that's a lot to do with only twenty thousand dollars.'"

I bit my lip. "Well, of course I wouldn't be able to do everything. But I could use it as seed money. I thought it would be a great angle since the judges will likely be looking for the business that will bring the most tourists into town."

Maggie smiled sweetly up at me. "If anyone can do it, it's you, Mom."

"Thanks, honey. But seriously, is there anything you think I should change?"

"Not a thing. Hey, how's it going with Luna? I've been meaning to carve out some time with her, but we've been booked with doctors' visits this week."

I pressed my hand to my forehead. "That's right. Isaac's checkup yesterday. How did it go?"

"His numbers are great."

"Thank God." My grandson had been diagnosed with type 1 diabetes three years ago. Though Maggie, Josh, and especially Isaac, handled the disease like pros, we always breathed a big sigh of relief when he aced his checkups.

"Luna?" Maggie's eyebrows rose. Luna was upstairs as we spoke, cleaning the Alcott room. I planned to help her as soon as Maggie looked over my application for the grant.

"She's a big help. We're adjusting to one another, of course, and I think things will be easier as she settles in and makes friends, but—"

"Settles in, huh? This is going to be a long-term deal?"

"I don't know. But I can't see myself kicking her out. I'll take one day at a time and see where the Lord leads us."

Behind us, the slightly squeaky swing of the butler's pantry door sounded. "You will not believe what Lizzie just told me."

I turned to see Josie. "Morning, sunshine."

She wrinkled her nose at the term of endearment.

"What's up?" Maggie closed out of the grant application on her laptop.

"Lizzie just told me that Ashley told her that Ashley's aunt told her that Jolene Andover is applying for the hospitality grant."

Maggie's mouth twitched. "Wow, sis, for a bestselling author, you certainly do have a way with words."

Josie playfully slapped Maggie's arm. "This is *serious*."

"Honey, Jolene has as much right to apply for the grant as I do." Jolene Andover opened the Red Velvet Inn shortly after we opened The Orchard House. Josie insisted Jolene had stolen my five-course breakfast idea. Honestly, I didn't harbor bad feelings about it. She'd had a terrible crush on Amos when we were in high school, though he'd never given her the time of day. Still, Jolene had never been much of a fan. Not that any of that mattered. We were adults, now. Time to move past childish grudges.

"She has a right, of course, but Ashley told Lizzie that Ashley's aunt told her that Jolene's new boyfriend just happens to be the CEO of the Chamber of Commerce."

Oh. Well, that might have the power to ruin my chances. "But surely they'll have a board or something—more than one person to decide?"

Josie shook her head. "I don't know, Mom. It just seems like wherever that woman is, there's trouble. Ever wonder who started the rumor we had rats last winter?"

I laughed. "This is the first time I'm hearing about it."

Josie exchanged a look with Maggie. "We tried to keep it from you. Figured you'd get worked up over nothing."

"Over nothing is right. I don't remember our bookings suffering last winter, do you?"

"Well, no."

I smiled. "Josie, I'm not going to lose sleep over Jolene or her boyfriend or the grant. If it's meant to be, it will be."

A shrill scream came from above us. The guest rooms? Luna?

"Speaking of adventure," Josie muttered as we all raced up the stairs.

10

I rounded the red-carpeted landing of the stairs and hurried up the last section, Maggie and Josie hot on my heels. I reached the top step to see Luna backing out of the Emerson room. "Mr. Emerson—I—I mean, Mr. Ellis, I am so, so sorry."

She shut the door to the Emerson room and dropped the basket of clean linens, her hands flying to her face.

"Luna, what happened?" I rushed to her side, keeping my voice low so as not to disturb the guests.

Not to disturb them *anymore* that is, considering Luna's screams had just accomplished that.

"Oh, Miss Hannah!" she wailed, her breaths coming in short puffs.

I led her toward the second-story entrance to our private quarters. Digging a key from my pocket, we slid through. Josie grabbed the basket of linens and Maggie followed, closing the door behind us.

Luna entered her bedroom and sank onto Lizzie's old flowered bedspread, tears streaming down her cheeks.

"Luna, what happened?" I asked, though I had my suspicions.

The Emerson room hadn't been cleared to be cleaned yet. I'd told Luna to clean the Alcott room after I'd ensured that the Tavares couple had left the premises, likely for the day. Not everyone used the "Do Not Disturb" signs.

"I—I finished cleaning the Alcott room and I thought you'd be happy if I got a head start on the others. I knocked before I unlocked it, I swear I did, but he mustn't have heard me from the bathroom. And when I came in, he was walking out of the bathroom . . . naked!" She ended on a wail and Josie muffled a giggle into her sleeve. Maggie elbowed her.

"Oh, honey." I sank beside Luna. "Remember I told you I have to make sure the rooms are clear first?" I felt like I was speaking to a toddler. The girl's heart was in the right place, but her brains sometimes, not so much.

"I—I know. But I thought I knew what car the Ellis's drove and I wanted to surprise you, but I guess I made a mistake."

"It happens," I assured her, although it had never happened *here*. I prided myself on making our guests as welcome and comfortable as possible. I wasn't sure the Ellises would ever come back after this mistake. I sighed. "We'll learn from it, is all. Someday, we'll be laughing about it."

But this only caused Luna to wail louder.

Josie cleared her throat. "One time, we didn't stock enough toilet paper in the Frost room and a guest screamed bloody murder until I went in and rolled her some across the bathroom floor."

I furrowed my brow. Huh. I'd never heard *that* story. Maggie wore an expression that must have been identical to mine.

Luna sniffed. "But at least you didn't see her naked. I'm sorry, Miss Hannah. I'm so sorry. I'll do whatever I can to make it up to you. I'll do thirty loads of laundry—I'll do dishes for the next three weeks, anything!"

Three weeks? So, Luna did appear to be making this stay long-term after all.

"Honey, we all make mistakes. We'll write Mr. and Mrs. Ellis an apology note and give them a discount on their stay. That's all that can be done."

"But then you're losing money."

"Not much. It's okay, Luna. Really."

She rubbed her stomach. "I'm not feeling so well. Would it be okay if I lay down for a bit?"

"Of course. I can handle things from here." We walked out of the bedroom and closed the door, bustling back downstairs to the kitchen.

"She's a nervous one, isn't she?" Josie opened the refrigerator and grabbed an apple, tossing it up in the air and catching it.

Maggie grimaced. "Poor thing. I think I'll make her some tea and bring it up to her in a bit."

"I'm sure she'll appreciate that." I placed the basket of clean linens on a barstool chair before turning to Josie. "You never told me about the toilet paper roll incident. We're normally so careful about stocking enough."

Josie shot me a sheepish grin. "Oh, that. Well, it was more a scene I'm writing in one of my books than something that actually happened."

"Josie!"

She shrugged. "I just felt bad for her, you know? I couldn't think of anything to make her feel better until I remembered that scene."

I shook my head. I may not be able to get on board with telling untruths, but I could get on board with Josie trying to console Luna. If compassion could overrule Josie's stubbornness, then perhaps there was hope for my children to form a relationship with Amos's daughter after all.

KEVIN CLAPPED A HAND ON OWEN'S SHOULDER AS THEY looked at the clean siding of the Victorian. It had been a long day, but Owen had surprised him by not complaining once and only taking out his phone when they took breaks. Though the teenager had been unsure about the power washing at first, Kevin had guided him, and to his surprise, the boy had heeded his advice.

"It looks great!" Hannah emerged from the bookshop, laptop under her arm, hair pulled back in a low ponytail.

By now, Kevin was accustomed to his stomach doing flip-flops in her presence. Ever since their fireside chat earlier in the week, he could think of little else than how to go about asking his neighbor on a date.

"You guys did amazing."

Something that resembled a smile pulled at the corner of Owen's mouth. Before Kevin could appreciate its presence, though, it vanished. "He worked hard."

Hannah fished a wad of cash out of her back pocket and handed it to Owen. "I can't tell you how happy I am to have this checked off my list. Thank you, Owen."

Owen took the money and glanced at Kevin. He nodded.

"I hope you guys are hungry. Lasagna's in the oven."

"We'll go get cleaned up and come back over." Kevin pulled his damp t-shirt away from his chest. Hannah's gaze followed his movement.

Hey, he might not be twenty-five anymore, but a guy didn't work in the logging industry for almost forty years and come out looking like a flabby fish. Maybe he could still catch the ladies' eyes, after all. Only, he had to admit, there was just one lady whose eye he was interested in catching in that moment.

Hannah met his gaze and a spark passed between them. She felt it too, didn't she?

She smiled, her teeth white against her slightly tanned skin. "Sounds good."

"See you soon, then." But he needed to make his feet move. He needed to pull himself away from that captivating smile.

She cocked her head, a bemused grin on her face before she walked toward the Victorian.

Man, he had it bad. Not since he'd started dating Katherine had he been this smitten with a woman.

He turned toward his property, keeping in time with Owen's slow steps. "You did a great job today."

"It was all right." The boy's shoulders slumped. He held up the wad of cash, still tight in his fist. "How much of this are you gonna let me keep?"

Kevin eyed the boy. "All of it."

Owen blinked. "What? Why?"

Kevin shrugged. "I don't much need it and between you and me, I kind of have a crush on our new neighbor. Wouldn't feel right taking the money for myself, but she wouldn't hear of us doing the job unless she paid."

Owen shoved the money in his pocket. "Sam used to make me give him seventy."

Kevin forced his legs to keep moving, forced himself not to show surprise at this first piece of voluntary information Owen gave him about his former life. "Seventy . . ."

"Percent. When I worked grocery pickup at Walmart."

"Who's Sam?" Kevin strove for a casual tone.

"Thought Ms. Bridges would have told you about him."

"Can't recall that she did."

Owen shrugged. "It's nothing. I don't have to see him again, so it doesn't matter." The teenager opened the door of their house and stepped inside.

No way. A door with the boy had finally opened, and Kevin had every intention of pushing through it. Before his nephew could run and hide upstairs. "Owen, it matters to me. Who's Sam?"

The kid sighed, took his phone out of his pocket, and began

scrolling mindlessly. But even Kevin could see it was a nervous reaction—that whatever was on the screen was not what captured the boy's attention. "Mom's boyfriend."

Of course. "You didn't like him?"

Owen let out a humorless laugh. "Oh yeah, he and I were chums. So close I made real good friends with his fists."

A surge of hot anger welled up within Kevin, spreading down his arms and to his own hands, which he clenched. "Ms. Bridges never said anything."

Another shrug. "Maybe she didn't know. I thought Mom had told her, but maybe she didn't care enough."

"No one should have to be treated like that, Owen."

"Yeah, well, Mom didn't do anything about—" He shook his head. "Whatever." He started up the stairs. "What time do I need to be back down?"

"Can you do ten minutes?"

The teenager grunted.

Kevin followed the boy up the stairs where he entered his own bedroom. He stripped off his wet clothes and jumped into the shower. As he scrubbed away the dirt and sweat of the day, he tried to keep his anger toward his sister at bay. Why would she put her son in such danger?

Then again, why had Deidra done any number of things she'd done the last twenty years? Drugs, most likely. For the first time, he wondered if a reunification between Deidra and Owen was possible. What would happen if Deidra kept missing her scheduled visits? Owen could certainly stay here. Sure, it wasn't the picture he'd had in mind for retirement, but maybe it was the plan God had. A better plan, even.

If only the good Lord would help him navigate how to get the boy to continue opening up to him.

I navigated toward the picnic benches near Lake Megunticook, hummingbird cake in hand. Luna had helped me bake it yesterday afternoon, and with the exception of a possible broken eggshell or two, I expected it to be a hit.

As we walked toward the crowd of familiar parishioners, Luna seemed to shrink inside herself. Again and again, it amazed me how a twenty-one-year-old woman could be so entirely unsure of herself, so entirely naïve. Yes, I'd seen high schoolers act this way, but it was as if Luna lacked surety in everything she did, which in turn made her more nervous and prone to social gaffes.

I thought back to the night before when Kevin and Owen had come for dinner. I noted the visible effort Luna made to be friendly and outgoing. She seemed to sense Owen's own insecurity, and even attempted to draw him out of his shell, somewhat successfully I might add. Why so bashful now?

"Mom!" Lizzie waved from where she sat with her friend Ashley and a couple members of the worship team. Not too far away, Asher played volleyball in his wheelchair designed for maneuvering in the sand.

When I reached her, I bent to give her a hug, squeezing her

tight with one arm while balancing the cake plate with the other. "How are you feeling?"

"I'm good." She beamed. "I'm feeling better than I have in a long time, actually."

"I'm so glad." IVF treatments had been rough on her. Both physically and emotionally. "I've been praying for you guys like crazy," I whispered in her ear. She'd be going for the embryo transfer next week.

"Thank you." Lizzie turned to Luna. "I heard you've been a big help at Orchard House."

Luna's face colored. "I don't know about that, but I'm trying to learn."

"She's doing great. Better every day." I gave Luna a wink. "I'm going to find a place for this cake. I'll catch up with you later, Lizzie?"

"Sure thing." Lizzie pushed over on the bench to make room. "Luna, let me introduce you to my friends."

Thank you, Lizzie.

I walked over to find the dessert table, stopping to chat with several people I hadn't seen in a while. I missed this. Though I tried to attend a Wednesday night Bible study, worship on Sunday mornings was a challenge with breakfast to serve. It was the only part of running the bed and breakfast that I sometimes resented.

I placed the cake on the table and laid a serving spatula alongside it. A presence came up beside me, leaning over the table. "When's it okay to dig into that?" My blood ran hot in my veins. Kevin.

I elbowed him. "I don't think there's any hard and fast rules, but I'd assume before the hamburgers and hotdogs are served is frowned upon."

He snapped his fingers. "Church picnics are all about timing. It's almost like a game. A game I'm bound to lose."

I squinted, the corners of my mouth tugging upwards. "How so?"

"You see all these people here?"

"Yes."

"How many would you say are in attendance?"

"I've always been bad at this game—the game where you guess how much candy is in a jar?" I shrugged. "Seventy-five? One hundred?"

"I think that's about right. Now, how many slices of cake you think are under that glass dish?"

I tapped my chin, playing along. "Depends who's cutting. Twelve, maybe fifteen."

"So, you're telling me that my chances of getting a piece of cake could be as low as twelve percent. That's why I'm voting for having a piece now."

I laughed. "Don't be silly. There's dessert enough for everyone."

"But after eating your lasagna, homemade sourdough bread, and that strawberry shortcake that I'll be dreaming about until the cows come home, I'm betting that your cake is going to be gone."

"Hmm, this is a dilemma. There's only one solution, I suppose." Was I *flirting* again? I was. And I was thoroughly enjoying it.

He stepped an inch closer and the scent of him—aftershave and woodsmoke and eucalyptus wound around me, making me dizzy. "Cut the cake now?" he said, his voice all low and sultry.

"I think in the case of a serious dilemma such as this one, it's only wise to ask ourselves what Jesus would do in such a predicament."

Kevin swayed forward. "Has Jesus ever tasted your cake?"

I burst into laughter and swatted his chest.

"Fine, fine. First shall be last and all that. I can take a hint, Hannah Martin. If I really want to impress you, I'm going to need to let all these other fine folks have first dibs at that cake, aren't I?"

I shrugged, raised my eyebrows. "It might seem so."

"Whatever it takes." His smile faded. "I had a really nice time last night. In fact, I was wondering if—"

"Hey, Mom." Bronson walked up beside me and slung an arm over my shoulder. I loved my son. Loved him to death.

But his timing couldn't have been worse.

Hmm. Or better, if Bronson had his way.

Kevin took a step away as Bronson pulled me in tighter, scanning my neighbor from head to toe.

"Hey, Bron." I squeezed an arm around his waist. "Where's Morgan?"

"Oh, she's already chit-chatting with Lizzie and her friends. When I saw you two over here, thought I'd come say hi." He held out a hand to Kevin. "How's the neighborhood treating you?"

Kevin shoved his hand into Bronson's. The men didn't take their eyes off one another. Oh boy. "Good. Real good. A beautiful town." Kevin glanced at me, and Bronson turned in my direction. "Mom, could I talk to you for a minute?"

"Of course." I smiled at Kevin. "I'll catch up with you later?"

"I hope so."

I swallowed and followed Bronson off to a secluded spot away from the beach in the shade of a pine. The scent of the tree calmed my racing heart. What had Kevin been about to ask me?

"Mom, what's going on?"

"What do you mean?"

"Oh, don't act like you weren't getting all cozy-cozy with that guy right in the middle of the church picnic, no less. You barely know him."

I folded my arms in front of myself and raised my eyebrows at my only son. "Honey, I am a fifty-two-year-old woman who's raised five children and survived the love of her life by five years now. I hardly think I should be made to feel guilty for enjoying another man's company in the middle of a social gathering."

"But what do you really know about this guy? He seems awful

into you for knowing you for what, a week? And the fact that he's right next door all the time . . ."

I breathed deep, seeking compassion for my son. It was only because he loved me that he showed concern. I placed a hand on his arm. "Bronson, I consider myself a good judge of character. Don't you trust me?"

Bronson sought out Kevin in the crowd. "It's men I don't trust."

I laughed. "Do you have something against your own sex?"

"I'm one of the good guys, Mom. How do you know your new neighbor is, too? Anyone can hang at church picnics, you know."

"Oh yes, all the crazies show up to church picnics. Honey, you're acting like I'm some hormone-addled teen."

He wrinkled his nose in disgust—I supposed at the thought of his mom having hormones. Heaven forbid.

I continued. "I've been around the block a time or two. I've had some great conversations with Kevin. From what I can tell, he's a good guy. Besides, we're only neighbors. He hasn't even asked me out yet."

"You won't mind me having a chat with him first, would you?"

"I would in fact mind, thank you very much."

Bronson grew quiet. Finally, he opened his mouth to speak. "I just wonder if all this stuff with Dad and Luna . . . I wonder if it might make you emotional and more susceptible to falling for the promises of the first man who shows interest."

I tapped my foot on the ground. "You think Kevin's the first man who's shown interest?"

Bronson's face reddened. "Well, no. That's not what I'm—ew, gross, Mom. Can we not talk about this?"

I squeezed his forearm. "Bronson, I love you. And I'll admit, Luna is a bit of a plot twist. But I'm stronger than I look. I'm not running to a man because I feel suddenly betrayed by your father. Remember, I knew about his affair."

My son winced, and my heart spilled open.

"How are you holding up?" Though I'd sent him a couple of texts, we hadn't really spoken since the revelation about Amos and Luna.

He shook his head, brushing me off. "I'm fine. Just worried about you." But the way his shoulders slumped, the way he avoided my eyes, told me otherwise.

"Bronson." I gentled my tone, attempting to pull my son out of himself—something I had a lot of practice doing throughout his teenage years.

He shoved his hands in his pockets and stared out towards the lake. Though our crisp Maine temperatures hadn't quite reached *hot*, some of the children bounded toward the beach in their bathing suits.

"I hate how this changes the way I feel about him," he finally said.

I stepped toward my son, placing a hand on his arm. "I'm so sorry." I closed my eyes, wishing my words were enough, wishing I could do something to fix the pain radiating from him. "He loved you, honey. He loved all of us." If I had my way, my kids would have never known the extent of their father's sins. Not because I wanted to build a fairytale of Amos's character, but because I hated to see them hurt by his actions.

"He had a funny way of proving it." Bronson's bitter words littered the warm spring air.

I dragged in a deep breath. Part of me was tired of defending my late husband—to my kids, and to myself. How many times had I made excuses for Amos? He was away from his family because he wanted to do good in the world. He didn't help around the house because his distracted, brilliant mind was too busy with more important things. He didn't spend enough time with the kids while they were growing up because he was off building a bigger, better world for them.

Who had I been kidding?

I prayed for wisdom to saturate my next words. "Bronson, like all of us, your father was undeniably human. Prone to falter. Believe me when I tell you how remorseful he was over the affair."

My mind raced back to that awful night, to Amos in tears as he sat on our bed, confessing his transgression. As his words sank in, as I came to grasp them, the first emotion that filled me when I pictured him being intimate with another woman was anger.

What right did *he* have to be emotional? As if *I* should be the one to comfort him. And why was he sitting on our bed—the bed where we'd made love countless times. We'd shared our secrets and dreams there. It was supposed to be a sacred space.

But Amos had allowed another in.

I'd asked him to leave that night, and he had. To this day, I still don't know where he went. To Aunt Pris's home? To his office? To the mission? To *her*?

By the time he returned the next morning, I'd already known I would forgive him. Not because I was convinced it was what God would want or even that it was what was best for my marriage, but for one reason and one reason only. Well, five reasons.

Our children.

If Amos and I separated, the kids would see him less than they already did. Just imagining the pain and confusion on their small faces as I told them their father and I were getting a divorce was enough to make me suck in my own pain and seek reconciliation with my husband.

We sought counseling and although it helped to dig deeper into our problems, after a few months Amos's schedule again became busy. He missed dinners. It was a year before we shared the same bed.

Was it wise to have stayed with him for the sake of our children? I can't honestly say I didn't question myself over and over again throughout the years. Not until the day of Amos's funeral, when his absence made me miss his presence all the more, when I consoled my kids and they did the same for me, could I honestly say I was glad we worked through the tough times. I had no regrets. I'd given my marriage my all. I *loved* my husband. And our love had helped to grow the most precious people I knew.

Now, I reached out a hand to my only son, who reminded me of his father in every way—from his tall stature to his deep-thinking ponderings. "Honey, you're going to have to forgive him just like I did all those years ago." I shook my head. "No. You don't have to forgive him, that's your choice. But it would kill me to see you carrying this pain around. Please, give it over to God. It's the only way toward peace."

Bronson's jaw softened a bit. "I'll try. I'm sorry about what you went through all those years ago. You never spoke badly about Dad—I never would have guessed."

I smiled. "That was God's strength, too." I straightened. "Looks like they're starting an official volleyball game."

He gave me a side-hug. "Right, don't want to miss showing up Pastor Greg on the court." He started to walk away, then turned. "I love you, Mom. You've done a great job with us."

Tears pricked my eyelids, but I swallowed them down. "I love you too, honey. Thank you. That means the world to me."

He left and I stood beneath the pine tree, gathering myself, counting my blessings, and looking forward to what the future might bring.

12

Kevin finished the last bite of his hamburger as he listened to Lizzie's husband, Asher, talk about the hiking program Lizzie headed up based out of his store, *Paramount Sports*.

Wait a minute. "*Paramount Sports?* You're the manager?"

Beside Asher, Lizzie smiled broadly. "He's the creator and owner. All of the Paramount stores are his."

Asher gave her a look that said, "Stop bragging on me," but she just shrugged.

"It's your store? That's amazing. Do you know how much I've spent on fishing equipment there? I can't stay away. All your products are top-of-the-line."

Asher smiled, angling his wheelchair in Kevin's direction. "Glad to hear it. Next time you plan on going out, let me know if you'd want some company."

"I would love some company." He'd never had time for fishing buddies with his business. It'd be great to find some guys who enjoyed the sport.

Bronson jogged down from where he'd been speaking to Hannah. "You guys in on this game?" He gestured to the volleyball net.

Wow. Bronson was actually including him? The way he'd elbowed in earlier with Hannah and practically dragged her away . . . well, he wouldn't have expected an invitation.

Unless Bronson planned to spike the ball in his face . . .

"I'm in." Asher began rolling his wheelchair onto the court. Kevin wasn't certain, but this wheelchair looked different from the one he'd seen him play flag football in the other night—wider tires, likely made for sand. Asher turned toward Kevin. "You in?"

Kevin searched the picnic area for Owen. There. On his phone beside a boy about his age who was also on his phone.

Before Kevin had a chance to answer, Josie bounded up to Asher. "I don't want to hear any claims that you can't move fast in the sand this time, Hill. You hear me?"

Asher pretended to brush lint off the arms of his shirt. "Are we still a wee sour over last year's volleyball game, Colton?"

Josie scowled at him. "Oh, please. I had just had a baby. This time, you're going down."

"Excuses, excuses." Asher rolled his eyes, but a smile tugged at his mouth.

"Mags, where are you? I need my setup partner!" Josie called.

Maggie ran over, dark hair bouncing in her ponytail. "Here! Hold up for Josh, though. He has a vendetta against Pastor Greg from last year."

"Man, you guys take your church sports seriously around here," Kevin said.

"You have no idea." Josie's husband—Tripp, Kevin thought his name was—bounced their son a safe distance from the sidelines before turning to Asher. "Go easy on my wife, okay? If not, I'll have to hunt you down."

Lizzie brought over a lawn chair and set it beside Tripp. A pretty redhead, Bronson's wife, did the same. "We'll watch Amos and Eddie if you want to play, Tripp."

"Not going to turn that down." Tripp handed Eddie off to Lizzie, who smiled in adoration at the infant.

They divided into teams, Lizzie's friend Ashley joining in alongside a woman who'd handed out bulletins when Kevin had attended church that morning. Pastor Greg and a couple other guys joined in.

"Wait, we're down one." Bronson looked around the court, counting the players.

"Yeah, better make it even or we'll never hear the end of it from the Colton crew over there," Asher teased.

Josie stuck her tongue out at him.

Kevin spotted Hannah near Lizzie, leaning over to tickle Josie's small son on the cheek. "Hannah!" he called. "Help us out? We're short a player."

Josie laughed loud enough for the entire court to hear. "Don't think Kevin here knows who he's talking to."

"Yeah, Mom's not really a sports kind of girl," Bronson said. "But she wins the cooking competitions every time."

Hannah straightened. "I'll play." She kicked off her sandals and jogged toward Kevin. She moved more like a graceful ballerina on those tiny ankles than a volleyball player, but he didn't care if she moved like a robot. As long as he got to spend more time with her.

Bronson's eyebrows drew together. "You will?"

"Sure." She shrugged. "It's been a while, but I'll try my best."

Kevin winked at her. "It's supposed to be fun."

"Have you met my children?" She spread her feet apart, searching out the ball. Looked like she might have a clue how to play, after all.

"Are we done yapping?" Pastor Greg teased. "Let's get this game going!"

Josie served first and Ashley returned it easily back over the net. Tripp set up Maggie, who, despite her best efforts, wasn't able to return the ball to the other side of the court.

"Next time, Mags." Maggie's husband clapped his hands.

"Come on, Mommy!" Maggie's twins yelled from beside Lizzie, where Luna had also settled.

Bronson served next. Pastor Greg slammed it back over. Asher hit it to a short guy with a man bun, then back over to Josh who returned it easily. Kevin lobbed it into the air, hoping to set up the front row.

"I got it!" Hannah called. She jumped higher than he thought possible for such a petite woman and spiked the ball over the net. It landed hard at Tripp's feet.

Their team erupted in cheers. Kevin high-fived his neighbor. "Great shot."

"Nice setup." Her face flushed from the exertion.

"Mom! Where did that come from?" Josie flung her arms into the sky, then placed a hand on her head. "Who are you and what have you done with Hannah Martin?"

Hannah laughed. "Didn't I ever tell you I was captain of the volleyball team back in college?"

Maggie and Josie exchanged looks of disbelief. Bronson clapped his hands. "All right. Let's get this thing done!"

A half-hour and a near shut-out later, the game finished— Kevin, Hannah, Asher, and Bronson's team winning.

They conducted a round of high-fives. "Way to go, Mom. You turned out to be our secret weapon. I had no idea." Bronson high-fived his mother.

"That felt good." Strands of hair worked their way out of her ponytail. Her face glowed. Man-oh-man, she was gorgeous.

"Another round?" Josie asked. "Mags and I got caught off guard. We need to redeem ourselves."

"You up for it?" Kevin asked Hannah.

She nodded.

Ashley hopped out of the game and with some persuasion, Luna took her place. Two games later, Josie was claiming the teams weren't structured evenly and everyone traded in volleyball for dessert.

Kevin approached the dessert table. Hannah's cake plate sat empty.

"Looking for this?" She sidled up beside him, her eyes twinkling, a piece of cake on a small white paper plate.

"I was, but there's no way I'm taking it from you."

"I got it for you. I'd much rather have Linda Snow's lemon squares."

"Well, who am I to—"

"Mom, no more cake?" Bronson stared in obvious disappointment at the empty cake platter. "I knew I should have ditched volleyball early."

Kevin held the plate out to Bronson. "Lucky for you, there's one left."

Bronson seemed to size him up. "You sure?"

"Absolutely."

Bronson took the plate, forking into it with gusto. "You know, Kevin, you're all right, man." He sauntered away, practically inhaling the cake.

Kevin met Hannah's gaze, her eyes shining up at him.

"What?"

"Oh, nothing. I think my son's right though. You're all right."

Though he didn't have much adrenaline left after the volleyball playing, Hannah's words served up a fresh surge flowing through his veins, pumping his heart. Maybe "you're all right" wasn't extraordinary, but for some reason, coming from her lips, it was more than enough.

❧ 13 ❧

I leaned back in my wicker chair on the patio and closed my eyes, my muscles aching even after the Epsom salt bath I'd taken. Oh, it felt good to sit.

The flames of the fire danced against the stone backdrop of the fire pit, casting shadows on my feet. What a good day. A very good day. The only thing that could make it better was some end-of-the-night company by the fire. But I still didn't have Kevin's number. Hopefully, we'd rectify that soon.

What had he been about to ask me when Bronson interrupted us? And how long would I have to wait to find out?

The sound of a door closing came from Kevin's property. My heart sped up.

His porch light turned on but I didn't see an approaching shadow.

Well, not all women had to wait for the man to make the first move. Ruth and Boaz and all that.

I pushed myself onto my sore feet and walked across the grass toward the stone wall to where Kevin sat in a long-sleeved flannel and jeans, rocking on his porch. "Howdy, neighbor," he called.

I smiled. "Howdy. Any chance you want to come and join me by the fire?" I asked.

"Big chance. Didn't want to push my luck by going over, though. Just in case you were sick of me."

"I'm not." My voice came out all sing-songy, and I scolded myself. *Tone it down a bit, Hannah.* I'd always been level-headed. Now was not the time to go boy—ahem, man-crazy. I cleared my throat. "No pressure, of course. You might be sick of *me*."

"I'll be right over."

I returned to the patio and a moment later I looked up to see Kevin holding a bottle of wine, two glasses, and a corkscrew. "Just for the record. I don't think I could ever get sick of seeing you," he said.

My pulse thrummed against my wrist, my neck, my temples—every single avenue of my body.

"Would you like a glass of wine?" He raised the bottle.

"Okay." I sat up, watching him uncork the bottle with a satisfying pop. He poured the red wine into two glasses and handed one to me, holding it up. "What are we toasting?"

"How about new beginnings?"

I smiled. "And maybe muscles that don't ache like the dickens tomorrow morning?"

He laughed a gusty baritone chortle that filled the evening air with joy and promise. "I wasn't going to say anything myself, but I will definitely drink to that."

We clinked glasses, catching one another's gazes as we drank.

"That's good," I said.

"Had it for a few years. Was saving it for a special occasion."

I raised an eyebrow.

He averted his gaze to the flickering flames. "I figured me asking a woman out on a date for the first time since I lost my Katherine was special occasion enough."

Oh. I blinked. *Oh.*

"So, what do you say? Will you go on a date with me?"

I smiled. So, that *is* what he'd been going to ask me earlier. "I'd love to."

He released a long breath. "Phew."

I laughed. "You did it."

"I did."

I brought my legs up beneath my body. "I have to admit, I didn't think I'd ever date again after Amos died."

"Really? You're beautiful, you're young—"

I laughed. "Tell that to my aching joints. That volleyball court kicked my rear end today."

"Oh, I think you showed it a thing or two. Your kids, too. You surprised them."

We grew quiet. My thoughts tangled in the events of the day. "You know, I think I've been a mother for so long—and now a grandmother—that I forgot there may be more. Don't get me wrong, being a mother and a grandmother is my favorite thing, and I love running this business, but somewhere along the way, I wonder if I haven't lost a part of myself, too."

I wondered if he thought me silly. Maybe this was more of a woman problem—losing ourselves in our family because we love them more than life itself.

"Your kids didn't know you played volleyball in college."

"I'm certain I told them at some point."

"Tell me. Tell me what you used to love. Tell me what you love now."

My face burned. "I'm really not that interesting."

"I'm one-hundred percent certain that's not true."

He searched my eyes with his and once again, I wondered what it'd feel like to be kissed by this man.

I shifted my legs, hugging my knees to my chest and savoring the cool breeze in the night air against my skin. "I was a book-loving, food-creating, volleyball captain back in college. Amos and I had been in love since high school. We married my junior year of college, and I had Maggie a few months after getting my degree. Other than working part-time at the library across the street, I've been a full-time mom. My kids are my life and my treasure. They helped me open this place. I never would have been able to do it without their encouragement." I pressed my lips together. What would my children think of me dating Kevin? Luna's arrival had thrown us into a tailspin. Was I being inconsiderate to give my kids more to handle?

But no. They were all adults, planning their own lives and futures. Was it not healthy for me to plan my own?

My worries softened beneath the blanket of an unspoken prayer. Almost as if God was assuring me before I could allow my anxieties to grow. One day at a time. To be content with each sunrise and sunset was a gift I was only beginning to learn. If only I could remember.

"What about you?" I sipped my wine, consciously going slow as I wasn't much of a drinker.

A soft smile curved his lips. "I went to a vocational high school down in Massachusetts. Ended up in the arbor program and knew I wanted to work with trees for the rest of my life. After high school I was hired by a tree service company in the Portland area, and I fell in love with the owner's daughter. We married and a few years later I started my own logging company. Spent too much time at work and didn't realize what a mistake I was making until it was too late."

I allowed his words to sift through the air. Everything about Kevin seemed laidback and carefree. With his tattoos and humor, I found it hard to believe he'd ever let work get the better of him.

"I'm so sorry."

"I sold the business last year. Too little, too late, maybe. But I needed a change of pace, a change in scenery."

"That's a big step. Do you miss it? Work, I mean?"

"I haven't let myself get bored enough to miss it. I'm not one for sitting around. I'll probably set up a small business here in town for tree jobs, but nothing like the shindig I ran before."

I hadn't realized it until now, but I'd been comparing Kevin to Amos. Thinking he was so very different than my husband. Yet, from the sounds of it, Kevin and Amos had been alike in their drive for work—Kevin with his business, Amos with his well-meaning charities and projects. No doubt, Kevin's wife's death had caused him to reconsider his life, as Amos's death had done for me as well.

For the first time, I pondered what would have happened to Amos if I had been the one to leave this earthly life first. Would he have changed? Torn himself away from work to spend more time with the kids and grandkids? I would never know. One only had the preciousness of each sunrise to build their legacy.

"How are things with Owen?"

Kevin smiled. "Difficult. But we had a small moment yesterday after we power washed."

"Glimpses of grace, I used to call them."

"Yup. No better word for it." He cleared his throat. "You telling me your kids weren't always the perfect people they are now?"

A laugh bubbled up in my chest. "Were you not part of the same volleyball game I was in today?"

"So, they're a little competitive. I like that. They have spirit."

"More than they sometimes know what to do with. But you're right, it keeps it interesting. Perfect, though? Far from it. We had some bumpy years with each of them, but I remember those moments where we'd find common ground."

Kevin took a sip of his wine, then placed it on the small table in front of us. "Owen spoke about his life before foster care. It's the first time he's mentioned my sister."

"That sounds like progress."

"I thought so. Too bad he clammed up as soon as I started asking questions."

"I'm sure it will take some time for you to earn his trust. He's likely been through a lot. Trusting doesn't come easy for kids who've been hurt every time they've tried to depend on someone."

"I never thought of it like that. You know, you're a pretty smart lady, Hannah Martin."

I shook my head. "You don't have to butter me up. I already said I'd go on a date with you."

"Speaking of which. How does tomorrow night look?"

I scooped up my phone from the table, tapping open the calendar app. "Oh, I'm at the mission tomorrow night. What about Tuesday?"

"What's the mission?"

"My husband's one successful venture." A smile softened my mouth as I remembered how Amos had openly joked about this fact. "It started as a place for the needy to get a hot meal, blankets, and winter coats but several churches got behind it and it quickly morphed into something bigger than any of us expected. Amos handed it over to a church in Rockport. They've grown it exponentially. Hot meals every day, a place for a limited number of residents to sleep, resources for them to obtain jobs. They're starting some classes in the fall. I help a couple times a month. I don't know, it makes me feel like I'm continuing Amos's legacy, you know?"

"That sounds awesome. I wouldn't be opposed to accompanying you if they need an extra pair of hands."

"Oh." The word left my mouth before I could stop it, Kevin's offer bringing up a plethora of surprise emotions within me.

"I'm sorry. That was presumptuous. It was your husband's project, and likely yours. It's foolish of me to think I could shuffle my way in. Forget I said anything. Tuesday is perfect."

I shook my head. "No, Kevin, it's not that. It would be wonderful for you to come sometime. It's just, I'm taking Luna tomorrow. I wanted to show her a piece of Amos."

In truth, it hadn't been easy for me to invite the young woman in the first place. What was this crazy need to shield Amos's mission from Luna? I couldn't understand it, felt it was not honoring to Amos's memory, and so I cast it aside and invited Luna. She'd eagerly accepted.

It wasn't as if I didn't want Kevin to join us, but it felt insensitive to Luna. Yet, why did I feel I owed the girl so much? It was not my fault she didn't know her father. It was not my fault her mother died so tragically last Christmas Eve. I'd brought her in, given her food and support and an opportunity to know her half-siblings. What more must I give?

The bitter thoughts stalled me.

No. This was not the woman I wanted to be—a woman consumed with what her fair share in life would be. I'd vowed to live by grace and faith, not fear and selfishness.

"I'm sorry," I whispered to Kevin.

"Don't be. I can't imagine all the feelings Luna's arrival has brought up. And now here I am, asking you out, elbowing in on your husband's mission. If you want to wait to go on a date until things settle down, I'm okay with that. Whatever makes you comfortable."

My heart softened, melting in my chest. "That's very sweet. But if I've learned one thing with my family, it's that things don't settle. I *want* to go out with you. Tuesday still okay?"

Those green eyes landed on me, drawing me in, threatening to take me under. "Tuesday is perfect."

14

I pulled into the parking lot of the mission and unbuckled my seatbelt. Luna stared up at the large building. Her gaze caught on the bold sign at the top.

"It's named after him. I didn't realize . . ."

I looked at the sign, trying to see it through Luna's eyes. *Amos House.*

I folded my hands in my lap, curling my fingers around my keys. "We've gotten into the habit of calling it simply, 'the mission.' The church that took it over renamed it. I think in part to honor my husband"—I swallowed—"your father. But it's a twofold meaning. Are you familiar with the Amos in the Bible?"

She shook her head.

"Amos was a prophet. Among other things, he spoke against those who loved religion but ignored the poor. Those who clung to social differences as a means of God's approval."

Luna didn't speak at first, but simply stared at the sign. "So, Amos wanted people to show love through action."

"Yes, that's exactly it." While I didn't know if she spoke of the prophet Amos or my husband Amos, it made little difference. Their heart for the poor had been the same.

Luna glanced at me and smiled. A large gap was present in the middle of her two front teeth—a trait Josie and Amie had shared before braces. "I like that." She looked out the window but didn't move for the door handle. "Do you think . . . do you think if he knew that—I mean, it's not like we were homeless or anything, but we got food stamps and I had free lunches at school. Do you think if he knew Mom had trouble paying the rent, he would have helped us?"

A muscle in my chest cramped. "Yes. I can say without a doubt Amos would have helped you." Even if that meant Bronson would have had to scour the thrift store for basketball shoes, that we'd have to live off beans and rice a couple nights of the week, that I would've spent even more hours on the phone trying to reduce Lizzie's medical bills . . . I could say without a doubt that Amos would have helped Luna and her mother. Because that's what he did. Went above and beyond, even if it meant his family suffered.

But no. Luna *had* been Amos's family, too, even if he hadn't known it.

I wet my lips. "Luna." The girl looked at me expectantly. "Did your mother say why she never told Amos about you?"

She bit her lip. "She didn't, but I have a feeling it had to do with him already having a family. I don't think she wanted to screw you guys up by bringing me into it." She laughed, a humorless sound. "Guess I took care of that this past week, didn't I?"

I placed my warm hand on her cold one. "It's good that you came. No one should be alone. Especially when they have family."

She swiped at her nose. "Thank you, Miss Hannah. You taking me in, bringing me here, letting me help out at the bed and breakfast, it's the nicest thing anyone has done for me."

"Oh honey." I squeezed her hand. "I'm happy to do it. And while we're at it, how about if you call me Hannah?"

She smiled that wide, tooth-filled grin. "Okay."

I placed my hand on the car door. "Are you ready?"

She bit her lip and nodded.

When we entered the building, I greeted the woman behind a desk in the office off the lobby. "Hello, Martha."

The woman pushed aside a long, graying braid of hair. "Hannah! Has it been two weeks already?"

I stepped to the side so Martha could have a better look at Luna. "This is Luna. She's come to help today."

I'd decided not to volunteer Luna's association with Amos. I didn't want to make the girl uncomfortable. Not that revealing the fact would make me feel all warm and cozy, but in time, if Luna decided to continue the work at the mission and if she wanted to uncover her relationship to my husband, I would leave that to her. While it pained me to imagine Martha or Robert looking down on Amos, I'd leave the truth in Luna's hands.

"Well, we can always use the extra hands. They're serving chicken pot pie for supper tonight."

"We'll head down."

The mission kitchen and dining area was in the basement. We rounded the corner and started down a dim, curvy staircase that spilled out into the kitchen.

"Hannah!" Marie, a forty-five-year-old recent empty-nester looked up from where she cut carrots. Food safety gloves covered her hands. "So glad you're here. Larry and I were just debating how best to roll out this pastry dough for all these pies."

I introduced Marie, Larry, and Clara to Luna before washing my hands.

"You want to help me make sandwiches, honey?" Clara, a retired schoolteacher who'd been recently widowed, asked Luna.

"Sure." Luna went to the sink to wash her hands before pulling on the plastic gloves.

While I helped Marie and Larry with the pastry dough, I listened to Clara explain to Luna how the mission gave out bagged lunches in addition to a hot dinner.

An hour later, residents and guests began filing into the room, sitting at the long rectangle tables. We served coffee and plates of salad. Larry and Clara dished out the chicken pot pie while Luna, Marie, and I served them up.

Amos House consisted of men and women of varying ages and situations. Addiction played a big role for many, but others had simply fallen upon hard times or had never been taught important life skills like basic communication or how to fill out a job application.

"Hey, Miss Hannah." A woman in her early thirties with pale skin and haunting brown eyes looked up at me as I set a piece of cake in front of her.

"Missy." I gave her a warm smile. "How are you?"

"I applied to four places this month."

"That's great. Hear anything back?" I'd guided Missy through the application process for a local Walmart when I'd come two weeks ago.

"No. But I'm close to the top of the list to get into the bunkhouse here. Maybe after I have an address, my chances will be better."

"I'm sure they will be." I'd thought of Missy often this past month. And though I'd momentarily considered hiring her to clean rooms at Orchard House, her constant struggle with drugs caused me to brush the idea aside. I wanted to help. But the reality was Missy still had a long journey ahead of her. Getting a bed at Amos House would be her best bet at finding a job. Many of the men and women who came to the mission found themselves in a catch-twenty-two; they couldn't acquire jobs without a residence to put on their applications, but they couldn't find a residence without a job.

That's where Amos House tried to fill in, although the demand for beds greatly outweighed the space and staffing needs of the mission.

"You gonna help me today, right, Miss Hannah? You promised last time." A young man about Luna's age looked up at me with hazy eyes.

"Yes, Calvin. After dinner, let's meet upstairs."

Calvin shot Luna a long look from where she served cake on the other side of the room. "New girl?"

A prickle of something akin to mother-bear protection traveled through me. Well, well. Now *that* was a surprise.

"Yes, that's my friend Luna."

"She going to help me too?"

"I think it will only take one of us." I opened my mouth to tell Calvin to eat his cake, but thought better of it. Luna had survived twenty-one years without me protecting her. While Calvin could be considered handsome, no doubt the girl would be able to see past his looks to the troubled young man who made his home at the local jail as often as at Amos House.

We finished dinner service and after the residents and guests filed out, we cleaned up. As I wiped off one of the long tables, I noticed Calvin stop at the foot of the stairs to say something to Luna. She smiled and nodded at him, but didn't seem to be bowled over by his attentions.

Good. Maybe I needed to think more highly of Amos's daughter. She certainly proved herself in her efforts, if not skill, in helping me with the bed and breakfast. Just because a part of my subconscious mind assumed her mother's character to be less than admirable did not mean Luna had inherited those traits.

I swallowed down my thoughts and worked to refill the saltshakers. Luna's mother was likely an intelligent, honorable woman. Though it was easier to think of her as a tramp, something about her must have caught Amos's attention. My husband was captivated by brains and brilliance just as much as he was by beauty.

After we finished cleaning, I led Luna upstairs to the main gathering room. The space was utilitarian and simple—folding chairs, a couple desks along the side, a bathroom off to the left, and a stand at the front with a simple wooden cross hanging on the wall behind it. Services were held every night, and I usually stayed. Until then, I tried to connect with the residents.

"Would you ask Martha for the iPad?" I asked Luna.

A girl of about ten smiled up at me from where she played with a doll. Beside her, a young woman stared into her phone.

I lowered myself to the seat beside them. "Hello."

The woman's dark eyelashes fluttered, and she quickly put the phone in her pocket. "Hello."

I held out my hand. "I'm Hannah."

"Julie." The woman smiled, her white teeth perfect against her dark skin. She lightly tugged on the younger girl's braid. "And this is Angelina."

I held my hand out to the girl. "Angelina, it's nice to meet you." I turned to Julie. "I don't think I've seen you here before. Is this your first time at Amos House?"

"Oh, yes. I have an apartment up the street, just running tight on groceries right now."

"I understand." And I did. How many times had I made a meal out of a loaf of bread and four eggs when the kids were growing up? Sure, they loved the French toast, but it wasn't exactly the most nutritious dinner to fill their stomachs before sending them off to bed.

"Here you go." Luna appeared beside me and handed me the iPad.

"Thank you." I introduced Luna to Julie and Angelina.

Luna's gaze landed on the doll Angelina played with. "Is that a Cabbage Patch doll? My mom got me the Dancer Doll when I was little. I think I still have it somewhere." Luna crouched next to Angelina.

"Her name is Daphne. She's dressed like a duck," Angelina said.

I stood, placing a hand on Julie's shoulder. "It was nice to meet you. If you ever need anything or want to talk, I'm around."

Sometimes, the offer didn't seem enough. Who was I to

presume a woman who'd obviously fallen on hard times would seek out a virtual stranger like me for help? More often than not, the relationships I built at Amos House took time. The ones who weren't shy coming for help—like Calvin—often expected me to lead them by the hand to a perfect situation—whether it be a job, a home, or a drug-free life.

I sighed. Maybe I needed a break. Maybe I was getting too cynical in my older years. Or maybe, I was simply burned-out.

I bit back a groan as I walked to where Calvin sat in a chair, scrolling through his phone. I prayed for patience and wisdom, for God to give me His heart for this young man. I'd never struggled in this area before. Why now?

I sat down beside Calvin, who took a few seconds to part with his phone. "Now, where do you think you'd like to apply to first?"

15

Kevin wiped his sweaty palms on his dress pants and tugged the rolled-up sleeves of his button-down shirt an inch lower to hide his tattoo. No denying he was attached to his ink—he'd gotten the compass after Deidra had run away from home, a beacon of hope and faith that she would one day find her way back to them. On the other arm, was Isaiah 41:10 in Hebrew. He'd bought that ink when Katherine was going through chemo. He'd hold her hand often in those days and point to his arm, a constant reminder that God had told them not to be afraid, that He was with them every step of the way.

He didn't regret either of his tattoos, but there were times—like when he was about to take a beautiful woman on a first date to a fancy restaurant on a balmy late spring night—that he wished they were a bit easier to cover up.

He shifted from foot-to-foot before the main front door of Orchard House. Truth be told, he felt as awkward as a teenager on a first date. Bad enough he wore this getup—something he hadn't worn since his cousin's wedding two years ago—he had a horrible feeling that he might just blow it this night.

He shook off the negative thoughts. Since when did he suffer such a lack of confidence? Was it the pants that fit a little too snug around the waist? More likely it was the sulking sixteen-year-old at home who, rather than outright defying his request to help with stacking wood from the old elm, simply did the worst job possible. Kevin had stacked ten logs in the time it had taken Owen to do two. When Kevin suggested they might get their job done faster if Owen put away his phone, Owen shrugged and continued staring at his phone.

It took all the restraint he could muster not to rip the blasted electronic device straight out of the boy's hands and hurl it into the woods.

He'd been all too happy to get the majority of the stacking done himself and release the boy to his room.

Kevin pressed the doorbell of Orchard House as he attempted to shove aside the events of the afternoon. Friday was another scheduled visit with Deidra. He could only pray she showed. How long would it take for mother and son to reunite? How long would Kevin be responsible for a kid who wanted nothing to do with him?

And the question at the back of his mind—was Deidra staying away not because she didn't want to see her son, but because she didn't want to see her brother?

He stood at the door for several minutes. He rang the bell again, questioning whether to perhaps use the side door and ring the bell at the front desk. It *was* a bed and breakfast after all. Guests were going in and out all day.

But then the door opened, and there was Hannah in a sleek black dress and heels, her shoulder-length hair loose in waves.

"Oh, wow," he said.

She curled a strand of hair behind her ear, which made her all the more alluring, if that was possible. "Were you waiting long? I'm not sure I heard you right away." She smiled. "You could have knocked on our back door."

"I know. I thought about it, but it felt too casual. I wasn't waiting long." He wanted to treat her with the utmost respect and admiration. Although, now that he thought about it, making her run across the huge Victorian in those heels probably wasn't the best way to show his admiration.

She grinned, and it melted every last bit of his anxiety. Her earrings sparkled and he had the crazy urge to reach out and touch her hair, rub a strand of it between his fingers.

"You look beautiful."

She shrugged, a blush working over her face. "I don't get to dress up all that much. Feels nice, actually. And hey"—her gaze roamed over him, and he quite enjoyed the moment—"you clean up pretty nice yourself."

"I can be halfway presentable when I put in the effort." He laughed. "If only presentable didn't mean 'uncomfortable as the day is long,' I'd be golden."

Her pink lips turned downward. "Kevin, we can throw on some jeans and go for a picnic. I don't need fancy."

He wanted to kick himself for not holding his tongue. "No way. *Natalie's* it is. You spend all your days pampering your guests, it's time someone does the same for you."

She tilted her head. "That is the nicest thing anyone's said to me in a long time."

Something fierce welled up within him at her words. A need to take care of her, protect her, peel off those layers of strength she'd surrounded herself with and understand the real woman beneath it all. Yes, Hannah Martin was strong. There was no doubt about that. But was it right for a person to be strong all the time out of necessity? Surely, she held secret fears and doubts. Surely, she wouldn't be opposed to a man like him coming alongside her to offer support and care in the hard corners of life.

"I just need to grab my purse. Do you want to come in?"

He followed her through the small foyer and past the sitting area and front desk until they swung open a door that led to a pantry and Hannah's kitchen. He whistled low. "This is quite the place."

"Oh, hey, *Kevin*." Amie sat at the bar, her legs crossed, swinging one leg, a goofy smile on her face that almost matched the goofy inflection she'd placed on his name.

"Hello, Amie. Nice to see you again."

She closed a bridal magazine and hopped down from the tall chair. "Don't you two look ready for a night on the town. Where you kids headed?"

Hannah rolled her eyes, but a smile played at her lips. "*Natalie's*."

"Oooh," Amie crooned. "I knew I liked you, Kevin."

He gestured to the magazine on the counter of the bar. "How's the wedding planning coming?"

"Considering it's two weeks away, the planning part is pretty much done. Nothing but the seating arrangements and hair to think about. Oh!" Her eyes widened. "We have extra space. You and Owen should totally come."

I glanced at Hannah to gauge her reaction. No way was I inserting myself into her daughter's wedding unless Hannah herself wanted me there. "That's very nice of you, but maybe we should see how my date with your mom goes tonight before I crash your wedding."

She shook her head, wagging a finger at me. "I *definitely* knew I liked you." She gave her mother a quick hug before turning toward the stairs. "Show her a good time, Kevin. She needs it." Before disappearing up the stairs, she swung herself around the wall. "Not *too* good, of course. My mother will not stand for—"

"Goodnight, Amie!" Hannah waved her daughter away and scooped up a purse from the breakfast nook before turning to me. "Ready?"

Oh, yes.

❧

"YOU AREN'T SERIOUS?" I STOPPED MID SALAD-BITE, WAITING for Kevin to continue his story. We sat at a table on the oversized porch of *Natalie's*, starting in on the first of a four-course menu of exquisite food. The rolling green of Camden Hills sat off to my left while the naked masts of boats in the harbor could be seen through the tree line. The setting sun reflected bands of pale orange against the water. A perfect night.

And the company wasn't at all bad, either.

Across from me, Kevin smiled, those pine-green eyes at once mischievous and captivating. I could look into them all night. Maybe for the rest of my life.

Did I actually just think that? My blood froze. Where had that come from? Me, who never intended to marry again and who certainly didn't need a man to have a fulfilled life. I had my family, Orchard House, and God. Why did I need a man?

The answer was, I didn't. And yet, *this* man . . . what was so bad about wanting companionship?

Kevin chuckled. "I am completely serious."

"What did you do? I mean, no one was hurt, right?"

He shook his head. "My buddy—the one driving my truck— saw the tree falling and got out in time. Thank God. It could have been a lot worse. Now, it's mostly something I look back at and laugh upon."

"And how old were you?"

"Eighteen. Truth be told, I was a little cocky. Right out of school, ready for all the side jobs in the world. Felling a tree on your own truck has a way of waking you up to reality."

I laughed. "I bet. But I see it didn't deter you, either."

"Nah, my motto has always been to learn from my mistakes." He sat back from his plate of black bass. "Okay, enough about me. Why don't you tell me some embarrassing stories from your teenage years?"

I laughed. "There's one that stands out more than all the others."

He raised his eyebrows. "I'm on the edge of my seat."

"I was at a football game with some of my friends. We were in the top part of the bleachers and the guy I liked was down toward the front. Well, I started to feel a little nauseous. Right around half-time, when everyone was getting up for snacks and all that, I realized I was going to be sick. I tried to get down the bleachers as fast as I could, but the crowd was thick. I ended up vomiting right at my crush's feet. Needless to say, he never asked me out."

"Ouch."

"Yeah. I was 'Heaving Hannah' for the rest of the school year."

Kevin's smile disappeared. "Kids can be cruel."

I nodded. "They can. High school can be cruel. It's not easy being a teenager. Being one myself and then raising five of them has assured me of that."

The waiter brought our second course—Duck with Date Vadouvan, Mustard Greens, and Farro for me and a Rib-Eye with Caramelized Leeks and Beef Katsu for Kevin. We breathed in the delicious scents of the food as the waiter took our first-course dishes away. I tasted the duck, the nutty flavor of the farro combining with the moist sweetness of the meat. I groaned. "I definitely feel spoiled."

"Oh, come on. With all the cooking you do? I bet you make stuff like this on a regular basis."

"My specialty is actually breakfast, and the kids were more fans of spaghetti and meatballs than duck or beef katsu. Not much fun cooking a fancy meal to eat by myself."

He held up a hand. "Well, now that we're neighbors, I can certainly sacrifice myself by allowing you to serve me a fancy meal whenever you want. In fact, I might just consider it my civic duty."

I laughed. "I'll keep that in mind."

"So, any more embarrassing stories to help me get the bigger picture of who Hannah Martin is?"

"If my 'Heaving Hannah' story didn't satisfy you, I'm not sure anything else will."

"How about your parents? Are they around?"

I nodded. "Dad is, but Mom died when the kids were little. Dad's living in Florida. He remarried three years ago. He's never been good about keeping in touch, but I call once in a while. I wish we were closer, but . . ." I shrugged. "My parents never approved of Amos. I suppose they saw his faults better than I did. Still . . ." I didn't finish my sentence. Saying I wouldn't change a thing would be a lie. I raised my gaze to his. "What about your folks?"

"Alive and kicking. They live just down in Glen Cove, actually. They're one of the reasons I made the decision to move here. Camden's just far enough away to keep my privacy but not too far that I can't be there for them. With Deidra—Owen's mother— out of the picture and with them getting on in years, I wanted to make sure I was around."

"No other brothers or sisters?"

He shook his head. "You?"

"No. Just me."

"Wow. I never dated an only child. I've heard it's a recipe for disaster."

"You have, have you? What else have you heard?"

"That only children are some of the most selfish on the planet."

I opened my mouth, pretending to be appalled.

"But I think you've blown that theory out of the water. Far as I can tell, you are one of the most giving women I've ever known."

A blush worked up my neck. "I'm sure that's not true."

"Did you always want a big family?" he asked.

I nodded. "I hated being alone growing up. Siblings can be complicated, but they're the people you can always count on—" I stopped, realizing my blunder. "I'm sorry."

"Don't be. I'd like to think that's how siblings should be, but I guess me and Deidra are the ones to blow *that* theory out of the water."

"I'm sorry," I said again.

"I'm still hopeful Deidra and I can make a connection. If she ever shows up to one of Owen's visits, maybe we will."

"That must be hard on him."

"Do you really want to spend our dinner talking about my sullen teenage nephew?"

My mouth tightened. "That sullen teenage nephew is a big part of your life right now. And isn't the point of spending time together to share parts of our lives with one another, to get to know each other?"

He chewed a piece of his rib-eye carefully. "I like the sound of that on your end, but I'm afraid you'll think poorly of me if I open up about mine and Owen's relationship. Or lack thereof."

I inched my hand across the table to him until our fingertips brushed. "Kevin, you are doing a *great* job with Owen."

His mouth pulled into a thin, firm line, causing his cheeks to tighten. I glimpsed a small dimple beneath his close-cropped beard. "You saw us together one day—and that was the best day we've had. If you'd seen us this afternoon, you might have a different assessment." He shook his head. "But I refuse to have a pity party on our date. Change of subject is in order. How's Luna?"

I laughed. "So, you want this to be *my* pity party?" I teased.

The waiter brought over our third course. Smoked Salmon for Kevin and Ancient Grains with Zucchini, Tahini, and Citrus for me. I sipped my champagne as the waiter retreated to check on a couple parallel to us.

"Amos used to say—" I started before cutting myself off.

"Go on." Kevin gave me a kind smile. "Hannah, he was a big part of your life for a long time. I don't expect him to never make his way into our conversations. Just like I'm sure Katherine will come up on occasion. It'd be weird if they didn't. What did Amos say?"

My insides melted like hot wax. And then, out of nowhere, a sense that I was betraying my dead husband sneaked up on me. Because here I was with this amazing guy trying to remember what I'd been about to say, thinking of Amos, and realizing that I wanted to be with Kevin in that moment more than anyone else. Maybe even more than my dead husband.

I bit my lip, forcing the guilt away. "It was a quote, from Fred Rogers, I think."

Kevin nodded encouragement.

"He said, 'there isn't anyone you couldn't learn to love once you heard their story.'"

"Your husband must have been a pretty remarkable guy to go around spouting stuff like that."

I smiled as I gazed off at the hills. "He was. Not perfect by any means, as you've probably gathered, but yes. He was remarkable."

Kevin forked into his pink salmon. "The problem is, Owen won't tell me his story. Sure, I know a little bit from the social worker but I'm getting the feeling even she doesn't know the half of it."

"She probably doesn't. But you're doing all the right things, Kevin. You sense there's more. Whether you realize it or not, you *are* getting to know him better. That's a start."

"I almost lost my temper with him today."

"Almost?"

"He was helping me with wood—or not helping, is more like it. He had his face in his phone and I almost hauled off and chucked the thing in the woods."

I closed my eyes. "But you didn't. Do you want to know how many times I lost my temper with my kids? More than I want to remember. But the important thing is to apologize, to own up to our own frailty. Not that it sounds like you have any," I teased. "You know, since you didn't actually hurl the phone."

"Only by the grace of God," Kevin breathed before giving me a warm smile. "Thank you. You've made me feel like I might not be failing miserably at this guardianship stuff after all."

We finished our meal, talking about everything under the sun. The mission, our faith, Kevin's late wife and his logging business, Luna and all my uncertainties regarding our future. By the time we'd both had our dessert of Persimmon Cake with Mascarpone and Cranberry and the waiter had brought our check—which Kevin refused to allow me to chip in—I was feeling like I was on Cloud Nine. Good grief, how had the most perfect man ended up right on my doorstep . . . literally? Surely, there was a catch. Surely, this couldn't be happening.

I studied him as we waited for the waiter to grab his card. "You said you haven't dated since Katherine died. I find it hard to believe women haven't been clamoring after you."

"Hard for them to clamor when I've been hiding out in secluded forests or my shop for the last few years. But even if they were, I wasn't ready, you know?"

I nodded. Was I ready for this? I thought I was. I'd been all too ready to go on a date with Kevin, to spend time with him. But as I realized the possibility of a real future, the question remained. Was I ready? "This is a little scary for me. Is it okay that I say that?"

This time, he reached for my hand. And it was more than just brushing fingers. He wound his fingers around mine, creating a gentle intimacy. "Hannah, I want you to say whatever is in that beautiful brain of yours. Because it means I get to know you better."

I shook my head, a smile curving my lips. "How do you know all the perfect things to say? Do you listen to romance podcasts while you're in your trees, or something?"

"Nothing all that logical." His eyes searched mine. "It's you. You inspire me."

"See. There you go again." This time, my blush dove in with the ferocity of a hot flash.

A couple walked onto the veranda, and a loud, shrill voice echoed in my ear. "Hannah Martin, is that you?"

I cringed as I looked up, already recognizing the voice but hoping beyond hope I was wrong. But no. There, in a sleek green, knot-sided wrap dress with hair so blonde it mirrored Malibu Barbie's, was the owner of The Red Velvet Inn and my very real competition for Camden's Hospitality Grant—Jolene Andover.

16

"Hannah, what a coincidence to see you here!" Jolene rushed over and scooped up my hands.

"Jolene, how are you?" I tried to keep my smile from tightening, but there was no use. This woman had never been kind to me. No doubt, she was putting on a show now.

"I am absolutely peachy! I just can't get over you all dressed up. And here I thought you *never* got out." She turned to Kevin, holding out a perfectly-manicured hand. "And *who* is this?"

I would have laughed at Kevin's deer-in-the-headlights look if I didn't have to answer my fellow innkeeper. "Jolene, this is my new neighbor, Kevin. Kevin, this is Jolene Andover. She runs a bed and breakfast down the street."

"What a pleasure to meet a new face around here." She turned to me and held up a hand to block Kevin's view of her mouth, as if she were telling me a secret. "And a *handsome* face at that."

Kevin shifted in his seat. I made to stand. "We were actually just leaving." We could pay at the front desk, couldn't we?

But Jolene was touching my arm, turning behind her to where a man about our age with black-framed glasses and a tie that curved around a full stomach stood. "Oh, wait. Before you go, I have to introduce you to . . ." She paused, trying to create a dramatic effect. "Robert." She let out a breathy sigh as she said his name. "You haven't met before, have you?"

I shook my head and held out my hand. "Nice to meet you, Robert. I'm Hannah Martin."

Robert gave a friendly nod. "Likewise." He held his hand out to Kevin, all of us exchanging enough germs to require a good Purell dose.

Jolene leaned against Robert and fiddled with the collar of his dark blue button-down shirt. "*Robert* is in charge of the Chamber of Commerce. You've probably seen him at town meetings or such."

Yes, he did look familiar.

"Oh!" Jolene lightly slapped her date's chest, as if remembering something. "You've probably seen Hannah's application for the hospitality grant come through the office, right honey?"

Robert cleared his throat, averting my gaze. "I'm not really supposed to talk about work, *honey*."

And yet how would Jolene even know I applied for the grant, unless Robert did indeed talk about work outside the commerce office.

Jolene waved a hand through the air. "Oh, pish-posh. Isn't it nice to place a face to a name now? If anything, I've helped you."

Robert laughed stiffly. "It's good to meet both of you."

"Hannah, we'll have to get together soon to talk about the parade. I'm on the committee this year, you know."

My head literally hurt at the thought of the Fourth of July parade. I usually headed up the celebratory efforts. Partnering with Jolene would be a special kind of community service indeed.

"We'll have to get together soon, then." I forced the words through my lips.

"You know how much I *love* serving our little Camden community." Jolene wrinkled her nose and laid a hand on Robert's arm.

I racked my brain for the last time Jolene had done anything for the community. No, that wasn't accurate. When Hurricane Bob hit in 1991, I think she brought over a can of expired pigeon pâté to the high school gymnasium to help the hungry.

I sighed, ordering myself down off my high horse. People could change. Even Jolene. Although I had an inkling that her sudden desire to get involved in community service had more to do with looking good for the grant committee than her desire to serve the community.

Whatever. If good was being done, who was I to judge Jolene's motives?

"I'll be in touch soon!" Jolene called as we bid goodbye. The waiter grabbed the bill pad and the host finally led Jolene and Robert around the corner of the veranda.

"That has to be the most passive-aggressive woman I've ever met," Kevin said.

I looked after Jolene, her hips swinging as she walked in her wrap dress. "We have a . . . special history."

"Special, huh? As special as your history with the football bleachers?"

I laughed. "More so, if possible." I bit my lip. "We did go to high school together, actually. She liked Amos, but he never gave her much attention. She's not used to that, if you can tell."

"I was starting to get a hunch."

"Josie insists she stole my five-course breakfast idea, but it's not like it's a complete novelty among bed and breakfasts."

"What's the grant she was talking about? You never mentioned anything."

I shrugged. "Camden's Hospitality Grant. It's a twenty-thousand-dollar grant that will go to a Camden inn to be used for the improvement of services. I'll admit, I was excited. *Until* I found out Jolene's boyfriend is heading up the process."

"Seems he should take himself out of the equation for the sake of impartiality."

"That would be the gracious thing to do. And who knows, maybe he will. But not if Jolene has her way."

The waiter returned the bill pad and bid us goodnight.

"What would you do with the grant?"

"A few things. But mainly I'd hire more help. When we opened Orchard House, all my kids were home and behind the idea of helping with the business. Now, after Amie's wedding, it'll just be Josie running the bookshop, Maggie manning the front desk and web side of things, and me left with everything else."

"Sounds like you definitely need to find some good help. But can't you do that now?"

"It's in the budget. I suppose I've been waiting to see how this entire situation with Luna will play out. She's been a big help, and I don't want her to feel as if I'm kicking her out of a job. She feels it's how she's paying me for room and board. Not that she couldn't get another job if she wanted to."

"Why not talk to her about it?"

I blinked. "Whoa. Now, who's the insightful guardian?"

He chuckled. "Hey, maybe I have my moments after all."

I rubbed my temples. "I guess I've been tiptoeing around the idea. I don't want her to feel like I'm kicking her out, you know?"

"Tell her that. There's nothing wrong with wanting to know her plans."

"You're right. It's just, she's still so young to be an orphan. And I feel a responsibility for her. Does that sound crazy?"

"Not at all. But she is a twenty-one-year-old woman. And she's not your responsibility. You want to help her—I get that, I respect that. But what's the harm with some open communication?"

I leaned my chin on my hand. "Anyone ever tell you you're really cute when you're showing off your wisdom?"

He leaned back in his chair. "No, but let's see what other wisdom I can dish up. Did you know that the invariable mark of wisdom is to see the miraculous in the common?"

I snapped my fingers. "Oh, no. You are not taking credit for that one. I think you forgot you're dealing with a former librarian who has done intensive research on classical New England authors for the rooms of her bed and breakfast. That's Ralph Waldo Emerson."

He shot me a sheepish grin. "Can you blame a guy for trying?"

When we left the restaurant a short time later, he asked if I wanted to take a walk.

I did. We strolled down Bay View Street to the rocky beach of Laite Memorial Park. "I'm afraid I didn't wear the proper shoes for a beach walk," I said.

Kevin studied the bits of rock and sand that made up the beach. "Not exactly barefoot walking sand." He pointed to a bench at the grassy hillside. "Do you want to sit instead?"

We picked our way over to the bench and sat, staring up at the moon just beginning to glow as the sun dipped below the horizon.

"Beautiful night," I murmured. "Thank you. I haven't had this much fun in a long time."

"Well, it's about time you *finally* got out," he teased.

I elbowed him. "I'll have you know, I get out. It just usually happens to be because one of my kids is getting married or the church is having a women's event, or the mission needs help on a project." My mouth turned downward. "Wait. I *don't* get out. I'm pathetic."

He laughed, sliding his hand in mine. "You are the farthest thing from pathetic, Hannah Martin." His gaze dropped to our joined hands. "This okay?"

I smiled. "You're not like any other guy I know."

"I feel like that should be a compliment, but since we've already established that you don't get out, I'm wondering how many guys you actually know. Maybe I'm the bottom of the barrel."

I shook my head. "There's something you don't know about me that makes that highly impossible."

He turned to me, those eyes dim beneath the moonlight, our shoulders touching. "What's that?"

"I'm an excellent judge of character."

Something smoldered in his eyes. He slowly lowered his mouth to mine, and when our lips met, I felt like I was taking a long, cool drink after walking in a desert for a year. He was gentle and slow, as if asking and testing my willingness to go deeper. When I responded, he continued with tender restraint, his passion building like the slow burn of a wood-burning fire. We sank into one another, his arms coming to my waist.

When we finally parted, I breathed as if I'd just finished a short sprint. "Wow."

He tucked an arm around me and pulled me close. "Wow, is right. I sure hope we can do that again real soon."

I giggled, snuggling into him. "I think we should schedule it in before the end of the night, at least."

He breathed deep. "That has my vote."

❧ 17 ❧

In all the world of kinship care, Kevin wondered if there'd ever been a guardian more nervous than him in this moment.

For the tenth time in the last two minutes, he peered down his driveway, willing a car to appear.

Nothing.

It wasn't that he was nervous about meeting with his sister, a woman he hadn't seen in almost twenty years—okay, he was a little bit nervous about that—but more so, he was anxious about how this visit, or lack of a visit, would affect Owen.

No matter how inept Deidra's parenting, the boy needed his mother. Whether Owen would admit it or not, he wanted his mother. The question was, would Deidra step it up or would she forfeit being in her son's life forever?

And if that happened, what role would Kevin play?

His phone dinged, signaling a text and causing a surge of adrenaline to rush through him. Would it be Rita Bridges, telling him Deidra cancelled?

He walked across the kitchen and scooped it up.

Praying for you guys.

Hannah. He'd told her last night during what had become their nightly fireside visits that they were supposed to see Deidra today. Seemed he told Hannah everything of late. And the same for her. Ever since their date at *Natalie's* on Tuesday, they'd quickly become an integral part of each other's lives. Every day he asked her about speaking to Luna. And every day she admitted she needed to, but hadn't. She promised she would today—said that if he was doing a hard thing by reuniting with his sister, she could also do a hard thing of sitting Luna down for that serious conversation.

Simply thinking about Hannah tied him up in knots. The good kind of knots. The satisfying kind he hooked himself to a tree-climbing harness. He knew it was too soon. He knew it might be irrational. But then again, he was fifty-six years old. He knew what he wanted.

And right now, he wanted Hannah Martin.

Not just in a physical sense, although there was no denying his attraction to her, but in a til-death-do-us-part sense. He loved her.

After he kissed her on Tuesday, he'd returned home, shut his bedroom door, and prayed into the dark night. Though he sensed Hannah was his new way forward, he couldn't deny that kissing a woman besides Katherine, while thrilling, had felt a tiny bit traitorous to his dead wife. And yet, in the days leading up to his wife's death, she'd urged him to love again. Told him he had so much love to give, it couldn't end with her. The remembrance had him swallowing down tears, but then, he felt peace. As if both God and Katherine would approve of his decision to build a relationship with Hannah.

Problem was, it *was* too soon. And if he told her how he felt, she might run off. The last thing he wanted to do was scare her. Better to take things slow, continue to get to know her, and her kids.

Something he'd have a good opportunity to do at Amie's

wedding next weekend. Hannah had invited him last night and he'd suffer those constricting clothes for more time with her and her family.

Thank you. I think we'll need all the prayers you have.

He sent the text, then reread it. Man, he sounded like a real downer. He added a smiley-face emoji, then sent that.

He was so lame. Either that, or so in love. When did he start sending smiley-face emojis via text?

He shoved the phone across the counter and turned his attention to the cloudless sky outside his window.

God, give Owen a new start with his mom. Give me a new start with my sister.

He was willing to bet that Owen was as anxious as he was, although the boy, as usual, was hiding in his room. Not that Kevin blamed him. The kid probably didn't want Kevin witnessing his disappointment if his mother didn't show.

He tidied the kitchen for the tenth time. The digital clock on the oven panel continued to count off the minutes until finally, it was fifteen minutes past eleven—fifteen minutes past their agreed appointment time.

Should he call Rita Bridges? Report the missed visit? Or see if she'd heard anything from Deidra?

As he picked up his phone, he heard the sound of tires rolling over the gravel driveway. He glanced up to see a beat-up Honda Civic lumbering toward the house, making more noise than any small car had a right to. He put down his phone, his heart battering his chest.

Deidra.

"Owen!" he called up the stairs. "Your mom's here!" The boy wouldn't hear him if he had his earbuds in, but Kevin didn't want to go upstairs when he should be outside greeting his sister. He also wasn't Mr. Speedy Fingers on texting, either. In the end, he decided to step outside to welcome his sister as the first order of business.

He wiped sweaty palms on the thighs of his jeans and opened the side door off the kitchen. The Honda rumbled to a stop and the motor finally quieted. From the inside of the window, his sister's blonde head looked down at what he assumed to be a phone.

Kevin stood, vacillating between walking up to the car and waiting for Deidra to finish with her phone, or going back inside until she stepped out of the car.

Turned out, he didn't have to wait long. His sister pushed the door of the car open and placed one skinny-jean-clad leg and stiletto heel onto the gravel.

He stepped forward. "Deidra." He spoke her name softly, affectionately, as if anything else might scare her away.

She stood and tossed long hair over her shoulder to finally meet his gaze.

She'd aged a lot since he last saw her. Then again, she'd been twenty years old. She was forty now, and every year seemed to show around her heavily made-up face. She wore a tight black t-shirt that read in white letters: *R—Restricted—May Contain Content Considered Offensive* and a small bag hung over her shoulder.

"Hey, big brother. It's been too long."

Was he imagining it, or was there a slight slur to her words? His heart lurched at the presence of his little sister. He'd been sixteen when she was born, so of course, he hadn't been around much. But he'd always tried to stay involved in her life—giving her piggy-back rides when she was a girl, bringing her presents when he visited Mom and Dad.

He last saw her a week before she'd run away with an out-of-towner twenty years ago.

He stepped forward again, wanting to hug her, but unsure if she'd welcome it. With sudden decision, he wrapped his arms around her and squeezed. "I've missed you, little sister."

She stiffened in his arms, and he released her, not wanting to be just another guy in her life who didn't know boundaries.

"You have my boy?" She glanced at his humble house as if assessing if it were good enough for Owen.

"He's been here for the last few weeks, yes. I'm happy to have him." Was that a lie? Owen had been a wrecking ball to his comfortable, solitary life. But sometimes comfortable needed a wrecking ball. Sometimes comfortable meant stagnant. He'd be here for the boy as long as Owen needed him. That much he knew.

"Come inside. I made coffee and picked up some cheese Danishes this morning."

There. Something softened in her gaze. Surely, he couldn't be imagining it? "They still your favorite?" he asked.

She stepped over the threshold. "Yes. Though these days they go right to my hips."

He smiled and took two mugs down from the cabinet. "Cream and sugar?"

"Might as well." She glanced around the kitchen. "Cute place."

"Thanks." He turned to his phone. "I'll let Owen know you're here. He's right upstairs."

She pressed her lips together as she took a tentative seat. "You take him to see Mom and Dad yet?"

He swallowed before pushing the *send* button on his text to Owen. "I was tempted. They know he's here, and Deidra, they want to meet him something awful. But I wanted to talk to you first. See if you wanted to be a part of their meeting." He held his breath, praying she'd respond positively.

It'd been hard to convince Mom and Dad to wait on seeing their only grandchild. Even now, Kevin wasn't certain of the wisdom of waiting. And after Deidra missed her first scheduled visit, he'd nearly caved. But what if his parents meeting Owen could be an important piece of reuniting Deidra back into the family as well? Perhaps both Owen and Deidra would be more open to a familial bond if they came into it together.

Deidra shifted in her seat, crossing her legs, and swinging one foot back and forth. Like a pendulum, or a time bomb, waiting to explode. He couldn't be sure.

Finally, she opened her glossed mouth, foot still swinging. "I'm sure Mom and Dad don't have any interest in seeing me."

Kevin stopped pouring coffee. "Dee—are you serious? They've been praying to see you for the last—"

Footsteps sounded on the stairs and he cut off his words, unsure of the wisdom of carrying on the conversation in front of Owen. Then again, Owen wasn't a little kid who needed to be kept away from the reality of important decisions.

Deidra turned and stood, holding out her arms for Owen. "Baby."

Kevin didn't miss the glance Owen cast his way before stepping into his mother's arms. Though he allowed her to hug him, his arms hung limp at his side. After a moment, Deidra parted from her son, holding his arms and staring into his eyes. "You okay, baby? Your Uncle Kevin taking good care of you?"

Owen nodded and Kevin noted the faint dark mustache on the boy's upper lip. Past time to introduce him to shaving. He should have thought of that before the visit with his mother.

"Well, you sure as anything grew a couple inches."

Kevin pulled out a chair for Owen. "You want a Danish, son?"

Owen shot a glare at him, and Kevin could have kicked himself from here to Kingdom Come. What in tarnation possessed him to call the boy "son" now, for the first time, in front of his mother? Was he trying to pretend a relationship that didn't exist for Deidra's sake?

Owen slumped in the chair, grabbing for a Danish and a napkin on the center of the table.

Kevin cleared his throat. "I'll give you two some privacy, then." That wasn't against the visitation rules Rita Bridges sent, was it?

Surely not. How could Deidra build a relationship with her son if she felt Kevin watching and assessing every word? "You mind if I take a peek beneath your car, Deidra? Sounded a little loud coming in."

She glared at him. "My car not good enough for you, now?"

Shoot. "No—that's not what I meant. Happens to the best of cars. I just thought—"

"I don't need you looking at it. Sam takes care of my car."

Sam. So, her boyfriend—the one Owen said hit him—was still in the picture. Turns out separating Deidra from her son hadn't been reason enough for her to leave the jerk. But what if she couldn't?

He nodded, heading out the door, but not before catching Owen's quiet words. "He's just trying to help, Mom."

Kevin sucked in the warm air, fighting the temptation to stay close enough to the kitchen window to hear their conversation. Instead, he trudged to the last of the wood at the base of the felled elm tree and took up his axe, taking a small amount of pleasure that Owen made an effort to defend him. And then, kicking himself for feeling that way when every fiber of his being should in fact, be rooting for mother and son to draw close. The last thing he wanted to be was a stumbling block in their relationship.

He positioned a log on top of the stump of the elm and raised the axe overhead before allowing it to crash down, sending two neat pieces of wood flying on either side of the stump. He reached for another log, finding solace in the physical exertion, in the manual labor.

After a period of time that couldn't have been more than twenty minutes, Deidra emerged from the house, purse slung over her shoulder. She waved at him as she headed for her car. "Thanks for the Danish, big brother."

Wait. That was it? The meeting was supposed to be an hour. "You heading out already? I could put more coffee on. I'd like to catch up a little, hear what you've been up to."

Well, if it involved drugs and prostitution, maybe he didn't want to hear so much. And yet, wasn't that part of reconciliation? Wading through the hard of it all? Hearing things he might not want to hear?

She shook her head. "I have a hair appointment. These roots are yelling at me."

A hair appointment.

Kevin closed his eyes, tried to anchor himself, separate himself from his anger. He opened them as Deidra swung open her car door. A fierce need to stop her before she rolled back down that driveway welled up within him.

"Wait. I—have you thought about visiting Mom and Dad with Owen? I can talk to Ms. Bridges. Maybe our next meeting—"

She shook her head. "I don't think I'm ready for that. And I doubt the parents are, either. But you go ahead and introduce them to Owen. Who knows? Maybe he'll get on with them better than I did."

A sharp pain split like lightning down his chest. "Deidra, he's their only grandson. Don't you want to be a part of this?"

She slammed the car door she'd just opened and whirled on him. "You know what? I'm sick of everyone telling me what I should want. The social worker, the cops, the courts, Sam, and now you. Maybe all I want is to be left *alone*."

He didn't break her gaze, felt if he did, he'd lose her for good. Again.

"Deidra." He spoke softly, trying to hook her eyes and soul with his own. Hook her with his words. Hook her like he'd hook a fish. If only it were that easy.

This was the sister who used to give him big, toothy grins when he walked through his parents' front door. She'd throw her arms around him, and he'd patiently braid gimp cords for her, help her with homework, and buy her new copies of the Sweet Valley Twins book series.

Where had that girl gone?

He's your son, he wanted to say. Instead, something else came out together.

"Are you trapped with—with Sam? Or with someone else? I have enough room here. Do you want to stay with me? For as long as you'd need. I—I'm here for you."

She held his gaze for two long seconds. Then she looked up toward the sky, shook her head, and blinked fast. Was she hiding her emotion, or was that only wishful thinking on his part?

"I can take care of myself."

And then she was gone. Taking away all his hopes that this might be a new beginning, not only for Deidra and Owen, but for Deidra and Kevin as well.

❧ 18 ❧

Some days with Luna felt effortless. The young woman was becoming more and more proficient at helping me run the bed and breakfast, and I found myself thanking God for her. Yesterday, I'd taught Luna how to make coffee cake—one of my five-course staples—and it had warmed my heart to see how proud she'd been to take out the perfectly crispy cinnamon crunch-topped cake from the oven.

And then there were days like today. Days Luna drew into herself. Sullen and quiet. Carrying out her tasks without the least bit of joy.

We worked in the kitchen together preparing a dinner of spaghetti pie. I formed the buttered spaghetti into a pie plate and Luna stirred the meat sauce on the stovetop.

"I've been thinking about our visit to the mission. Angelina seemed to really like you. You had a way with her."

A soft smile curved Luna's face. "She reminded me of me, you know? I sensed her dad wasn't in the picture and—" Her gaze flew to mine. "I'm sorry. I didn't mean to sound like— you know. I just understood a little bit about where she's at."

There'd been many single mothers who had come into the

mission over the years. Though I didn't always know a lot about the missing fathers, I'd certainly formed my opinions. Dads who were caught up in drugs and addiction and selfishness, unwilling or unable to care for the people who needed them most. Dads who perhaps hadn't known their own fathers, who had several children from different women.

Now, as I realized Amos had been one of those fathers and hadn't fit the description I formed in my head, I was instantly chastened. What did I know about any of those missing dads really? Nothing. I'd been too busy playing the martyr, rushing in to help the poor while ignoring my husband's favorite quote—the one about how you could love anyone if you knew their story.

I sighed and reached out a hand to Luna. "I understand. And don't ever feel like you have to walk on eggshells around me when it comes to Amos. He wasn't there for you when you needed him. That couldn't have been easy. In fact, I can't imagine how hard it was for you."

Luna gave the sauce one last stir before placing the wooden spoon on the spoon rest beside the stove. "I survived, right?" She lifted her chin, as if acknowledging Amos's absence by snuffing her nose.

I smiled and nodded, searching for the right words to wiggle my way into this girl's world. Whether I had them or not, now was the time. I'd promised Kevin, and I'd promised myself today was the day I'd have a good heart-to-heart with Luna.

"You did survive. You and your mother must have been incredibly strong."

"We did what we had to do."

My mouth tightened. "I want to let you know how helpful you've been here. I think it's only right that if you continue your work at the inn that you be paid more than room and board."

"Oh, Miss Hannah, I'm not sure I'd feel comfortable with that."

"Luna," I began slowly. "I want to let you know you're

welcome here, for as long as you like. I realize you came here hoping to know your father, and what you got was me—a woman who doesn't share an ounce of blood with you. Is that—I mean, how are you feeling about all this?"

Luna blinked slowly. "I like getting to know you. In a way, it makes me feel closer to him."

I swallowed down the unexpected emotion bubbling in my throat. "I can understand that," I managed. "And I think Amos would approve of us getting to know one another. There's just a lot of dynamics here. I'm wondering if you might want someone else to talk to."

"Like who?"

"Like a counselor, maybe."

Luna shook her head with force. "I don't do shrinks."

I straightened. "Okay. Well, what about talking to me?"

"We already talk."

"I mean really talk, Luna. About how you're feeling about all this. About what your future might look like. About finding out Amos was dead and that you have five half-siblings you've never known. There's so much to process."

Luna grew quiet.

I placed a hand on her arm. "I think we need to be more open with each other. I don't even know what you went to school for, what your dreams are, what you believe and think, what your mom was like. We've been living together for a couple weeks now, and yet we still don't know one another."

She didn't speak, and I pushed a loose strand of hair behind my ear to hide my frustration. If she didn't want to have a relationship, I couldn't force one upon her, and neither did I want to. Maybe I needed to heed my own advice—the advice I'd given Kevin. Give it time. Pushing too hard too fast wouldn't accomplish any progress.

"I'm sorry. You've been through a lot. None of this has to be rushed."

And so what if I couldn't plan for how much help I needed to hire in the future for the bed and breakfast? Luna was here now, and that was enough help for today.

"How was yoga class this morning?" I asked to disrupt the sudden quiet that had come upon us.

"I didn't go. Amie had to meet with the wedding venue. Last minute stuff."

"It will be a beautiful day. Oh! Do you have something to wear? We could go shopping together if you'd like?"

I should have asked before now, but I'd been caught up in helping Amie, in giving my input on the bridesmaids' dresses and florist and menu that I hadn't thought to ask Luna about her dress. How would she feel seeing all of her half-sisters walk up the aisle and stand alongside one another? Would it make her feel sad, left out, or maybe simply grateful to be there with them?

I didn't have a clue.

Luna stared at the bubbling meat sauce, her fingers fiddling with the spoon she'd just placed down. "I—I don't think I'm going to go."

"What? I thought you were excited?"

She shrugged, her thin shoulders almost disappearing inside her retro tie-dyed t-shirt. "I—I was, but I think it might be too awkward. Not just for me, but for all of you as well."

My insides lurched. "Honey, Amie *wants* you there. We all want you there."

She scrunched up her face and gave me a sidelong glance. "I'm not sure *all* is quite accurate."

I gritted my teeth, knowing she hinted at Bronson and Josie. Though Josie had made an effort with Luna the day she walked in on our guest in his birthday suit, that had been the extent of any reaching out. Same went for Bronson. And yet I wasn't convinced the two wanted to push Luna away so much as they simply didn't know how to go about creating a bond—a bond they might not even want.

I leaned against the counter and folded my arms across my middle. "Bronson and Josie . . ." But what was there to say? They were my two stubborn children? They didn't know how to play nice? They were busy with their own lives? They were hurt their father had betrayed us and the only way to deal with it was to push Luna away?

Anything I said would sound like an excuse. And all my kids were adults. It wasn't my place to make them feel things I thought they should feel—things that I myself had trouble feeling. But still, Luna was their half-sister—didn't that mean anything to them at all?

Luna's phone rang out and she glanced at it, her face growing red. "Sorry. I have to take this." She dove out of the kitchen and headed up the stairs, but not before I heard her first words. "I asked you not to call me."

Who was she talking to? Someone from her past life, no doubt. And yet, she'd told us she had absolutely no one.

৩৯৫৩

I SLOWLY TURNED THE HANDLE ON THE FISHING POLE, allowing the line to reel in closer per Kevin's instructions. He told me the movement of the bait would lure the fish.

"Try not to look like you're having so much fun." Kevin raised an eyebrow in my direction, eliciting a laugh from me. He wore a navy-blue t-shirt that boasted his old company's logo—*Williams Woodworks*—jeans, and a backwards Red Sox hat. He looked so incredibly and ruggedly relaxed and sexy that a pull of attraction had me already anticipating the end of our night. So far, we'd spent almost all our nights together the last week, each one ending in a steamy make out session that made me feel like a young teenager again.

I wanted more of Kevin, in every way. If I were one of my daughters, I would have cautioned myself to slow down, to come up for air and assess the situation and the relationship. It was too soon to feel so strongly for a man I'd known less than a month. My relationship with Amos had taken months to grow into love. Everything had been slow and methodical and proper.

There was nothing methodical about me and Kevin. Nothing methodical about how he pulled me close and kissed me as if his next breath depended on it. Nothing methodical about my response to him—my own boldness in returning his kisses, my own desire to have more of him, all of him.

I was not my daughters. I was a fifty-two-year-old widow who was tasting a second chance at life and love. Was it wrong that at this stage in my life, I knew what I wanted?

"I'll say it again." This time, he poked me in the ribs. "Try not to look like you're having so much fun."

I scrunched my nose. "I'm sorry. Is it that obvious I'd rather be sitting on my back patio with a fire?"

"You've barely even given it a try." Kevin gestured to my pole. "At least give it an hour."

"An hour? If a fish hasn't bitten that plump worm on the end of my line in an hour, I'll think they're on strike."

Kevin readjusted his hat. "Wow, this is a side of Hannah Martin I've never seen."

"One that doesn't like to kill fish for sport, you mean?"

"No. One that doesn't have a ton of patience."

I rolled my eyes and dug in my heels, reeling my line in to see the plump worm still on the end. I cast it out like Kevin showed me earlier, but it didn't go far. "My patience for maiming God's innocent creatures when we likely know we won't eat them, is indeed limited. In fact, the more I think about it, I can't believe my boyfriend even participates in such a heartless activity." My mouth twitched as I realized how like Amie I sounded.

Kevin set down his rod and came beside me, wrapping his arms around me tight, pressing close. "Oh, I'm your boyfriend, am I?"

My face heated as I continued to clutch the rod, wishing very much my hands were free so I could turn into him and run my fingers up his tattooed, muscled arms. The thought alone made me dizzy.

"'Boyfriend' sounds a bit foolish for people our age, doesn't it?"

His arms tightened around me. "Speak for yourself. When I'm with you, Hannah Martin, I feel like a teenager again."

I giggled.

"But you know what? You can call me whatever makes you comfortable. Manfriend, Honey, Hot Stuff, Lovebug, Booboo Bear, Good-looking . . . need I go on?"

"Booboo Bear?"

"Okay, I don't know where that came from. Please don't call me that."

"Oh, I think a guy with all your arm ink absolutely needs a nickname like Booboo Bear."

"Hannah . . ."

I shook my head, feigning pity. "It's too late now, the damage is done. I will from now on think of you as Booboo Bear."

"Oh, really?"

He wiggled his finger into my side and I laughed, realizing how very teenager-ish we were acting and caring not a whit. It felt wonderful to release all the cares of life—Amie's impending wedding, Lizzie's struggle to get pregnant, Josie and Bronson giving Luna the cold shoulder, Luna's mysterious phone call earlier in the day. To release it all and simply enjoy the presence of Kevin's company. To play together like this. Had Amos and I ever done this? Laughed with carefree abandon over pure silliness? Surely, we had. Had I forgotten? Or had we been so busy with the deep thoughts of life to engage in such behavior?

I cast the notion aside, hating myself for comparing once again. Why did I have to rob my time with Kevin by thinking of all the could-have-beens with Amos?

A hard tug came at my line. "Wait. I think I have a fish!"

Kevin straightened, sliding his hand to the pole. "Seems so. You ready for this?"

I firmed my jaw and nodded.

"Okay, reel him in."

"How do you know it's a 'he'?" I asked as I slowly spun the crank on the fishing line. "What if it's a poor mama fish trying to get food for its baby fish and she just got a hook in her mouth?"

"You really know how to zap the fun out of this, don't you? Even Jesus helped the fishermen."

"They needed it for their livelihood. Are we going to eat anything that comes out of this lake?"

"If it's big enough we will."

I continued reeling, faster and faster until I finally pulled up . . . a big clod of seagrass. I burst out laughing at the sight of the slimy green grass, dripping large drops back into the water. I put my hands out behind me to fall onto the patch of grass. "Oh, I'm so relieved it's not a mama fish."

Kevin held up the seaweed, staring at it dubiously. "Yes, this is *so* much better."

I covered my mouth to hide my laughter. Kevin dropped the seagrass and sat beside me, leaning over to kiss me soundly on the lips. I inhaled his scent—eucalyptus and the faintest woodsmoke and sawdust before he pulled away. "I guess I need to accept that you're not a fishing girl."

"I'm sorry. But I love being out here. I'm happy to come and sit with you whenever you want to fish—and if holding a pole above water and waiting for hours for a fish to bite will make you happy, I'll try my best to pretend I'm having the time of my life."

He shook his head and stared at the ground, a slight smile on his handsome face. "It's your company I'm interested in, Hannah. You don't have to hold a fishing pole to make me happy."

I curled my arm around his and leaned my head against his shoulder. "Thank you."

"Any hobbies you're fond of that you want me to try my hand at?"

"Unless rolling out fondant interests you, I think we might be better off finding new hobbies we can do together."

"Fon—what?"

I laughed. "Nothing. What about kayaking?"

"I'm up for some kayaking."

"We could rent them from Asher's store. You think Owen would want to come? Maybe Luna, too."

"Sounds like a plan."

We grew quiet for a minute, simply taking in the sunset view of Megunticook Lake, the sound of birds singing the sun to sleep, muted laughter of kids on the beach, the distant sound of church bells tolling the hour.

"I'm sorry things didn't go how you wanted them to with Deidra today," I said, still leaning on his shoulder.

He sighed deep and put an arm around me. "It's not how I envisioned it, that's for sure. But who knows, maybe it's a start."

More quiet before he spoke again. "It is making me realize that this road might be longer than I was prepared for. If Deidra doesn't leave Sam, I can't imagine social services ever placing Owen back in her care. *I* wouldn't want him back in her care."

I nodded. "Sometimes it's easy for us to see the obvious choices when we're on the outside looking in."

An almost imperceptible stiffening of his arm around me served to tarnish the moment. "If she's in trouble, why would it be so hard for her to ask for help?"

"I don't know," I whispered. I didn't want to tell him I'd observed over and over again similar situations in the fifteen years I'd worked at *Amos House*. The people most likely to change were those who could be reached by young adulthood. Very seldom did someone more set in their ways—someone closer to Deidra's age —choose a different path. And yet, as soon as the thought flitted across my mind, I chastised myself.

Did I or did I not believe in a God who could do anything? A God of second chances and miracles? When had I become so cynical?

"I know it's been a long time. I know we're practically strangers. But I'm still her only brother."

"It's hard when we don't know the full story," I whispered.

He sat up straighter and I moved myself off his arm.

"That's not my fault. I'm doing all I can. She's the one who ran away without leaving a number or a place to find her. Do you know what sort of pain she caused my parents? How many nights they wondered if she was half-dead in some back alley, hurt or raped? If she was warm enough, if she had enough to eat?"

I placed a hand on his arm, attempting to bring him back to our present. I'd never seen him so upset before and though it pained me, I was glad he felt he could open up to me. "Kevin, I'm so, so sorry. What Deidra did is inexcusable. I didn't mean to make you think I was validating her actions."

The lines in his face softened. "And I didn't mean to jump down your throat. I guess I want to deal with her like a reasonable human being, only I can't. If she's got drugs in her system, that might not be possible."

"Keep trying. It's all you can do. With both her and Owen. Keep showing up for him, prove to him you're not going to be one of the adults in his life who's going to walk out on him. Even if you can't get to Deidra, it's not too late for your nephew."

He placed his arm around me again, nuzzling his chin into my hair. I sank into his warmth.

"You think I should take Owen to see my parents?"

He'd told me about Deidra's refusal to reunite on the ride to the lake. "Yes, I do. I think Owen needs all the connections he can have right now. Grandparents can be huge. Deidra may never come around to the idea."

He nodded slowly. "I admit, I had it all perfectly planned in my head. A big ol' family reunion. But it's not right to hold off any longer. I'll take him over tomorrow."

We sat in silence until the sun dipped below the horizon. After another long, tantalizing kiss that assured me Kevin didn't harbor any ill feelings about anything I'd said regarding his sister, we packed up our fishing poles.

"Next date, rolling out fondant."

He wrinkled his nose. "I thought we were trying kayaking?"

I winked at him. "Oh, yes, that's right. Completely slipped my mind."

He squeezed me to him as we walked toward his truck, and I snuggled beneath his arm as the moon glowed above us. "Just so you know, Hannah Martin, I'd roll fondant for you. I'm starting to think I'd do near anything for you."

My skin heated with a rush at his words. And while they thrilled me, the practical part of me wanted to stomp on the brakes. Sure, we were older, but that didn't give us an excuse to rush things. If anything, we should be wise about the fragility of relationships, of letting down those we loved.

I thought of Luna at home in Lizzie's old room. I, for one, should learn from the past. Human love—no matter how good it looks—always had the potential to fail.

❦ 19 ❦

"The trick is to bring the razor straight down. You get the nicks when the blade slides side to side." Kevin demonstrated with his own razor in front of the bathroom mirror as Owen watched carefully—something Kevin considered a victory.

With puffs of shaving lather on both their faces, Kevin began to demonstrate how to shave in smooth strokes.

"Wait. You're shaving off your beard?"

"I'm thinking I need a change. It'll grow back if I don't like it." He wondered what Hannah might think. But more so, he hoped this snapshot in time of bonding might stick in Owen's head better if Kevin shaved off his comfortable beard.

Owen maneuvered the razor down his face with slow, careful strokes. He opened his mouth and curled his top lip under his teeth to gain better access to his upper lip area.

"There. You're a natural." Kevin continued with his shaving, his heart beating slightly faster at the thought of broaching the next topic of conversation. He studied their dual reflections in the large bathroom mirror, trying not to be obvious. It struck him how, with both their right hands raised, they held a similar stance. Almost as if Owen could pass for his son.

He swallowed, pushing the thought aside. Not something to dwell on at the moment.

"What do you think of paying your grandparents a visit after church?"

Owen's hand slipped and a thin red welt appeared to the left of his mouth. Kevin stifled a curse. "That happens." He turned to the toilet paper roll and staunched the small flow of blood. "Just leave that on there for a few minutes and you should be good as new."

Owen took up the razor again, but this time, his hand trembled. Kevin reached out and placed his fingers on the boy's, lowering the blade. "Better wait until you're steady."

Owen tossed the razor on the countertop. "Forget it, this is dumb. I'm going to cut up my whole face."

"No, you're not. You got this." Kevin held the razor out to him. He took it and Kevin turned back to the mirror to focus on his own face. "So, what do you think? About meeting your grandparents."

Owen worked his tongue around in his mouth before answering. "I heard you and Mom talking yesterday. Why doesn't she want to see them?"

"I don't know, actually. Could be lots of reasons. Maybe she's mad at them about something. Or maybe she's feeling kind of ashamed, you know? That it's been so long since she's seen them."

Owen nodded. "I didn't know I had grandparents until I heard you guys talking yesterday."

Kevin's eyes closed. He wanted to shake his sister. It was one thing to leave behind everything you'd ever known when you were twenty, but to pretend as if none of it mattered? To not even tell your son he possessed living and breathing grandparents who would give their right arms to meet him?

"I guess that means you didn't know you had an uncle until

relatively recently too, huh?"

"No, Mom talked about you all the time."

He blinked. "She—she did?"

"Said you were some big football hero in the town you guys grew up in."

A soft smile curved his lips while at the same time his heart lurched like a fish caught on a hook. Deidra had spoken about him to her son. That had to mean something, didn't it? But why then didn't she talk about their parents?

He turned back to the mirror, thinking this heart-to-heart may be easier if they could avoid direct eye contact. "I want you to know, Owen, that if I'd known you existed—if I'd known where to find you—I would have found a way to see you. To be a part of your life."

Owen's bottom lip trembled. "I wanted to meet you, but whenever I asked Mom, she said it wasn't possible." He shrugged.

"I'm sorry, but it's possible now. And so is getting to know your grandparents. What do you say? You think you're up for it?"

"More than shaving, anyway." He wiped his mouth with a towel and presented his face to Kevin. "Did I miss anywhere?"

"Just one spot." Kevin carefully ran Owen's razor over the very corner of his mouth. "There. Looking sharp."

Owen gave himself a once-over in the mirror and nodded before exiting the bathroom.

Was Kevin wrong, or did the boy have a slight swing in his step? He prayed he was making the right decision introducing him to his parents without Deidra. He prayed nothing about this day would serve to block the small bit of progress he'd just made with Owen.

Two hours later, Kevin parked his truck in his parents' driveway. The small white ranch was neat and tidy with window boxes boasting red geraniums that matched the front door. Bird-feeders sat before the picture window of the living room, all sorts of suets and feeders to attract not only birds, but other wildlife too.

Kevin turned to Owen. "You ready?" His words ended on a false high note, as he'd felt the urge to call him *son* or *buddy* or some other nickname he'd previously deemed harmless before Deidra's visit.

"What if . . . " The boy paled.

"You okay? You need some water?"

Owen shook his head.

"What if what?"

"What if they don't like me?" He croaked the words, and Kevin's soul nearly cracked in half.

He placed a firm grip on the teenager's shoulders. "Owen, look at me, son." He chanced the nickname, felt the boy needed it now even if he didn't want it. He waited until his nephew raised dark eyes to his. "They are going to *love* you."

He could only pray his father wouldn't say anything about the large gaping holes in Owen's ears. The man had made it known how much he'd been opposed to Kevin's tattoos, and that had been when Kevin was in his twenties. Never mind deformed earlobes. But he'd have to trust his eighty-year-old father to behave himself in that regard.

He once again clapped Owen's shoulder. "Let's do this."

They jumped out of the truck and Kevin led the way up the front walk ahead of Owen, pointing out a large maple to the left of the house. "Your mom used to love to climb that tree. I let her try my climbing harness when she was old enough."

Owen scrunched up his face, as if having trouble picturing his mother climbing any trees, much less using a harness to do so.

Kevin gave two hard raps on the red door before pushing it open to the scents of lasagna and—if his nose didn't deceive him —cake. "We're here!" he called.

His mother came around the corner, wiping her hands on a dishrag and flinging her arms around Kevin. "I didn't even hear you drive up. Dad's making so much racket in the garage—" She stopped short at the sight of Owen behind Kevin, her hand fluttering to her throat. "Oh my lanta. Why, he looks just like Deidra." His mother shook her head, tight gray curls barely moving. "I'm sorry. I mean, it's wonderful to meet you, Owen." She held her hand out, blinking back tears.

Owen took her hand. "It's nice to meet you, Mrs. Williams." He spoke in a voice that sounded clearer than anything Kevin had yet to hear from the boy's mouth. In that moment, he was proud of this kid. This lost teenager who was trying like the dickens to build a tentative relationship with grandparents he'd only just found out existed.

She kept a firm grasp on his hand with both of her own. "Please, don't call me anything as formal as that. Call me . . ." Her gaze flew to Kevin's. "Well, what should he call me?"

"They here, Doris? I can't get that headlight to work for anything." His dad came around the corner. He gave Kevin's hand a firm shake. When he spotted Owen, he gave a sharp nod and stepped forward, extending his hand. "Son, good to meet you."

Kevin held his breath. Owen shoved his hand into his grandfather's. "Nice to meet you, sir."

Sir. Well, well, well. Turned out Owen had been holding out in the manners department. Kevin raised his eyebrows at the teenager, but the kid's attention was firmly on the sturdy frame of his grandfather.

"Doesn't he look like Deidra, Paul?" Kevin's mother grasped his father's arm.

His father grunted. "Got the earrings, anyway."

Kevin winced, silently pleading with his dad to behave himself. To his relief, though, Owen forced a small laugh. "Mom was pretty mad when I came home with these."

"I can see why. But never mind all that." He placed his hand on Owen's shoulder. "You like cars? I have a 1963 Chevy Corvette in the garage. Most beautiful car you'll ever see."

His mother rolled her eyes. "Dinner's almost ready, Paul."

But his father was ignoring his mother, ushering Owen toward the garage door. She looked at Kevin and shrugged. "How's he doing?" she asked as soon as the door to the garage closed.

"We had a bit of a rough visit with Deidra yesterday."

His mother nearly dove at him. "You saw her?"

He nodded. "I did. She's . . . " How to finish that statement? *Good* wasn't exactly accurate. And yet, somehow Deidra was standing on her own two feet. She'd lost her son, of course. Was tied to an abusive scoundrel who may very well serve as her pimp, but other than that, he supposed Deidra was fine enough.

"Did you tell her we want to see her?" His mother fiddled with her fingers and his chest burst with pity. His mom didn't deserve this. She'd been the best. When you pour everything into your kids, wasn't it fair to at least expect some sort of return on investment? A chance to see your only grandson grow up, at least?

He nodded. "I did, but she's not ready yet, Mom. I'm sorry." Even as the words left his mouth, he questioned whether he should give his mother that much hope. And yet, deep down, it was his hope also—that Deidra would be ready one day. That somehow, they could be a family again.

His mother blinked back tears. "Okay. Well, at least you saw her, Kevin. Keep telling her we love her, will you?"

"I will, Mom." His voice cracked and he cleared his throat. "You need help setting the table?"

She turned toward the kitchen. "Already done. Just need to wrangle your father in here long enough to say grace and eat."

Kevin opened the door to the garage to see Owen pointing to something beneath the hood of his father's antique car. He watched for a minute as Owen asked about drum brakes and commented on the split window and wheel trims.

Kevin gave himself a swift mental kick. Of course. The kid

was into cars! Why hadn't he realized that before? A sixteen-year-old boy, into cars. What a novelty. He chastised himself for all the times he tried to get Owen involved in tree work or whittling or fishing—all things he himself liked. He'd thought the kid's interests ended at video games, but once again, he'd been proven wrong.

He cleared his throat. "Dinner's ready."

His dad slapped Owen on the back. "How about we take her for a ride after dinner? I'll even let you drive."

Kevin's mouth fell open. "Dad, you never even let *me* drive the Corvette."

His dad jerked his thumb in Owen's direction. "This kid knows his cars. I can tell just by the few minutes we were in here." He turned to Owen. "What do you say, son? Take her for a spin after dinner?"

Owen's gaze flew to Kevin's before dropping to the ground. "I actually don't have my permit yet, sir."

Kevin's temples squeezed. His driver's permit. He hadn't even asked, hadn't even thought about it when sending Owen off to the bus every morning for school. What kind of a guardian was he? And yet, Ms. Bridges hadn't mentioned anything either. Was Owen even allowed to pursue his license while in foster care?

Kevin's dad looked from Owen then to Kevin. "Well, why on earth not? You're fifteen, aren't you?"

"Sixteen, sir."

There it was again. *Sir.* Just what had Kevin's dad done to earn him that title in the space of a few minutes?

Kevin's father raised his eyebrows at Kevin. "Why haven't you taken this young man to get his driver's permit, then?"

Owen stepped forward, shaking his head. "We could never afford it when I lived with Mom. I didn't want to bother Mr. Williams about it."

While Owen's pleasant tone lifted Kevin's heart, the *Mr. Williams* at the end of his sentence made him pause. He'd introduced himself as *Kevin* to Owen, and now the name the kid used sounded so distant and impersonal. As if all of Kevin's efforts with Owen were for nothing.

Blimey, he needed to get a hold of himself. The kid was going through a lot. He needed a sturdy rock. Not someone who had his own issues to work through—which clearly, Kevin did.

He shook his head. "I'm sorry, Owen. I didn't even think about it. Of course, we can take you to get your permit. Tomorrow, first thing after school, after I run it by Ms. Bridges."

Kevin's father nodded once, hard. "And then you two come over here so we can take my girl for a spin."

Kevin raised his eyebrows, deciding it was time to make use of his "legal guardian" title. "Thanks, Dad, but Owen's first time driving isn't going to be behind the wheel of your prized possession. Why don't you take us for a cruise after dinner, though?"

"You don't have to twist my arm." His father grinned and gestured for Owen to head back into the house. "Good thing you came over here, isn't it, son? You might have been seventeen without a learner's permit before my knucklehead of a son realized it. Don't be afraid to speak up, you know? You're almost a man. Sometimes no one's going to stand up for you if you don't do it yourself."

Kevin watched them enter the house, but the scent of his mother's cooking wafting out into the garage wasn't the reason for the twisting deep in his belly. He'd been trying to show Owen that *he* would stand up for him when no one else would. Being a man wasn't always about standing on your own. Sometimes, it was about depending on others.

And yet, the permit thing had completely gone over Kevin's head. Of course, he needed to speak to Rita Bridges, but maybe teaching Owen to drive would be just the thing to bond the two of them.

20

I f there was ever a perfect bride, my youngest daughter would be it.

Okay, I've said that about every one of my daughters, but seeing my very last one on the arm of my son, about to walk down the aisle to the love of her life and leave me an official empty-nester, was a different experience altogether.

"She's gorgeous," Luna breathed beside me, reminding me that I wasn't quite as close to being an empty-nester as I may have liked to imagine.

I smiled at Luna, beautiful in an emerald-green dress that complimented her pale skin. I squeezed her arm. "I'm glad you're here." I sought out Kevin and Owen a few rows back and blushed when Kevin winked at me. He looked absolutely dashing in a suit that I had an inkling he'd rented special for this day. And when I'd seen him earlier in the week with his face all shaven, I'd practically swooned like a silly schoolgirl.

That face.

As handsome as he was with his short beard, to see the smooth lines of his jaw and the area around his mouth made me want to map every square inch of his skin with my eyes until Jesus returned. It didn't hurt that Kevin looked about ten years younger with the smooth face, and although he didn't look old to begin with, for the first time I could picture him as a more youthful version of himself. And if that wasn't enough to churn my insides into sweet butter, kissing that flawless face and the corners of his smooth mouth certainly was.

I blinked, forcing myself back to the present. My baby girl was getting married and I refused to miss a second of it because I was googly-eyed over my neighbor.

There'd be plenty of time to stare at him on the dance floor later that evening.

The ceremony was beautiful. Amie and August had chosen the very elegant venue of the Samoset Resort in Rockport, a short drive from Camden. As soon as the vows had been said, guests were ushered to a large, tented pavilion complete with a dance floor, white linen tablecloths, and sparkling stemware and silverware overlooking the shimmering Penobscot Bay.

I turned to Luna. "We won't be long with the pictures. Would you mind showing Kevin and Owen where our table is?"

I hoped this would include her while not rubbing her nose in the somewhat sensitive fact that she wouldn't be a part of the wedding photographs. What a horrible conundrum that no family should have to endure. Certainly, if Luna had been a part of our lives for longer than a month, Amie would have thought to include her in at least one picture. At least, I think she would have.

But who was to say how long Luna would be among us? Though I felt we had made some headway the other night, we still seemed a long way off from a true, healthy relationship. And what kind of relationship did a wife have with the daughter her late husband had conceived with another woman, anyway?

It was enough to make my head ache.

But not tonight. Tonight was about celebrating with the people I loved more than anything in the world.

Even by the bay, the evening hung hot and stuffy. As soon as the pictures were completed, the guys in the wedding party traded in their jackets for their button-down shirts and rolled-up sleeves. We made our way back to the tent, a thin line of sweat breaking out at the base of my breastbone.

I fanned myself with the program still in hand. We'd broken up our family into two wedding tables, creating enough room for Luna and my guests, Kevin and Owen. At our table also sat Maggie and her family, as well as Lizzie and Asher.

I studied my second youngest daughter over the Tuscan salad. She looked better than I'd seen her in a long time. Glowing, even. I noticed how she avoided the champagne at the table—and yet that wasn't anything out of character. And then, I *knew*. I wanted to drag her to the bathroom and pump her with questions, but of course Lizzie wouldn't say anything until Amie had her wedding night. Never in a million years would she want to steal her sister's thunder.

Still, the thought of my Lizzie pregnant made me nearly giddy. As the waiters served up grilled lobster tails and deep-sea Maine scallops and Josh quietly joked how far this was from the poor man's wedding he'd given Maggie, I sat back and soaked in the moment.

"Where did you two get married?" Kevin asked Josh. The two men hadn't spent much time together, but I had a feeling that, if given a chance, they would get on well.

"In my parents' backyard," he answered after reminding Davey to settle down in his chair. The boy looked about ready to bounce out of his seat.

"Which is no poor man's venue, if you ask me." I turned to Kevin. "Josh's parents own a beautiful home on the water."

Maggie curled her hand around her husband's elbow. "Besides, it didn't matter where we got married. I got the man I wanted. That's all that mattered."

I smiled. Luna gazed at them as if they were an anomaly. For the first time, I wondered if she'd ever had a father figure in her life. Just because Amos hadn't been around didn't mean her mother didn't have a boyfriend or hadn't gotten married. And yet she'd implied they'd been alone.

I turned to Owen. He'd taken out the large hoops that stretched the bottom half of his earlobes to unimaginable proportions. Though they looked a bit loose and malformed, I wondered if he was making an effort for the sake of Amie's wedding. He looked quite handsome in khaki pants, a white button-down shirt, and a pale blue tie. "How are driving lessons coming along, Owen?"

Kevin had told me they'd gone to the RMV to obtain Owen's permit after getting the okay from his social worker. Though he'd had to take a written test, he'd passed with flying colors. Turned out all those hours Owen spent up in his room on his phone weren't spent playing video games—they were spent watching car videos on YouTube.

"Good, I think." The teenager glanced at Kevin, as if for assurance.

Kevin nodded. "The kid's a natural. I have to admit, I never thought I'd feel safe putting my life in the hands of a sixteen-year-old, but Owen's changed my mind. Dad's even going to let him drive his antique tomorrow, and I can't say I have any qualms about it."

The boy beamed and my heart burst with happiness for Kevin over the obvious relationship beginning to form between the two of them. "That's wonderful."

After we finished our meals and ate the vanilla cake topped with sweet cream frosting, and after Amie and August danced together as husband and wife for the first time, the DJ opened up the dance floor for the guests. Etta James crooned out "At Last" over the speakers, her strong voice spilling out into the tent and towards the rolling green grass that ended at the bay.

Kevin pointed to Luna and Owen walking onto the dance floor. "You think that's okay?"

"I don't see why not. Luna knows how old Owen is. She's just being nice, although he really cleaned up good tonight, didn't he? Just like his uncle." I bumped him with my shoulder.

Kevin smiled and I took in the dimple on his right cheek, much more pronounced without his beard, and with his skin glistening from the warmth of the night.

"So, are we going to sit here and talk about how handsome I am while everyone else has fun on the dance floor, or are we going to dance?" He moved to get up but I placed my hand on his arm and he sat back in his seat, brow furrowed. "You don't want to dance?"

"Kevin, every other guy has taken off their suit jacket and rolled up their sleeves. It has to be eighty-five degrees beneath this tent, probably ninety on that dance floor. I can't help but wonder if you're hiding something." I tapped his forearm where I'd practically memorized the faded ink outline of the compass tattoo.

He slid his hands off the table. "This night means a lot to me. I don't want to give any of your family a bad impression."

"My family has already seen your tattoos, as far as I can remember. Flag football night? Besides, it doesn't matter what anyone else thinks. I love you for you, tattoos and—" I cut my words short, realizing what I'd just said, trying to catch my mouth up to my brain. "I mean, I like you just the way—"

He placed a finger over my lips, leaning close. "I love you too, Hannah. Unless you want to take it back?"

My breath grew ragged in my chest, my brain dizzy from his words. This man—this beautiful, amazing, caring man that God had all but dropped into my life—loved me. I'd made peace with the fact that I would never know romantic love again, that once with Amos was enough. But it wasn't. There was no way I could settle after spending these last few weeks with Kevin.

I shook my head and blinked back tears. "No. I don't want to take it back."

"Good." He gently kissed my lips. "Because neither do I." He stood and peeled off his jacket before pushing his shirtsleeves up to reveal the inky lines of his tattoos. I realized then that I loved those tattoos. Every centimeter of ink. Not because I was drawn to them in and of themselves, but because they were a part of the man I loved, a part of his history that I wanted to know more about. These were the arms that drew me onto the dance floor. These were the arms that held me close in their sure embrace. And these were the arms that I was coming to believe, would never let me go.

⚜

Though almost nothing could tear Kevin away from Hannah and the dance floor, a bladder about to burst would do the trick. After the *Cupid Shuffle*, he and Hannah broke away from the dancing bodies and headed for the restrooms, laughing at themselves along the way.

"You're a great dancer, Booboo Bear."

Kevin scrunched up his face. "For a minute there, I thought you were serious about my dance moves."

"Oh, I am."

He slid an arm around her slender waist, pulling her closer, wanting to drag her behind the bushes where he could kiss her good and proper, away from the eyes of her children.

And maybe he would. After he took care of business.

They parted ways and after Kevin exited the restroom, he turned at the sound of a voice calling his name. Standing below the light of the pool house where the restrooms were housed, Bronson stood, his white dress shirt bright in the moonlight.

Kevin slid his hand into Bronson's, giving it a firm shake. "You make it a habit of lurking outside restrooms?"

He squeezed Kevin's hand a little harder than necessary. "I was waiting for Morgan when I saw you duck in. I—I wanted to tell you that I haven't seen my mom this happy in a long time. Maybe in forever." He shrugged, a sheepish grin on his face. "I think that's because of you."

His breath loosened in his chest at the unexpected compliment.

"Thank you. That means a lot to me. She makes me happy too."

The shadows of Bronson's mouth grew firmer beneath the outside light. "I'd hate for her to get hurt again. My dad, he left her with a lot of pain, you know, not the least being Luna's arrival."

"Bronson, believe me when I tell you I care very deeply for your mom. I know we haven't known one another long, but some things you don't need long to know. And I'm trusting this is one of them. I can promise you I will never, ever intentionally hurt your mother. I plan to treat her with the utmost care—all of her, including her heart. She doesn't deserve anything less."

He breathed deep, only half doubting if he should divulge these next words to the young man. Without thinking too much, he went for it. "And when I'm ready to ask her to marry me, I'll be asking for your permission to do so before I pop the question. Does that sound like a deal?"

Bronson's jaw fell open. "Um—yeah. Wow. I didn't realize you guys were that serious."

Kevin shook his head. "I plan to take things slow. The last thing I want to do is scare her. Can you keep my secret?"

Hannah's only son straightened to his full height until they were eye-level with one another. "Yes, sir. Yes, I can."

Kevin broke out into a grin. "Good. Thank you."

And though he hadn't known until tonight that one day soon he'd ask Hannah to be his wife, he couldn't imagine being more certain about anything else in all the world.

21

"Hannah Grace, you best be spilling your guts because I haven't heard you this giddy since—oh my, are you in love or are you still feeling the effects of the champagne from the wedding last night?"

I tucked my legs up onto the chair of the bookshop as I listened to my best friend's voice. The bookshop was closed Sunday afternoon, and I had sought its solitude in order to call Charlotte. The last thing I needed was Luna witnessing my *giddiness*.

"Am I crazy, Charlotte? Tell me I'm crazy. I mean, I'm a grandmother for goodness sake. I'm menopausal. I'm not thinking straight. Is that it?"

"Honey, you may be a grandmother and you may be menopausal, but you're not *dead*."

I laughed. Okay, it was more like a giggle. I was *giggling* now. Lord, help me. "I certainly don't feel dead."

Just thinking about dancing in Kevin's strong arms the night before, remembering his confession of love, was doing all sorts of strange things to my insides. No, I hadn't felt this alive in a very long time.

Charlotte's voice grew soft. "Hannah, it's not wrong to be happy, or in love. Stop doubting it."

I swallowed at the sudden change in tone of our conversation. Charlotte was my oldest and dearest friend. Though more than a decade older than me, we met when I was a teenager and we worked together at the Bar Harbor Inn. I'd been hired as a chambermaid initially but became an assistant chef in the years before marrying Amos. During that time, Charlotte and I had become fast friends. Though she'd been through her own heartaches, including the loss of her husband and a painful estrangement from her daughter, Charlotte was my rock. My truth-teller. My faith-friend. In some instances, she was the mother I no longer had.

I sighed and gazed out the large floor-to-ceiling windows toward the orchards in full bloom. Bronson and Morgan's first week of summer camp would begin next week. I looked forward to a group of young kids running around the orchards again.

"I guess I am doubting it. As happy as I am about how things are going between me and Kevin, part of me feels it's too good to be true."

Charlotte allowed the silence that came next, most likely sensing my need to process my own thoughts. She was so good like that. "Is it strange that I feel a little bit unfaithful to Amos?"

Even as I voiced the words, a vicious thought cast itself into the depths of my mind. For why should I feel unfaithful to Amos when I'd been faithful to him from the time I was a lovestruck teenager and beyond the grave? It had been five years. He was the one who'd been unfaithful. He was the one who'd left me with a lonely young woman whom I still hadn't a clue how to deal with half the time.

And yet, those thoughts were poisonous. I knew it before they even entered my head. If my relationship with Kevin was the blessing I hoped for, I refused to allow it to be motivated by anything but love. Not by guilt or a twisted justice. No. I owed

Amos everything. He'd been my world. He'd given me the five most beautiful gifts of my life. I would not hold one terrible indiscretion—an indiscretion I had forgiven him for while he was still very much alive—over his grave. It wasn't healthy. It wasn't what God would want for me, and Kevin was most definitely worth more than such a thought.

"Hannah, I can understand. But marriage is for the living. And you are alive, as we've already firmly established." Charlotte laughed softly. "Amos would want you to share your life with another."

I sniffed. "What about you? You've been alone now for what, seventeen years?"

"Eighteen next month."

"Why haven't you ever remarried?"

"I suppose I might have if God dropped the perfect man to be my next-door neighbor. But seeing as I'm stuck with crotchety old Simon Andrews, I suppose the good Lord isn't ready to play matchmaker for me quite yet."

I smiled. If anyone deserved a companion, it was my friend. I at least had all my children around me.

"Now, don't go feeling bad for me. I can hear it in your thoughts."

"I wasn't—"

"I have the Beacon and its guests. I have this beautiful piece of land, and most importantly I have the Lord. It's taken some time and lots of prayers, but I am content, Hannah." Charlotte ran the Beacon Bed and Breakfast, a beautiful inn on the coast of Acadia National Park. With an old lighthouse keeper's cottage and a working lighthouse attached, it was one of the most picturesque places in Bar Harbor, Maine. And that was saying something.

"You are an amazing lady, Charlotte."

"Is my life really all that bad?"

I shook my head. "You know it isn't. I miss you."

"I miss you too. Maybe one day I'll tear myself away from this place long enough to pay you a visit."

"Oh, Charlotte, anytime. I'd love to have you." Out of the large window, I glimpsed Josie's minivan pull up the drive. Out spilled Lizzie, Maggie, and Josie, practically bouncing around each other as they ran to the back door of the bed and breakfast. "Hmm, I could be wrong, but I think my girls just arrived to tell me some good news."

"You had a wedding yesterday. How much good news can you take?"

"If it involves another grandchild, I'll take all the good news I can get."

"Oh, Hannah. Lizzie?" Her voice hitched up in a hopeful twinge and my heart burst with gratitude, not only for the news I suspected my girls came to tell me, but for Charlotte, who celebrated each and every wedding and grandbaby with me despite the trials that had made it impossible for her to know her own grandchild.

"I think so," I whispered. "Can I call you back tonight?"

"You better."

"Love you."

"Love you, too. Enjoy every moment."

We hung up, her words clinging to the air surrounding me.

Enjoy every moment.

Those words were the reason I waited an extra two seconds in the bookshop, though a part of me wanted to run into Orchard House to search out the girls.

The anticipation only lasted the two seconds, however, before the bell above the bookshop jingled and the girls poured into the shop. "There you are!" Josie sang. "Is this your hideout these days?"

"I'm not hiding. I just got off the phone with Charlotte." I hope my daughter didn't think I needed to escape Luna, even though I had sought out the quiet of the shop to have some privacy. "And to what do I owe this pleasure?"

Josie flopped on the couch while Maggie and Lizzie perched on two chairs near the gas fireplace. Josie flipped her long chestnut hair over her shoulder. "I'm going to be straight with you, Mom. We have a lot of ground to cover and not a lot of time." She looked at her phone and placed it face down on the small coffee table.

My insides dropped. Maybe I'd been wrong about Lizzie? "Okay . . ."

Maggie waved her hand through the air. "We'll talk about Mom and Kevin later, Josie. Right now, Lizzie has some news." Maggie nodded at Lizzie, as if to encourage her.

Yay! My heart danced at the sight of Lizzie's glowing face. Though I'd known they'd had another round of IVF, I tried to give her space and not hound her about pregnancy tests. The last thing she and Asher needed was more pressure from well-intentioned loved ones.

"I'm pregnant!" Lizzie burst out.

I squealed, tears filling my eyes. Not just because this was another grandbaby to love and cherish and cuddle, but because Lizzie and Asher's road to pregnancy had been one of failure and heartbreak for too long. I threw my arms around her, then tempered my embrace, almost scared to break her.

I inhaled the scent of her lavender shampoo and gently squeezed. My sweet Lizzie, a mother. A ball of emotion worked its way in my throat. I pulled back to gaze into her eyes. "Honey, I am so very happy for you."

Her eyes shone. "Asher is over the moon. Seriously, if we lost power, he could light the way. He's so happy." She licked her lips. "We're not telling too many people yet . . . you know, just in case—"

I squeezed her arm, not allowing her to finish the thought.

"This baby is going to be healthy and beautiful and such an amazing blessing."

Lizzie smiled, a sly look on her face. "And that's not all . . ."

"Oh my, should I sit down?"

"I'm pregnant, too," Maggie blurted out.

I fell on the couch, covering my mouth with my hands. "Maggie! I had no idea you and Josh were—"

"We weren't! But it happened, and we couldn't be happier. I'm two months along, but I wanted to wait until after Amie's wedding to announce it. Then when Lizzie told us last night, I couldn't contain it anymore. We told Amie right after the reception. She said it was perfect news to end a perfect day."

I hugged my oldest daughter. "Seems the blessings are pouring out left and right around here. These kids are going to be the best of friends growing up. I always wanted tons of cousins." I was so glad my girls were close to make it so. I gave Josie a sidelong glance. "Any other surprises I should know about?"

Josie's eyebrows shot up. "No way, not for me. There's one of Tripp and one of me, that makes two. My rule is to never be outnumbered by my own children. The rest of my babies will be book babies."

I laughed. That reminded me, I needed to catch up with her on her latest manuscript. But there was plenty of time for that.

I stood. "This calls for a celebration. Have time for tea? I'll whip up some apple crisp in no time."

Josie vacillated. "I planned to write while the boys finished their naps, but apple crisp always wins. *And*, we still need to talk about you and Kevin getting down and dirty on the dance floor."

My face burned.

"Josie!" Maggie admonished. "They were *not* getting down and dirty. My goodness, you can be so crude sometimes."

"Thank you, Maggie." I tried to keep my composure as we exited the bookshop and crossed the driveway to the back patio of the bed and breakfast.

"They were absolutely adorable, is what they were." Lizzie held the door of the Victorian open for me.

"Girls, you're embarrassing me."

Josie hopped up on a bar stool. "Hey, if you're going to flaunt it, we have to talk about it."

Maggie elbowed Josie, shook her head and gave her a look that said, *What in the world is your problem?*

I studied my second-oldest daughter, taken aback by her abrupt shift in attitude. Yes. What in the world was her problem?

But I knew, didn't I? The same question I had wrestled over with Charlotte just half an hour earlier was probably the same question that troubled Josie. She and Amos had always shared a special bond. No doubt, it bothered her that I was trying to move on. And yet, five years? Would no time ever be enough?

"Josie, I'm sorry if it was hard for you to see me enjoying myself with Kevin, but—"

"Mom, you do not need to apologize," Maggie cut in.

I bit my lip and straightened. I supposed the apple crisp would have to wait. "I'm not apologizing for being with Kevin, although I can understand why it might make you feel uncomfortable, Josie, and for that, I am sorry."

I reached out a hand to cover hers, surprised that it remained a bit stiff beneath my palm. "Honey, I loved your father. I still love him, will always love him. But my heart is big enough to move on, to entertain the notion of sharing it with another man."

"Are you sure this isn't all because of Luna?" Josie asked.

"Luna was a surprise, of course, but me falling in love with Kevin has nothing to do with Luna."

"Mom, you're in love?" Lizzie made a face as if she'd just seen a cute stray kitten to cuddle.

I smiled, a bit cautious not to flaunt my happiness in Josie's face if the fact would pain her. "I am." I turned to Josie. "I love you girls—all my kids—more than anything in the world. I respect each of you, and if you had major concerns about Kevin's character, then of course I would listen. But I don't think that's the problem. And I'm not going to live like I'm half alive because I'm scared of offending you. I love you. I want you to be happy for me, and I hope one day you can."

Maggie threw her arms around me. "Of course, we can!"

"Yeah, Mom. We're behind you." Lizzie squeezed me tight.

I chanced a glance at Josie, drumming her fingers on the bar top. "I'm sorry, Mom. I do want you to be happy. I just didn't expect how hard it would be to see someone replace dad."

I went to her side, smoothed her hair out of her face, sensing she'd allow me the pleasure in this moment. "No one could *ever* replace your father. We knew the same Amos Martin, didn't we? The man who'd stay up late trying to solve world hunger? The guy who taught his children compassion and kindness and faith? The man to whom I owe everything"—my voice broke—"because he gave me the world when he gave me you kids, when he taught and instilled in you the things of utmost importance."

Josie smiled, but a tear meandered down her cheek. She swiped it away. "He was pretty amazing."

"And no one made pancakes quite like he did." Lizzie grinned.

Maggie groaned. "Those things had enough baking powder in them to float across the Atlantic."

Josie giggled. "And they tasted like a basket of sidewalk chalk."

I smiled at the remembrance of the time I'd been sick in bed and Amos had set out to make "The World's Best Pancakes." The guy had tried to solve world hunger, but he couldn't follow a recipe to save his life. "You all shoveled them down like champs."

"Enough maple syrup can disguise even the worst baked good," Maggie said.

I sighed. "My point is, if I could have spent the rest of my days with your father, I would have. Kevin will never replace your father. Not for me, and certainly not for you kids. But I'd like to think the Martin clan has big enough hearts to let others in.

Whether they be more grandkids or a half-sibling . . . or a man your mother really, really adores."

Josie swallowed and nodded. "I love you, Mom. I want you to be happy. I'm sorry if I acted like a spoiled brat. I am one sometimes, you know."

I laughed, squeezing her tight, relishing her thin arms returning my embrace. "I know. And I love every bit of you, even the sometimes-spoiled parts." We dissolved into giggles.

"And you know. . ." Maggie tilted her head to the side. "Josie might never admit this, and Amie isn't here to say it, but Kevin is *hot*. Especially now that we can see his whole face."

Lizzie reddened, giggling behind her hand and I pressed my lips together, chancing a glance at Josie, who, to my satisfaction, cracked a smile.

Around the corner, I heard soft footsteps on the stairs and the sound of a bedroom door closing.

Luna.

I hated that I wondered how much of our conversation she heard, how my mind backtracked, thinking if we'd said anything that might offend her. Josie had mentioned Luna . . . I groaned and turned to Lizzie. "Would you like to invite Luna down for our celebratory apple crisp?"

"Absolutely." Lizzie started around the corner and I prayed that somehow, our hearts—all of them—would indeed find themselves large enough to encompass all that God placed in our paths.

❦ 22 ❦

Later that afternoon, after the girls had left, I headed upstairs and lightly knocked on Luna's door.

"Come in," came the soft reply.

I inched open the door to see Luna laying on Lizzie's old bed, phone in hand.

"Hey," I said softly.

"Hey."

If it were one of my girls, I would have sat on the bed, touched their arm, a leg, something. But with Luna, I found myself monitoring everything, unwilling to scare her off. Not exactly sure of my place.

I sat at the desk chair beside the bed.

"Lizzie said you weren't feeling great?"

Luna had never come down for apple crisp, and I found myself raking the coals of my mind for details of my conversation with my three girls that could have upset Luna if she had indeed overheard us.

Luna shrugged. "I'm okay. Just tired from the wedding yesterday, I guess."

"You had fun?" I scolded myself. Not an open-ended question

that would make way for deeper conversation.

"It was a beautiful wedding." Her voice took on a wistful tone.

How did I reach this girl? Suddenly, I was exhausted. Exhausted from the wedding and the good news of Kevin's feelings. Exhausted from the excitement of knowing that Maggie and Lizzie would be birthing babies within weeks of one another. Exhausted from Josie's hurt over seeing me with Kevin. Exhausted over wondering about the hospitality grant and the silence from the Chamber of Commerce. Exhausted thinking of my upcoming meeting with Jolene to finalize parade plans. Exhausted trying to figure out how to better include Luna in our family, how to make an attempt at healing the wounds of her past.

Suddenly, it all felt like too much.

I closed my eyes. *God, I don't have strength—help me lean on You. Give me Your strength, Father.*

I opened my eyes to see Luna staring at me, a hurt expression on her face. "You were praying, right?" she asked.

"Yes, I was."

"Praying because you don't know about me."

I let out a puff of air, a small laugh. "More like I don't know about me."

She sighed, her chest rising and falling with the exhalation. "I think I might be overstaying my welcome."

"Luna—no. Did you hear something downstairs today that upset you? Josie . . ."

She shrugged again. "Kind of. But that's not it. It's more like just a sense that it's time for me to move on, you know? I don't really belong here."

"Honey, where do you think you belong?"

"I don't know." Her voice cracked and her eyes shone.

That was enough to cause me to make my way over to perch on the bed. I placed my hand on the young woman's arm. "Luna, I know we don't have a roadmap or manual for this entire situation, and I'm sure by now you realize that your arrival did most certainly throw me for a loop, but believe me when I tell you that I want to be here for you. And you've been such a help, you are not a bother. In fact, I'm becoming quite fond of you."

As I said the words, I realized just how much I meant them. I enjoyed teaching Luna the ropes of the bed and breakfast. Though her blunders had been aplenty, she seemed more interested in the day-to-day running of the inn than any of my other children. And that went for the baking as well. The girl could bake. I looked forward to our time together in the kitchen. To the way she would lightly hum an old song under her breath, how she would glance up at me before she added a teaspoon of vanilla to the coffee cake recipe, looking for my go-ahead. So unsure. So ready to please.

Amos's daughter. And, in some crazy way that didn't entirely make sense, now my daughter as well.

"I'm fond of you, too." Luna sniffed. "But if you marry Kev—" She stopped short, her eyes wide. "I mean, when you marry—"

I shook my head, my face heating at her words. "Kevin and I only just started dating. What makes you think we're getting married anytime soon?"

She didn't meet my gaze but shrugged. "I don't know." Then her thin mouth inched up into a sly smile. "He likes you a lot."

I shot to my feet, my skin heating to epic proportions. I grasped for a stray piece of paper on Luna's desk to fan myself. "Thank you. I'm fond of Kevin, too, but honey"—I stopped the fanning, forced myself not to pace—"I am not marrying anyone anytime soon. And even if I was . . ."

I'd been about to say there would still be room in this house for Luna. But was that a wise thing to promise?

"Luna, I'm not going anywhere. I promise, I'm not going to abandon you."

Like Amos had done. Like she may even feel her mother had done, although by no fault of her own.

Without warning, Luna sat up and threw her arms around my

waist. I stood frozen for a moment before dropping my hands to rub her thin back.

"Thank you," she whispered.

"Of course." I squeezed her tight, feeling perhaps we'd made a new breakthrough in our relationship.

Out of the corner of my eye, her phone lit up on the desk. A flash of a name. Aunt Julia, maybe? I forced my gaze away and the screen blacked out. I'd seen it wrong, of course. Luna couldn't have an aunt. She'd told me that after her mom died, she had no one.

And she'd never given me one reason to believe she'd lie to me.

23

Kevin finished nailing a two-by-four in place before lowering his nail gun to the plywood floor of what would soon be his new woodshed. He inhaled the scent of sawdust and freshly-milled wood, his senses tingling.

It's not that he didn't enjoy retirement. Problem was, he legitimately loved working. Why did the two have to be autonomous? In his mind, they didn't have to be. As soon as he was done building the woodshed, he planned to try his hand at furniture-making, something he'd always wanted to do but never had the time. Well, now he had the time.

"Hello, Mr. Williams!" From Hannah's backyard, Luna waved, approaching a bit timidly.

He wiped his forehead with the back of his forearm. "Hi, Luna. What are you up to this afternoon?"

"I told Owen I'd help him with his math. He just texted me to come over."

"Oh. Well, that's nice of you. Come on inside."

"Yoohoo!" A shrill voice sounded behind Luna, and they both turned to see Jolene Andover, in a striped pantsuit and high heels, striding through the yard toward them.

Luna let out a soft curse under her breath and practically ducked beneath his arm toward the house, lowering her voice with her next words. "I'll just show myself inside if that's okay!"

Kevin looked after the girl, vacillating between following her or being polite and waiting for Jolene to reach him.

"Be sure to call Owen down, okay, Luna?" No need for the girl to go up to Owen's room. Not that he thought he had anything to worry about on Luna's end, but she was a pretty girl and Owen was a sixteen-year-old boy who Kevin had thought had been doing fine in math.

But Luna had already disappeared inside the house. "Luna?" he called. He waved to Jolene. "Be right with you."

He strode the few steps to the house and opened the door to see Owen shuffling through his backpack at the kitchen table. Luna stood beside him, back to Kevin. Okay, then. Nothing to worry about.

"Let me know if you guys need anything. I was quite the stud when it came to quadratic equations back in the day."

Owen rolled his eyes. "Sure you were, Uncle Kevin."

He inhaled a sharp breath at the title of *uncle* before his name.

Guess if you teach a sixteen-year-old boy to drive, miracles start happening. He'd have to thank his father for that breakthrough.

Kevin pushed the kitchen door open to see Jolene surprisingly close to the house, practically peering into the window. The woman clearly didn't know boundaries.

"Jolene, right?" He raised an eyebrow at her preoccupation with his window trim.

She glanced at him, obviously distracted. "Yes. I—I was looking for Hannah. We were supposed to meet to discuss the . . ."

"The . . .?"

She blinked, her brown gaze focused fully on him for the first time since she'd arrived. "The Fourth of July parade. Hannah invited me for tea." Again, the woman's eyes traveled to his window.

"Well, Hannah's usually reliable. I'm sure she'll be back from grocery shopping any minute." Yes, he knew where Hannah was on any given minute of the day. Not in a stalkerish sort of way, but in a they-talked-so-much-throughout-the-day sort of way that it made it impossible for him to *not* know where she was every second.

She shook her head. "I'm sorry. But that girl that was just here. Did you say her name was Luna?"

"Yes. She's helping my nephew with his math."

Jolene turned away, pressing a hand to her mouth. "It couldn't be . . ." she whispered.

"Is something wrong?" Silently, he prayed Hannah would turn into her normal parking spot *right* now.

"I—I thought she went out west." Jolene's tone took on a distant and faraway quality, and quite suddenly she was the furthest thing from the prim and polished lady he'd met at *Natalie's* on his first date with Hannah.

"Are you okay?" he asked.

His voice broke her from her musings. She shook her head. "I realize this is forward, but could I come inside? I'm almost positive that girl in there is my niece."

Kevin blinked. Oh, man. Surely, there was a misunderstanding. And yet, that might explain why Luna was so eager to avoid seeing Jolene. What tangled-up web were they about to discover? And for all that was holy, why did he have to be the one to sort it out?

He exhaled a long breath. If Luna was Jolene's niece, he didn't want the girl

to feel ambushed. And yet she'd told Hannah she didn't have any living relations.

Now, he could understand not wanting Jolene for an aunt, but turkey was turkey and bread was bread and if Jolene was Luna's aunt, she'd lied to Hannah.

"Let me ask her to come outside, okay?" Somehow, that seemed less intimidating than bringing Jolene into his small kitchen to confront the young woman.

He ducked inside to see Owen scribbling on paper and Luna hunched in her seat, the tips of her ears red as a beet.

"Luna, the woman outside thinks she knows you. You think you could come talk to her?"

The girl raked her hands along the sides of her head until they covered her ears. She released an exasperated groan and then flung herself upward and toward the door. Kevin stepped back. He and Owen shared a surprised look.

"I—I better make sure everything's okay." Kevin followed Luna outside, feeling a sense of responsibility for her while Hannah wasn't around. Perhaps it was misplaced, but he didn't care. Whatever was up with these two, he was beginning to think he couldn't trust either of them alone together.

"Luna Anne, how could you not tell me you've been in Camden this entire time?" Jolene held her arms out at her side as if pleading with the girl.

Kevin willed Hannah's car to round the corner of the bed and breakfast. No such luck. He stood just outside his door, unsure whether he should remain there. Did Luna need him? Jolene may be a bit of a flighty character, but her concern for the girl was evident.

Luna stood stoically, arms crossed in front of her, as if blocking Jolene's presence. She stayed silent.

Jolene paced in front of Luna, her high heels sinking into the soft grass near his driveway. She took out her phone. "Your mother has been worried sick."

Kevin's blood slowed within his veins. Luna's *mother*? She not only had an aunt, the girl had a *mother*? A mother that, from the sound of it, was quite alive.

Luna looked over her shoulder, her face sinking at the sight of Kevin. Her bottom lip trembled, and she looked about to cry.

"Can we talk about this somewhere else?" Luna's words barely reached Kevin's ears.

Jolene stopped pacing, kept right on talking as if Luna hadn't spoken. "And you're staying with Hannah Martin, of all people? What has gotten into you, girl?"

"Aunt Jolene," Luna pleaded. "Please."

Jolene flung her hands out at her sides. "What am I supposed to do now?"

"Will you just listen to me for two seconds?" Luna's strident voice came across clear this time. "I need to go. *Now.*"

"Come with me. We're going for a ride." Jolene grabbed Luna's arm and started pulling her toward the bed and breakfast, but Luna dug in her heels.

"No. I am not going anywhere with you."

"Yes, you most certainly are. I don't care if I have to—"

Jolene's words came to an abrupt halt at Kevin's gentle but firm hand on her arm. "Jolene, I think you should leave," he said.

Jolene narrowed her eyes at Luna but finally dropped her hand. "You're a selfish brat, Luna Anne, to put your mother through this."

Kevin cleared his throat. "Maybe when Hannah comes back you two could schedule a time to sit down and work some of this out."

Jolene sneered at him. "Hannah Martin is the last person I need snooping around in our family business. Lord only knows how Luna wound up here, anyway. But Hannah has always attracted the strays, hasn't she?" With that, Jolene turned on her heel and stomped past his newly-framed woodshed. When she was at the edge of Hannah's patio, she turned. "Tell Hannah I'm sorry to have missed her." She gave Luna one last once-over. "Real sorry."

And then she was sliding her grass-clumped heels into her sleek new Prius and driving off.

Luna whirled around. "Mr. Williams, you have to let me explain."

He grunted, starting back to his woodshed. "Seems the one you have to be explaining to is Hannah."

"Please don't tell her," Luna pleaded. Her eyes glistened.

Now, what in the world was he supposed to do? He couldn't very well keep such a big secret from Hannah, and yet hadn't Hannah been the one to tell him that sometimes, kids simply needed someone on their side? Yes, their very first chat by her fireside patio. He'd been asking for pointers about Owen.

We can stand by their side when no one else will.

Maybe this was just such a time for Luna.

But there was standing by Luna's side, and there was deceit.

He shook his head. "Luna, I can't lie to Hannah. It's wrong of you to ask me to."

"Not lie. I'll tell her. I promise. I just need some time. A few days. She has a full guest load including this nosy woman who keeps showing up in the kitchen. Please, Mr. Williams, I don't want to screw this up."

It was on his lips to tell her that, seems to him, she already had. But he could also understand Luna wanting to approach Hannah with the truth herself. The last thing he relished being was a tattletale.

He walked away from her a few steps, thinking, praying. He blew out a long breath through parted lips. "Okay. You tell her. But don't drag it on too long, okay? I really care for Hannah and I'm not a fan of secrets. If you don't tell her by the weekend, I will."

She grasped his hands. "Thank you. Thank you, Mr. Williams. You have no idea what this means to me. I'll make everything right. I promise."

Gently, he slipped his hands out of hers. "Luna, I don't know what you're up to, but I'm not sure this is going to be an easy one to make right. You told Hannah your mother *died*. That's a big lie. Was Amos even really your father?" He shouldn't have asked it, should have left well enough alone.

Her eyes grew wide, and she nodded emphatically. "Yes, of course, yes. That's why I had to come. That's why I had to find out for myself."

He bit the inside of his cheek, on the verge of asking more questions. But no, he didn't want to know. It would only complicate matters and really, it wasn't any of his business.

And yet, the woman he loved *was* most certainly his business. He was introducing her to his parents tonight.

"Tell her by Saturday, Luna." His voice came out in a near growl, and he tried to soften it. "She has a right to know."

24

"**H**oney, it is so nice to finally meet you!"

Kevin's mother slid cool, wrinkled hands into mine and pulled me inside their quaint home. Though it had been a long time since I had to meet a boyfriend's parents, Mrs. Williams made me feel right at home.

"Thank you so much for having me."

"Well, when our only son wouldn't stop talking about his pretty neighbor, and then when he finally shaved off all that hair—"

"No need to embarrass me *all* at the beginning of the evening, Mom. At least save something for dinner." Kevin smiled at her, and then at me, and warmth bloomed in my chest. Though he'd been uncharacteristically quiet on the ride over, I assumed he was nervous about Deidra's scheduled visit tomorrow. Either that, or me meeting his parents. Some things didn't get easier with age.

Mrs. Williams peered behind me. "And where is our driver?" She enveloped Owen in a hug. "How are the lessons going, honey?"

Owen shoved his hands in his pockets, a bashful grin on his

face. Wow, it was almost like the kid had transformed. Maybe Kevin's parents were miracle workers. "Going good."

"And did you try those muffins I sent home with you the other night?"

Kevin turned to me. "Mom loves to bake almost as much as you do."

"They were good," Owen said. "Never thought I'd like pistachio muffins, but I ate them up."

I raised my eyebrows. "Pistachio. Now, there's one I certainly need to try."

The older woman placed a hand on my arm. "I'll copy the recipe for you."

Again, a warmth—a kind knowing that Mrs. Williams was already accepting me into their small fold—rushed over me. I wondered if this was what helped draw Owen out of his shell. If so, I could see why.

"Now, let me go find my husband. Probably tinkering in the garage again." She walked with steps that belied her age to the opposite end of the home. "Paul! Our company's here!"

Kevin ushered me into the dining room, his hand gentle at the small of my back. He leaned down to whisper in my ear. "She likes you."

I shot him a sly grin. "What's not to like, right?"

He chuckled. "Right."

A moment later, Mr. Williams bustled into the dining room in a Red Sox hat and grease-splattered pants.

Kevin straightened. "Dad, this is Hannah."

Mr. Williams held out his hand and I reached for it. Warm and calloused, he gripped it firmly, as if he meant his next words with deep sincerity. "Very nice to meet you, Hannah. I'm Paul."

"Wonderful to meet you," I said, for some reason unable to call him by his first name. "Kevin says you're quite the mechanic."

Mrs. Williams swatted her husband lightly with a potholder. "Oh, don't go and give him a big head about it, now." Her eyes sparkled up at him and my heart pulled. From all accounts, these two were still very much in love. Though no doubt they'd been through plenty of pain, they'd found their way through it together, it seemed.

Paul nodded his head toward Owen. "You got your license yet, boy?"

Owen's face reddened but the grin he wore made him look more like a little boy than an embarrassed teenager. "I've had my permit for two weeks, Grandpa."

I exchanged a look with Kevin, whose parted lips showed his own surprise at the title Owen had given Kevin's father. And why shouldn't the boy call his grandparents by their titles? What was the sense in holding off on such endearments when they'd already missed sixteen years of one another?

Paul studied the boy. "I see you grew some sense and took those holes out of your ears."

"They'll take a while to close up, but yeah, I did."

"Now I hope you didn't let this bear here intimidate you into that, honey." Mrs. Williams poured water into glasses around the table, and I moved to help her. "In fact, I was kind of fond of those earrings."

Owen winced. "Not earrings, Grandma. Plugs. Or some people call them flesh tunnels."

Paul grunted. "Flesh tunnels. That's just the kind of thing you want decorating the side of your head. Gives me the warm fuzzies just thinking about it."

Owen laughed good naturedly, but I couldn't help but wonder if he removed the plugs to ingratiate himself with Paul. Not that I could blame the boy for wanting to please the grandfather he just met.

And from the looks of it, he certainly seemed to be.

He certainly seemed far better at integrating with long lost family than Luna who had once again claimed to feel ill when I invited her to come with us to the Williams's home for dinner.

Was the girl actually sick so often or did she wish to avoid meeting new people? For a twenty-one-year-old, she didn't seem to get out much.

Mrs. Williams carried a platter of turkey to the table, and Kevin and I pushed aside napkins and candles to make room. Then came mashed potatoes, a salad, and a medley of vegetables. We sat, and I inhaled the homey scents, relishing this glimpse into Kevin's life.

Paul said a simple grace and after we served ourselves, Kevin's mother turned to me. "Kevin says you run a bed and breakfast, Hannah. That sounds so interesting! How in the world did you start such a venture?"

I told them the entire story. How running a bed and breakfast had always been my dream but how I had never had the time or the means until Josie had come home from college and approached Aunt Pris with a crazy plan that we'd actually pulled off.

"So, do all of your children have a hand in running the business, or is it mostly you and Josie?"

"Oh, they've all been a big help. Although now that Amie and Lizzie are married and away from home, they've stepped back a bit. Maggie runs the business side of things and Bronson and his wife run the orchard and a summer camp."

"My, it certainly sounds like a busy place."

"I'll have you over for dinner soon and give you the grand tour."

Owen cleared his throat. "Luna helps a lot, too."

I nodded. "Luna is a young woman staying with me right now. She's sort of like a stepdaughter." That was the best way I could think of to describe our relationship without going into details. "Kevin told me I could invite her tonight, but she's feeling under the weather."

The corners of Kevin's mouth turned downward. "Did she tell you Jolene stopped by today?" He shifted in his seat. What was putting him on edge? Was it simply the visit to his parents? But we'd broken the ice splendidly, if I did say so myself.

Oh no. Jolene. That must be it. He'd had an encounter with that woman and something had unsettled him. A sudden unpleasant prick of memory stormed my mind. Senior year of high school. Rounding the corner near Amos's locker and seeing Jolene cornering him, practically pressing him up against the lockers. He'd squirmed against the locker, his wild hair in front of his eyes as he searched the halls for escape.

I had cleared my throat and charged straight for them. "Is there something you need with my boyfriend, Jolene?"

She'd jumped back but recovered quickly, flung bleach blonde hair over her shoulder. "Just conducting a little experiment." She allowed her gaze to roam over Amos's body. "It worked." Then she flounced off.

I remembered sneering after her, shaking my head at her as Amos and I headed to our next class. I'd never asked him what she'd meant by her running an experiment that worked. Back then, I'd written the entire thing off. My intelligent Amos was most certainly not interested in flighty Jolene.

Now though, with Luna's recent arrival, his unfaithfulness clung to the corners of my mind. Should I have been so quick to trust him? But no. One night of infidelity for which he'd been repentant did not a lifetime cheater make. Though my trust in him had been shaken for good, I was quite certain that Amos had never been enchanted by Jolene.

"Luna didn't tell me, but I was wondering why Jolene never showed." Not that I bothered to follow up with the owner of the Red Velvet Inn. We weren't exactly texting buddies.

"She said she had to leave early," Kevin said.

I scrunched my nose, wondering why we were spending so much time on the topic of Jolene at his parents' dinner table. "Oh."

Kevin studied his food. "Maybe you should call her."

My gut tightened. Something was definitely up. I'd have to talk to Kevin later. Now, I gave his parents a small smile from across the table. "Jolene is another innkeeper in the area. We're working together to coordinate the Fourth of July parade. Not that it needs much coordination. It practically runs itself at this point."

Kevin went on to tell his parents how I volunteered at the mission and attempted to employ some of the men at Orchard House.

"My, our Kevin seems to have found a keeper," Mrs. Williams said.

I rolled my eyes. "Believe me, he's making me sound more generous than I actually am. He hasn't told you about the temper tantrum I threw when he tried to take me fishing."

"Uh oh, not a fisherwoman, then?" Paul asked.

"Afraid not."

"He must really like you then, if he's still keeping you around." Paul shoveled a bit of mashed potatoes in his mouth, and I couldn't quite decipher if he joked or not. For the first time, I wondered if Katherine fished. If that was something they spent time together doing, if he'd fallen in love with her over smelly fish bait.

"We're going to try kayaking." Kevin winked at me, and I released my doubts. Turns out some insecurities would be tough to get past—didn't matter if I was seventeen or fifty-two—dating had its challenges.

Kevin squeezed my knee beneath the table, and I glanced up at him, melting in those pine-green eyes once again. It was okay. Everything was okay.

There weren't any challenges I wouldn't go through to make this man a part of my life.

Of that, I was certain.

"THEY'RE SO SWEET, KEVIN. I REALLY ENJOYED THEM." Hannah strapped on her seatbelt in the front seat of the truck while Owen settled in the back.

"They loved you."

Hannah twisted in her seat. "What do you think, Owen? Do you think I passed the parent test?"

Kevin glanced in the rearview mirror to see one side of Owen's mouth lift. "If I passed their test, I'm pretty sure you were a sure thing, Mrs. Martin."

They all laughed. But Hannah remained turned in her seat, her attention on Owen. "Honey, it's clear they completely adore you. And I doubt you had to pass some test. They love you simply because you're their grandson, and that's enough."

This is why he loved this woman. She had a way of seeing to the heart of things, of talking about the deep stuff of life without embarrassment or shame. He had an inkling Amos had been like that as well. Kevin could only hope she didn't find him shallow or lacking once the newness of their relationship wore off.

The ride home was quiet and when Kevin pulled up to his house and Owen headed inside, he took Hannah's small hand and walked her across the dew-filled grass to her backdoor.

"Another visit tomorrow, right?" She squeezed his hand, and he could just make out her pensive expression beneath the moonlight.

He nodded. "You remembered."

"Of course. I've been praying that you make some sort of progress with Deidra."

"Thank you." He leaned down and kissed her cheek, his mouth lingering against the softness of her skin. When she turned her head to give him a proper kiss, he sank into it, trying to lose all his worries by pulling her body against his, by pressing her soft curves into him with determined passion.

And she seemed all too willing to respond, matching his desire with her own. When they finally drew apart, she gazed up at him with dreamy eyes. "If that's what I get every time I go to your parents, we might have to do it more often."

He ran a thumb over her cheek. "Hannah Martin, you make me crazy. In all the best ways."

She laid her head on his chest and he held her close, feeling the slight movement of her breaths against his body. Smelling the now familiar, flowery scent of her shampoo. Oh, man. He had it worse than bad. He didn't want to leave her. He wanted to go to bed with this woman every night and wake up with her every day. Eat every meal together and when they were apart, anticipate being with her all over again. He didn't know how long to wait to ask for her hand. Certainly, they should date through the summer. See how things went with Deidra. And Luna.

Luna.

He straightened. "I think you should talk to Luna."

She lifted her head. "Oh? And why is that?"

"I saw her this afternoon—she came over to help Owen with math. She was upset. I think you should talk to her."

"Okay. If she's awake, I'll talk to her now."

God help him, he wanted to spill everything. But he was a man of his word, and he'd promised Luna time. But the last thing he wanted was to see Hannah hurt. What was Luna's motivation in lying to the Martins about her dead mother? What kind of a person even did that?

But, like Owen, clearly Luna had gone through a lot. She was still young. Didn't she deserve some time and space to explain? Hannah said the girl was a great help around the bed and breakfast. As long as she wasn't a physical harm to Hannah or the business, it was probably best to give Luna the time she requested. He thought of how Jolene had spoken to her niece. Far be it from him to add his name to the list of people who would hurt her.

"Okay." He stroked the tops of her arms.

She tilted her head to the side. "Did something happen with Jolene today? Did she make a pass at you or something?"

He chuckled. "That woman has claws, that's for sure. But I think she knows I only have eyes for you."

She grew serious. "She used to corner Amos at his locker."

He bent his knees to lower himself so he could look directly in her eyes. "Hannah, there was no cornering. And even if there was, I can handle her."

"I thought Amos could too . . ." Her tone turned wistful.

He ran a lock of her light blonde hair between his thumb and forefinger. Tugged gently. "I don't know what I have to do to prove to you I'm not going anywhere, but you name it and I'll do it."

A sly smile crept over her face. "You could kiss me again."

"That, ma'am, will be no problem." He lowered his mouth to hers and fell into the spell and charm of this woman. In her arms, he could forget about Luna, and even Deidra. In her arms, the world fell away and his load lightened.

Everything would work itself out. God hadn't brought him into Hannah's backyard to watch her life crumble around them.

No, this was just the beginning of all the wonderful.

❧ 25 ❧

Well, his sister certainly hadn't learned to be on time in the twenty years since she'd left his parents' home. Kevin glanced at his phone. Four-twenty. Deidra was twenty minutes late, but perhaps it was simply habit.

Unlike last time, though, this time Owen sat on the small porch with Kevin, wrestling through some math homework.

Kevin pushed his feet against the worn floorboards, sending his old rocker back and forth, back and forth. He listened to the birds in the trees, trying to relax.

He thought of Hannah at his parents' house last night and his insides warmed. Then he thought of their heated kiss on her back patio, and he grew even warmer. Then he thought of Hannah talking to Luna about Jolene's visit and it was like a hose of cold water being sprayed on his bare stomach.

Luna must have told Hannah the truth by now, but Hannah hadn't texted him. Probably didn't want to bother him with Deidra's impending arrival and all.

"How's the math?" He spoke with his eyes still closed.

"I think I'm getting it."

"Luna help you at all yesterday?"

"She wasn't here long enough. Whatever. Everyone's got their own issues, right?"

Kevin popped open one eye. "Suppose that's true. You want me to have a look?"

Owen handed Kevin the worksheet. Kevin brought it closer to his face, then twisted it sideways and then upside-down. "Usually, I can figure things out by looking at it from a different perspective, but I'm afraid this doesn't make sense no matter how I look at it."

Owen gave him a look that said, *Really?* He shook his head. "You are so corny."

He sounded as if he wanted to say *old*, but Kevin couldn't even try to be offended. He chuckled just as Deidra's Honda turned into the driveway, louder than it had been last week, if possible.

"What do you know, she actually showed up." Owen slipped his math paper into the bookbag beside him.

"You're going to play nice, I expect." Kevin raised an eyebrow in the teenager's direction, realizing just how comfortable they were beginning to be with each other. Owen spouting off sarcastic comments about his mother, and Kevin attempting to prod him to use his manners.

Kevin stood as Deidra stepped out of the car in the most inappropriate attire a mother could possibly wear to a state-induced visit with her son. A short black miniskirt left Kevin praying that she at least had underwear on beneath the thin fabric. A short-sleeved blouse dipped low and suggestively. Worst of all was how she swayed by the car, as if trying to focus on where—or how—to walk.

Kevin raked a hand through his hair, unsure whether to go to her, go inside and make coffee in hopes it would sober her up, or demand her to leave his property and find something more appropriate to wear. If not for his sake, then most certainly for her son's.

Owen slapped his back. "I thought about mentioning how

well-behaved Mom was last time but figured you could use a good surprise."

Kevin dragged his gaze to the boy. "This is funny to you?"

Owen's cocky grin drooped. "No, sir." The comment had been nerves, no doubt. Nerves and disappointment because his mom hadn't shown up for him. Again. "She spends Wednesdays with Sam most of the time. I thought this might happen."

"Why don't you go inside?"

For a minute, he looked as if he'd argue but then, thinking better of it, opened the door to the house.

"Owen!" Deidra yelled the one word, sending it slurring and hissing and slapping against the screen door where her son had just disappeared.

How did she even make the drive here?

"Owen! Come out here boy and give your Mama a kiss." She giggled and attempted a couple steps toward Kevin. Her gaze roamed over him, cold as the Maine Atlantic in January. "You gonna keep my boy from me, big brother? That how this is gonna play out?"

"This isn't good, Deidra. Better you hadn't come at all than show up for one of the visits like this."

She pouted and placed her hand against her mouth. "Is big brother going to tell the mean l-little social worker on me?"

He gritted his teeth. He didn't smell any liquor, so it must be drugs. Making a quick decision, he talked into the screen door. "I'm going to take your mom home, okay?"

Owen shook his head back-and-forth. "No. Don't go."

The boy's words stopped him. "I have to make sure she's safe. She can't drive like this. If I call the police on her, you won't get to see her again for who knows how long."

"Sam'll be there. He has guns, Uncle Kevin. When he and Mom are high, there's no reasoning . . ."

Kevin opened the door and stepped inside, placing a hand on

Owen's arm. The fear in the teenager's eyes was enough to drive him to his knees.

Owen gripped Kevin's arm, hard, as if his very life depended on Kevin's next decision. "Please, don't go. I know this is a bad idea."

While he wasn't afraid to face down a drugged-up boyfriend, Kevin was afraid of ruining the relationship he was just beginning to build with his nephew. Owen was finally learning to trust him. What would it say about their relationship if Kevin threw his nephew's warnings out the window, even if they were unfounded?

He made a quick decision.

"Can you go upstairs to my room? There's a heavy trunk in the closet on the floor. Can you grab a t-shirt and maybe some sweatpants?"

Owen took off up the stairs, stomping back down them in no time with a small pile of Katherine's clothes.

Kevin grabbed a blue V-neck t-shirt Katherine used to wear when doing housework. He'd slept with the thing for a solid six months after her death. Then he picked out a pair of black yoga pants.

"What are you going to do?"

If he could keep Deidra here, he would. But Rita Bridges had been strict about the short visitation times. He'd even mentioned asking Deidra to move in with him to the social worker, but she'd been deeply distressed, saying that if that were to occur, they'd have to place Owen in another home.

Just another among many mistakes he'd made in his journey as a guardian to a teenager.

But he hoped this was not one.

"I'm going to take her home."

Owen got that wide-eyed wild look about him again. "He won't think twice about shooting you. The only—"

Kevin shook his head, placed both hands on the boy's shoulders. "Grandma and Grandpa's home."

Owen blinked and bit his bottom lip. "I want to come."

"Owen!" Deidra's strident voice sounded through the screen.

"I'm sorry, son. I don't think that's a good idea."

"But—"

"Owen, my job right now is to keep you safe. Not just physically, but mentally and emotionally. I know you're a tough kid. I know you've had to handle more than most boys your age ever have to in a lifetime, but I'm making this decision with you in mind. The last thing I want to do is give Ms. Bridges a reason to think I'm not fit to take care of you. Can you understand that?"

Slowly, he nodded.

"Thank you," Kevin breathed. "I'll be back as soon as I can. I have my cell. If I'm not home for dinner, see if you can join Hannah and Luna."

"Okay."

Kevin pulled Owen in for a brief, firm hug. He slapped his back. "I'm proud of you."

Then he grabbed Katherine's old clothes and headed out the door, ready for the fight of his life.

⁂

GETTING DEIDRA INTO HIS TRUCK WASN'T THE PROBLEM. ONCE he told her he was taking her home, she'd quietly accepted the ride. He prayed all the way to his parents' house, hoping against hope that he was making the right decision.

Deidra was out of control. She needed rehab. Not two eighty-year-old parents who didn't have the physical or emotional energy to handle a drug addict.

He promised himself he'd call Rita Bridges tomorrow. Like it or not, he needed to be honest with her about Deidra's status. He needed her help. If for no other reason than for Owen's sake. He'd been naïve to think Deidra would pick up her life for the sake of her son, been naïve to think he could swoop in and be the hero that won her back to her right mind, to their parents, to her son.

Deidra opened her eyes ten minutes into the ride. "This isn't the way home."

"I have something else in mind, actually." He wanted to wait until the last possible moment to tell her their true destination. The last thing he needed was a full-blown tantrum in the truck.

Luckily, she seemed to black out again and didn't wake until they pulled up to their parents' drive. He put the truck in park a healthy distance from the house. Deidra bolted upright. "Where are we?" She looked around, horror spreading over her heavily made-up face. She lunged at him, hitting him hard, poking long fingernails into the skin of his face, his neck, his chest. "What do you think you're doing? Take me *home*!"

He opened his door to wiggle away from her piercing jabs. "This is your home, Deidra. Mom and Dad still want you."

She let out a string of expletives that would paint a blush on the crudest of sailors. "You can't kidnap me." She dug in her pocketbook for the phone. "I'm calling the police. They'll arrest y-you. K-kidnapping me against m-my will."

"Deidra." He gentled his tone. "Do you really want to do that?"

She stopped and her face crumpled. "I *hate* you."

He had no doubt she meant all the emphasis she put behind the word. "I wish it wasn't this way. I love you, Deidra. You'll always be my little sister."

She shot off a bunch of curse words again.

"You shouldn't have showed up today the way you did. What did you expect me to do?"

More curses. Did he really expect to reason with her?

"Take me *home*. My real home."

"The home where the guy you live with beats your son? That home?" He goaded her, he knew it, but frustration welled up within his chest. Why couldn't she see what was so obvious to everyone else?

"You don't know"—more cursing—"about my life or my home. Sam loves me and he loves Owen. He takes care of us."

"By selling your body to other men?" As soon as the words were out, he wished to take them back. In his mind, he was trying to get her to see reason, but in her mind, no doubt all she heard was judgement. "I'm sorry."

She started hitting him again, but this time he grabbed her wrists. "You have two options right now. Either I drive you to a rehab facility." He could ask Hannah for a referral. Maybe even Amos's mission had some sort of program. "Or we try this. No judgements. Mom and Dad will be so happy to see you."

She gave a huff of sarcastic annoyance before pushing open the truck door and sliding out. "Fine."

He winced as her skirt rode up. Well, on the plus side he could now be assured she did indeed wear underwear beneath the skirt. If he wanted to call that skimpy piece of fabric underwear.

She slammed the door. "I'm home, Mama and Daddy! Ready or not, here I come!"

Shouldn't have expected her to make this easy.

"Any chance you want to put a t-shirt on, little sister?" He called as he closed his truck door.

She whirled around and shook her upper body in a suggestive way. "Thought you said no judgements?" She shook herself again. "Are you judging me?"

He averted his eyes. "No, of course not," he ground out. Heaven help him. Heaven help his mother. He strode up to the house, hoping to get there first. Though how his parents hadn't yet come out to see who was shrieking was beyond him.

He reached the door and rang the bell all while Deidra kept up her yelling.

"Mama! I'm home! Daddy! Come see all your little girl's become!" She flung out her arms.

This was a mistake. A terrible, terrible mistake. The only thing he could do was pray his parents weren't home. Maybe they were out playing cards. The garage door was shut. Maybe it would be a small grace if he simply turned around and took Deidra to some halfway house or rehab center.

But a moment later, the door opened. And there was his mother, staring slack-jawed at Deidra. But she wasn't staring at her clothes. She was staring at her face.

And then she was falling toward her baby girl, moving faster than he'd seen her move in ages. "Deidra. Deidra, you're home. It's really you! My girl. My girl."

She wrapped her arms around her daughter, and wonder of wonders, Deidra allowed their mother's wrinkled, loose arms to grasp her. And for the first time that afternoon, his little sister was silent.

❦ 26 ❦

"**L**una!" I whisked the eggs for my baked Florentine omelet a bit harder than necessary. We had a full house this morning and one of the guests—a woman in her early sixties with a penchant for butterfly pins and livestreaming on social media—kept ending up in the kitchen asking if I needed help.

I'd just assured her once again that I had things under control and urged her to pour herself some coffee from the bar beneath the guestroom stairs when I considered calling Maggie or Josie to see if they could stop by to help with breakfast service.

Not for the first time this morning, I wondered how Deidra was doing. Poor Kevin. He'd been so torn between staying with his parents last night and coming home to Owen. Through texts, I'd offered to have Owen stay at Orchard House, but he told me it was against foster care protocol to place Owen in the charge of non-licensed caregivers. He'd come home late, and then went out again as soon as Owen climbed the bus stairs that morning.

From what I gathered, Deidra hadn't committed to anything. Last night, she'd passed out in her old bedroom. This morning, Kevin and his parents planned to talk with her. I'd given him several numbers and websites we used at the mission. I could only pray this would be a turning point for all of them.

Now, I needed to worry about breakfast. "Luna!" I called again, trying not to be too loud lest the guests wonder what the raucous was about.

Amos's daughter had hung out with Lizzie at Asher's store yesterday, and I hadn't seen her much. When I'd come in from my time with Kevin two nights ago, she'd been asleep. The few minutes I had seen her, she'd possessed a rather mopey attitude, and since I'd been busy with our full house, I'd chosen to stay clear.

"Luna!" I called again. I turned to my phone, ready to tap out a quick text because I didn't have time to run up the stairs.

"I'm here." Luna walked around the bar as she tied her hair back in a haphazard ponytail. The girl just didn't seem herself. I'd have to make it a point to have another heart-to-heart with her after breakfast.

"Good morning. All our rooms are full this morning and everyone has decided to come down to eat right at eight." I squinted at her. "You up for this?"

She nodded, tying on the apron and grabbing the order notepad we used for drinks. Though I wished she looked a bit more perky for our guests, I couldn't complain. On a morning like this, I needed to be in the kitchen preparing food. Maybe I *did* need to hire more help.

I looked over the breakfast order forms from the night before. Twelve guests. Seven Florentine omelets, five Belgian waffles. I heated up the waffle iron and added sprigs of lavender to the coffee cake plates.

A moment later, the pantry door slammed open. I straightened. "Everything okay?"

Luna tossed the notepad on the counter and opened the door of the refrigerator. "Do you have some sort of privacy policy here?"

I stopped in the middle of plating a slice of coffee cake. I cleared my throat. "Um, when the guests register, they're informed that I won't use or sell their information."

She blinked and poured a glass of orange juice. It sloshed over the side and I wet a clean dishcloth under the faucet to help with the spill. Luna moved on to fill a glass of cranberry juice, seeming not to have noticed the spilled OJ.

"I mean, are guests supposed to be filming inside the bed and breakfast?"

The woman with the butterfly pins. I swiped the dishcloth around and under the glass. "I don't have a policy against it, no. In fact, I suppose in some cases it might be good publicity."

Luna released a huff.

"Is someone bothering you out there, Luna? Because I can take care of table service."

She shook her head and threw back her shoulders. "I'm fine. I got this." She loaded a tray of glasses, and I cringed as she barreled through the pantry door.

What was going on? I remembered Kevin's admonishment that I talk to Luna. Was her uncharacteristic behavior part of the reason why he suggested I do so?

I breathed a prayer asking for wisdom and patience. Whatever was up with Luna would have to wait until the waffles and omelets were served.

I finished the coffee cakes and ran them over to the large butcher block counter near the swinging door to the guest area. I turned to check the bacon crisping in the oven when a loud crash and a scream tunneled toward me from the guest dining room.

Stumbling toward the pantry door, I pushed it open, unable to guess what I would find. All eyes were on a table in the corner alcove where the woman with the butterfly pin sat covered in orange juice. Luna stood above her, a smartphone on the floor a couple feet away.

The woman scrambled for the phone. Pointed it at Luna. "You did that on purpose."

"Your phone was in the way." Luna's voice was low and even.

"Well, what do you have to say for yourself?" The woman continued to point the phone at Luna. She was . . . recording?

Quick as lighting, Luna slapped the phone out of her hand until it was again on the floor.

I pushed through a younger couple that carried coffee to their table. "Excuse me, but what in the world is going on here?" I glared at Luna. No matter our guests' quirks, I always strove to treat them with respect. Luna slapping the phone out of the woman's hand was inexcusable—no matter how annoying her videoing might be.

The woman again crouched down to retrieve her phone off the hardwood floor. When she straightened, I tried not to stare at the offensive orange liquid spilled down the front of her white blouse, seeping straight through to her bra.

"Your *daughter* has been incredibly rude and is assaulting me. I have half a mind to call the police." This time, she faced the phone at me.

My thoughts ran amuck. First, that what the woman accused Luna of seemed to be true. Second, that she may indeed call the police. Third, that I needed to set things straight. This was not who the Martins were. This was not what our family or the Orchard House would be known for. I needed to fix this.

"She's not my daughter." The words came out hastily, and although I could practically feel Luna's gaze drilling into my back, I continued. "Please, ma'am. I'm terribly sorry for this incident. Please be assured I'll be taking over your breakfast service this morning and for the rest of your stay. If you'd like to change, perhaps we can talk after breakfast and see what we can work out."

I whirled away from the camera, giving reassuring smiles to the rest of the guests as I slipped into the pantry, Luna following.

"What in the world was that about?" I hissed as I grabbed the coffee cake plates.

"She wouldn't stop taping me. I have a right to my privacy, don't I?"

"Luna, I don't even know where to start right now."

Luna picked up coffee cake plates, but I shook my head. "Oh, no. You will not set foot out there again. I'm taking over."

She whipped her apron off and tossed it on the counter. "Fine."

"After breakfast, we need to have a talk."

"No, we don't. I'm leaving."

"Luna—"

"Don't worry about me, Miss Hannah. I'll be fine on my own. It's not like I'm your daughter or anything."

She stomped up the stairs and I closed my eyes, breathing around my frustration. In that slice of moment, I hoped she was going upstairs to pack her suitcase and leave for good. Life was simpler without evidence of Amos's unfaithfulness before me every day. Loving his daughter was too hard, especially in moments like this when she made things ten times more difficult.

Maybe it had been a mistake to invite her to stay at Orchard House in the first place. Couldn't I have supported her from a distance? Why did I have to feel responsible for her?

I released a groan of despair and leaned my hands against the counter, breathing deep through my nose as I uttered a silent prayer amidst the scent of burning bacon.

In that moment, more than anything, I wished for Kevin. But Kevin was trying to help his sister. And right now, I had breakfast to serve.

By the time I finished serving the coffee cake and apologizing to each guest individually, my head had cleared. After serving the main dishes to my guests, I grabbed up my phone and texted Luna.

Please don't leave. I really think we should talk.

I sent off the text and turned my attention to the dirtied waffle iron. Surely, this was just a misunderstanding. I'd speak to the lady with the butterfly pin—Mrs. Tippins—after breakfast, and then Luna and I would sit down and have a good heart-to-heart. That had always worked with my girls, right?

Although, if one fact was becoming apparent to me, it was this; Luna was far from a daughter of my womb.

⚜

THE MINUTE I'D FINISHED CHECKING OUT MR. AND MRS. Tippins—reimbursing them in full for their stay the previous two nights—and saying goodbye, my phone rang.

I scooped it up from the kitchen island, noting Josie's name flashing on my screen. "Hey, honey."

"Mom, what is going on over there?"

I straightened. "What—what do you mean?"

"I *mean* with Luna? It's all over social media. How horrible she was to that lady. She's tagged all of our accounts, including the Camden town pages. You need to get online and address it. It looks horrible. Probably has the power to ruin us."

Cold dread climbed up my insides. No. *No.* My guests. The reputation I'd worked so hard to build and preserve. Certainly, our faithful guests might overlook such an incident, but what about new guests? What about my reputation in town? My bottom lip quivered at that last thought.

What about the hospitality grant?

I shook my head. "I need to talk to her."

"Kathy Tippins? I don't know if that will help at this point. It's already getting more shares than a cold in flu season."

"No. Luna. I don't know what's gotten into her. I have to go, Josie." As much as I cared about the business, I couldn't shake the sense that something was terribly off with Luna. What if she left? What if she hurt herself or someone else?

"Mom, no. She's the one who got us into this mess."

"Can you call Maggie and have her jump online and try to clean things up?" Maggie took care of our social accounts. She'd prove much better with words than I in this situation. Besides, if I went online, I'd have to look at the video. I'd have to watch the potential destruction of the business I'd poured myself into for the last four years.

"Okay. I'll be over soon. Call me if you need anything."

I thanked her and hung up before jogging up the stairs. "Luna!" Once I reached Lizzie's old bedroom, I knocked on the door. No answer. I pushed it open. The shades were drawn, but a quick flip of the light revealed none of Luna's things in the room.

She was gone.

I scrolled to her name in my text messages and hit the *call* button. It rang hollow in my ear for several minutes before I started back down the stairs, unsure of my next steps.

Halfway down the stairs, a solid pounding met my ears. When I reached the landing and saw the woman on the other side of the door, I groaned.

And here I thought this day couldn't get any worse.

I opened the door. "Jolene. I'm afraid this isn't a great time."

She pushed her way past me, the scent of her floral perfume overpowering my kitchen. "I apologize Hannah, but this can't wait."

"I realize we're behind on the parade planning but if we could just email our thoughts, I think that might be a lot easier."

She glanced at the mess of my kitchen and wrinkled her nose. "Looks like you need to hire on more help."

I certainly did.

"Like I said, we're in a bit of a snag right now—"

"Oh, believe me, I know." Jolene spun around at the bar and crossed her arms, leaning against the granite. "I saw your little fiasco on Facebook. I came right over."

I rubbed my forehead. "You came over because . . .?"

"That girl is out of control, Hannah. Something has to be done."

I bit my lip. "I'm not entirely certain why Luna is your problem, Jolene." Couldn't the woman mind her own business for one simple Friday morning?

She stared at me as if struck dumb. Something I'd never seen, quite honestly. Then she laughed, a pitiful, mirthful sound. "Your boyfriend didn't tell you?"

My mind raced. "Kevin? What does he have to do with this?"

"Kevin saw the whole thing the other day. I could have sworn you'd be the first person he'd run to." A small smile pulled at her Botox-puffed lips. "Guess you guys aren't as tight as I thought."

I breathed deep around my pain. Whatever it was, it needed to be dealt with. I needed to know.

"Jolene," I ground out. "Just spit it out."

"Turns out your dear little Luna isn't exactly who she says she is. In fact, she's *my* dear little Luna. My niece. And her mother—my sister—is very much alive."

Kevin didn't know what was harder—watching his sister hurt his parents all over again or watching her hurt herself.

"There's a way out of this, Deidra," he spoke softly, as if anything too loud might frighten her. And indeed, with the effects of withdrawal already beginning to take root, it just might. "We want to help you."

Deidra rolled her eyes, but her hands shook. "This my intervention, is that it? I haven't seen you all in twenty years and this is how we're gonna start things off?"

"These are all the people who love you the most in one room trying to stop you from killing yourself." Kevin's mother wrung her hands. A single tear meandered down her wrinkled cheek. "Think of your son, Deidra."

His sister stood. "I raised him the last sixteen years without you, so don't pretend like you know anything about him."

"He's a good kid." This from their father.

Deidra looked up sharply at their dad in his old ballcap. "Oh, my son's a good kid, huh Pop? What'd you like about him the most? Was it the plugs, because God only knows if I came home with them all hell would have broken loose."

"Deidra," their mother started.

"No, Mom. You wanted me to come home all this time? Well, I'll be danged if I don't say my piece."

His mom wrung her hands as if they were a mud-filled mop she had to bring across a clean floor. "Okay, then. We want to hear what you have to say."

Kevin shifted in his seat. Yes, maybe this was progress. The beginning of healing. No doubt it would be hard, but if reconciliation and healing were at the other end, wouldn't it be worth it?

"You hated me," Deidra began. His mother looked positively pained. She shook her head, but Deidra continued. "I could never live up to your standards, could never be the perfect daughter like Kevin was the perfect son."

He winced at this new glimpse in perspective. His parents *had* been overly proud of him and his accomplishments. Had that dribbled down in a negative way to Deidra?

"I never wore the right clothes to school—and especially not church, never dated the right boys." She laughed, but it lacked any humor. "Oh, here's a good one. You want to go deep? Remember that time you sent me to church camp, hoping it would save my soul?"

Kevin racked his brain, but he'd been married and deep in his business by then, not always in touch with the goings on in his sister's life.

"You know what happened at *church* camp, Dad? One of the counselors got real friendly, that's what. Touched me in places I'd never been touched before. And you know what? I liked it. You hear that, Dad? I liked it. How's that for saving my soul?"

His mom was sobbing now and through his shock, Kevin reached for his sister. "Deidra—"

She shrugged him off. "Even you can't save me now, big brother."

"Why didn't you tell us?" his father croaked.

"Would you have believed me, Pop? You barely believed I did my homework every night, even when I did. Would you have believed that your perfect altar boy neighbor would have pulled the moves on me at a camp that was supposed to make me see Jesus in a whole new light?" She laughed with that sickly mirth again. "I saw the light, all right. But it wasn't toward God."

Kevin breathed deep, disgusted by his sister's crude manner and the way she vomited it onto his parents. So many emotions whirled inside him, he could hardly manage them all. Disgust, pity, and then . . . Adam, the altar boy? The kid he used to play ball with every spring and summer. He clenched his fists tight, ready to hunt down the little shortstop punk and give him what-for.

His dad seemed to be in the same headspace. "Adam Rollings?"

"Turns out he wasn't just knowledgeable in the Bible." Deidra cast a haughty look at her father.

"He should be prosecuted and held accountable." Kevin raked a hand through his hair. "You were a minor. Who knows how many other girls . . ."

Deidra waved a hand through the air. "There you go again, big brother, always thinking you can save the world. When are you going to learn it's no use?"

He gritted his teeth. "I don't believe that. And I do believe in you, Deidra. What happened back then was wrong and horrible. But I believe in you *now*. You can come out of this. You can do it for your son."

Through silent sobs, her mother slid to the floor at Deidra's bare knees. She groped for her daughter's hands, her gray head stooped and ancient. "Deidra, I am so, so sorry. Please forgive us. We—we never meant to hurt you. We were only trying our best."

For a split second, something in Deidra's gaze softened. And then it was gone. As if she'd seen the two paths before her and had made her choice. She stood, her hands trembling. "I have to go."

If Deidra walked out of this room now, he was quite sure they'd never see her again. Maybe Owen wouldn't, either.

He placed his hands on the sides of Deidra's arms. "This is your chance. Please. Take it. Is this the life you want?"

"It's the life I have."

"I drove you here, remember? You don't have a car. Why don't we find a place that can help you? I won't leave until you feel comfortable. I promise."

Her hands shook more, and she wriggled from his grip. "I don't want help. I need Sam. I need to go home."

He couldn't force her to make the right decision, and with the effects of withdrawal already starting to kick in, she likely wouldn't make a healthy one. She wanted her fix. She wanted her no-good boyfriend.

"Fine. But I'm not driving you back there. You'll have to figure it out yourself."

She dug out her phone. "Sam'll pick me up."

The last thing he needed was Sam coming to his parents' house. He shook his head. "Your car's at my place. I'll take you back there."

She smiled over her shoulder. "Fun times, Mom and Dad. Almost how it used to be, right?"

All Kevin could do was place a hand on his mother's quaking shoulder and squeeze. They'd tried. As much as he wanted to drag Deidra to a rehab center, what good would it do if she was set against it?

When they pulled up his driveway and he parked the truck, Deidra sat quiet, trying to clasp her shaking hands in her lap. "This is a nice place for a boy to finish his growing up years."

Kevin blinked. "A nicer place is with his mother."

She sniffed. "Not with the kind of mother I am. Not with what he has to see . . ." She shook her head. "You'd adopt him, wouldn't you, big brother? Or at least let him stay with you until he's old enough?"

It was the first time she'd shown any sort of vulnerability. His throat threatened to close as he sought the wisdom to answer. Truthfully, he'd sign the paperwork to adopt Owen in a heartbeat. But would that simply give Deidra permission to completely abandon him? Is that what she wanted? And if so, was it out of selfishness or the notion that she indeed wasn't the best thing for him?

And the reality was, she wasn't. If she refused to get help, refused to ditch the man who beat her son, the fact remained that Owen was better off with Kevin.

"He has a place to stay in my home for however long he wants." The words crawled up Kevin's throat in a croak.

Deidra nodded. "I'll talk to Rita right away, then. Get the paperwork started."

"Deidra—"

She shook her head so hard her large hoop earrings hit her neck. "Stop trying to change me, Kevin! This is who I am. The best thing you can do for me is take care of my boy. I—I can't change things. I can't."

"You can't. Not alone. But with—"

She pushed open the door. "Like I said, I'll call Rita."

And then her Honda was rumbling down his drive and a big, gaping hole took up residence in his heart. He hadn't been able to stop Deidra from running away all those years ago. He hadn't been able to give Katherine a baby. He hadn't been able to stop his wife from dying. And now, he hadn't been able to give Owen his mother back.

While he knew he didn't have the power to save the world, he liked to think he at least had the power to help those he loved. Now, though, he wasn't so sure.

He wasn't sure of anything.

28

I didn't know how I ended up in the bookshop again, but here I was, staring at the empty fireplace. Josie wouldn't be in until twelve. Maggie had hunkered down at home to deal with our social media fallout. And Jolene had left shortly after she'd reported her shocking news.

I hadn't been able to stand another minute in the mess of my kitchen, alone with my thoughts. Neither could I make myself clean up. Instead, I curled into the smallest ball I could manage on the couch in the bookshop and prayed no one would find me for a very, very long time.

Luna's mother was alive. Jolene's *sister* was Luna's mother. Amos had had an affair with Jolene's sister. Kevin had known all this, and he had not told me.

What an idiot I was. Trying to swoop in and help my husband's orphan child. Believing every word that poured out of her mouth.

Excellent judge of character, indeed.

I racked my brain for a mental picture of Jolene's younger sister. Her name was Lila. Jolene had refreshed me on that much. She'd been a student at the college where Amos had taught.

Jolene hadn't known Luna's father had been Amos until a couple of days ago.

I groaned, wanting to push it all away.

Amos, look what you've done to us. You've ruined us, all these years later, with your one stupid mistake. You were so smart, my love. So smart. Why did one woman have to be your downfall?

I thought I'd forgiven my husband. But with each new heartache that came in the present, I found the past harder and harder to forgive.

"Lord, help me move past this once and for all," I whispered into the still shop.

And yet, what would that look like? Luna's mother was alive. The girl had lied and cajoled in order to convince me to open my house and home to her. I shouldn't feel responsible for her, and yet somehow, I still did.

In some crazy way, in my head at least, my promise to be faithful to Amos extended to Luna. My answer to dilemmas had always been simple—love. Love, even in the hard. It's why Amos and I had worked through our problems. Why I'd been able to champion my kids even when they made foolish decisions or acted unlovable. It was why I did my work at the mission, why I was able to brush off the inconvenience of hiring some of the men at the mission who had, unfortunately, proved unreliable at times.

But what was the answer when it came to Luna, my husband's daughter? A girl who'd been raised without a father, who'd lied her way into our family, who may very well have ruined the reputation of all I'd worked for the last four years in a single morning?

And what about Kevin? Yes, I loved him, but what did it say about our relationship that he didn't tell me as soon as possible when he found out the truth about Luna? What excuse could he possibly have? And how could we begin a relationship when the trust I'd felt for him had already been broken?

Was I destined to fall for men who failed me?

The back of my eyelids burned, and I clenched them shut. For the first time in a long time, an intense ache for my mother overwhelmed me. I wanted her arms around me. I wanted to cry on her shoulder.

The bell above the door jingled and I didn't move, hoping whoever it was might go away. Surely it was too early for Josie . . .

"Hello? Hannah?"

The melodious tinkle of that voice strummed chords of hope across my heart. I sat up and turned, disbelieving my eyes at seeing the petite, gray-haired woman standing in my bookshop. A woman who should have been two hours away in Bar Harbor. "Charlotte?" I stood on wobbly legs.

"Now, Hannah Grace, what are you doing hiding out in this bookshop when your kitchen looks like a tornado's been through it?"

Tears coursing down my cheeks, I lunged into the arms of my best friend. "How—how did you know I needed you? Why are you here?"

She squeezed me tight before releasing me, her sea-blue eyes twinkling, somehow assuring me that everything would be okay in the end.

"I saw a bit of the debacle online, I'm afraid. I figured you could use some help with damage control."

I hid my face in my hands. "Was it as awful as it was when it was happening?"

The corners of her mouth turned downward. "I'm afraid so. But don't worry. Everything can be fixed."

"A reputation can't be fixed like a broken appliance."

She patted my hand. "I say, we start with the kitchen. Once we've cleaned up, I'll make us my famous chocolate cake and we'll sit down and figure how to sort this all out."

I cracked a smile. "Chocolate cake fixes everything, huh?"

"No, of course not. But it sure makes it easier to handle."

AN HOUR LATER, THE KITCHEN GLEAMED AND THE SMELL OF chocolate cake wafted from the oven and through the screen door onto the patio where Charlotte and I sat with glasses of sparkling water. I'd told her everything. About Luna's moodiness the last couple of days, about the debacle that morning, about Jolene's visit, my anger toward Luna, and my renewed anger toward Amos. I told her about my newfound uncertainty regarding my relationship with Kevin.

When I was finished, I leaned my head back on the chair and stretched my legs so my bare feet were in the sun. "Sorry to hurl all my problems at you."

Charlotte laughed. "I was counting on it."

I shook my head. "Charlotte, you shouldn't have come. How did you get away from your guests?"

"No guests today." She said it as if it wasn't a problem, but something about her tone caused a red flag to wave in my head. Before I could question her though, Maggie slid through the screen door and flopped onto one of the wicker chairs.

"I think I've done all I can do." She pushed back a strand of dark hair behind one ear.

"Honey, I can't thank you enough for handling all of that. I wouldn't have known where to begin. What a nightmare."

"All I could do was apologize and reassure the trolls and naysayers that this is our first incident, that we have stellar reviews otherwise, and that we were working to solve the problem from within." She shrugged. "That's all I can think to do. Though the timing is lousy, Mom, with the grant and all. I'm sorry."

I breathed deep and closed my eyes. "I *really* wanted that grant."

"Have you heard from Luna?" Maggie asked.

I shook my head. "I've texted and called, but nothing. I'm guessing she doesn't want to face me. And she doesn't even know that I know she lied about her mother."

Maggie crossed her arms over her chest. "I was really starting to like her, you know? But that video . . . I felt like she was someone else. Like, she really just lost it. That can't be happening when we're trying to build a business and serve guests."

Charlotte and I nodded.

The sound of a car pulling up the drive caught our attention. For a moment, my heart jolted, thinking it might be Luna. But no. It was an old Nissan Sentra—not a car of one of our guests either.

A tall woman in form-fitting jeans and a button-down blouse stepped out of the car. As soon as I glimpsed her face, I knew who she was. Aside from Amos's sharp brown eyes and wide brow, this woman was the spitting image of Luna.

I pushed myself up in my chair, unsure if I had the energy to meet the woman Amos had chosen all those nights ago. Couldn't she have at least come after we'd had cake?

Charlotte stood, placing a reassuring hand on my shoulder. "I'll go see to that cake."

Maggie leaned toward me. "You want me to stay, Mom?"

I stared at my daughter, the perfect combination of Amos's mysterious dark looks and my fair features. My goodness, how I loved this girl. All my kids. Was it even fair to Luna to try and hold her in my heart alongside them?

I patted Maggie's knee. "I'll be okay. Thanks, honey."

And then she was gone, and I stood to meet my guest.

Lila was a pretty woman, with softer, more natural features than her older sister. I could only hope they differed in more than looks.

She approached me with slow steps, forcing a smile. "Hello, are you Hannah?"

"I am." I extended my hand and she took it. "You must be Lila."

She cocked her head. "How did you . . .?"

"Jolene was here this morning."

Her mouth fell open. "I hope she didn't make a scene."

No more than your daughter did this morning. I bit my lip. "Would you like to sit?"

Lila sat in the seat Charlotte had abandoned. I couldn't help but study her. The graceful way she carried herself, how she crossed her legs and adjusted her blouse. Her figure was near perfect and she still possessed a youthful look about her, and even though Amos was long dead, even though what happened had occurred nearly twenty-two years before, I found myself fighting off jealousy. A feeling of lack.

"I don't know where to begin." The woman held out her hands, palms up. "When my sister called to tell me Luna was staying with you, I was shocked. She'd disappeared some weeks ago after an argument, but I tried to give her space. She texted me once to let me know she was okay."

It would be so easy to sit on my high horse and judge this woman who'd seduced my husband. Who raised a child who ran off after a single argument with her mother? A child who could fly off the handle at any minute and ruin all I'd worked for the last four years?

But the reality was, I knew what it was like to be a mother grieving a runaway child. Just last year, Amie had run off with one of our bed and breakfast guests, putting herself in a dangerous situation. And she'd been older than Luna. Josie, dear girl, had been lost to me for a year after Amos died. Deep in her grief, she'd run away in an altogether different manner—to college and New York to drown her sorrows in the arms of an older man.

No, I had no right to judge this woman.

I swallowed. "When Luna showed up, she said she was Amos's daughter. She told me her mother died last Christmas Eve. I thought she was an orphan. I told her she could stay here for a bit to get to know her half-brother and sisters."

Lila bit her lip and nodded. "Her showing up here couldn't have been easy. I'm sorry for that."

I dragged in a deep breath and took the plunge. Addressed

what we'd no doubt be dancing around for a good long time if I didn't go ahead and dive in. "Lila, I knew Amos had an affair all those years ago. He came home and told me. I just—I never knew there was a child that resulted from it. I can't help but wonder now if Amos knew?"

Ugh. I hated this. Hated how I needed to question this woman about my husband's knowledge of Luna. Surely, he would have told me something so important?

She shook her head, as if to assure me. "He didn't."

I breathed a sigh of relief. Not only that my husband hadn't kept a secret that big from me, but that who I thought he was still remained intact. "He would have wanted to be a part of Luna's life if he'd known. I hope you know that."

"I do. That's one of the reasons I never told him." She glanced at the pavers beneath our feet. "He wasn't the only one who felt badly about that night. Although, I don't regret what came from it. No matter our struggles, Luna is a blessing."

I forced a tight smile. "She said she doesn't have any brothers or sisters. She must be very precious to you."

"She is. We did okay, the two of us. Not well-off or anything, and believe me, there were times I wanted to knock on Amos's door and demand his help."

"Why didn't you?"

"It wouldn't have been fair to him. He had five children, a wife. I'm the one who came onto him. He was helping me with a project. One night, we just—"

I held up my hand. "Please, I don't want to know details."

"Sorry. Anyway, before Luna ran away, she demanded to know about her dad. She had just turned twenty-one. I didn't think it was fair to keep the truth from her any longer. So, I told her."

"She thought Amos was alive when she came here."

Lila's mouth turned downward. "She was angry when I admitted that I never told Amos about her. I think, in her mind, she always thought he was a deadbeat dad." She shrugged. "Probably because I let her think it. Easier that way. Easier to think it was me and my girl against the world. Harder for her to accept that I willingly chose not to inform her father she existed." She tapped her fingers on the arm of the wicker. Inside, the oven timer went off for the cake. A cake for which I no longer had an appetite.

"She left before I could tell her about Amos not being alive. She didn't answer my calls or texts and I didn't want to break the news to her over a voicemail. I had an inkling she might try to find him, but never in a million years did I expect her to stay with you after she found out Amos was dead. I didn't know it until two days ago, when Jolene told me."

"I wish she hadn't lied to me about you. There would have still been room for her to get to know my kids. We really did have a lovely time together most of the time."

"You have a big heart, Hannah, to let her into your family. I know we didn't know one another well. But I've watched the Martin family from a distance all these years. And secretly, I did wish for my daughter to be a part of it. But that . . . would never leave room for me."

Her vulnerable words caused my chest to twist. "Lila, I'm so sorry it had to be like this."

"Me too."

"Do you have any idea where Luna might have gone?"

"She's not here?"

"We had an incident at breakfast this morning. Luna's been helping me serve our guests, and she flew off the handle at something one of our more irritating guests did. It was caught on video and played on social media, and let's just say, it's been a rough morning all around."

Lila pressed her lips together. "I'm so sorry. Luna is . . ." She fidgeted with her fingers in her lap. "Not that I'm making excuses for her behavior, of course, but she probably didn't tell you . . ."

"Tell me what?"

"She has a moderate case of bipolar disorder. With medication, we've learned to manage it well. But she's been resistant to taking it sometimes. I'm wondering if she would have sought out a new pharmacy in the area."

I worked my tongue around in my mouth. "Not that I'm aware of . . ."

"Things like stress can make it worse. I suppose she's been under a stress of her own making, trying to keep up with the lies she's told."

I swallowed. "From what Jolene said, she was found out two days ago. But I didn't know until this morning."

Because Kevin had chosen not to share that with me.

Lila stood. "I need to find her. If she hasn't been taking her medication, there's no telling where she went or what she might do."

"We'll help any way we can."

"I'm going to see if she went back home. I stayed overnight in Camden last night, so we could have missed each other. I'll keep calling and texting her. Maybe you could do the same?"

I nodded, tapping on my phone. We exchanged numbers.

"Has there been anyone she's gravitated to in her time here?" Lila asked.

"Mostly me. Although she and my youngest daughter hung out a bit, but Amie's on her honeymoon, so she wouldn't have said anything to her. Oh!" I snapped my fingers. "There's a boy next door she's been friendly with. I'll check over there." The likelihood of Owen knowing something was slim to none, but it was worth a try.

"Okay, I'm going to head out. Will you let me know?" She gathered her purse and started for her car.

I nodded but couldn't quite let her go yet. "Lila."

She turned.

"I'm glad you stopped by. I'm sorry about all of this, but . . ." I pressed my lips together, wondering if I could admit vulnerability to this woman. If not now, when? "I hated you for a long time. I'm ashamed to admit that, but it's the truth. I didn't know you, and yet I hated you."

She stood, fiddling with the strap on her purse, waiting for whatever I would dish out for her. As if she deserved it.

"But now that I've met you, I can't make myself do it anymore. Thank you for that. Thank you for making me see you, a fellow human, struggling in life at times, but trying your best to love your child."

She smiled and reached forward to put a hand on my arm. "Thank you, Hannah. We'll talk soon?"

"Yes."

When she drove away, Charlotte stepped onto the patio. "You okay?"

I nodded. "You know what? I think I am."

"Up for some chocolate cake?"

I smiled. "I think so. But first, I need to pay my neighbor a visit."

Though I needed to speak with Kevin, that would have to wait. Right now, the neighbor I needed to speak to was Owen.

29

Kevin bit into his tuna fish sandwich and chewed carefully, replaying the conversation he'd had with Deidra that morning over and over in his head. As much as he wanted to force her to get clean, to make her see how much her son needed her, he didn't know how to go about any of it. And what was the best thing for Owen? Though he hadn't entertained a long-term situation with Owen, it seemed there was no way around it. And he would never question his decision to take in his nephew.

But that didn't mean that Hannah wouldn't. If their relationship progressed as he hoped it would, how would Hannah feel about having a teenager around again after just becoming an empty nester herself?

He sighed and swigged his glass of water, deciding not to worry about all the logistics until Rita Bridges called him. He wasn't looking forward to reporting the events of the previous day to the social worker.

A knock on his door jolted him from his reverie. When he saw Hannah on the other side of the screen, the weight he'd been carrying for the last day slipped from his shoulders.

"Hannah." He opened the door and welcomed her inside, drawing her into his arms. "Boy, have I missed you."

"I've missed you, too." But her arms didn't come around him quite as enthusiastically as he would have liked.

He pulled away. "What's wrong?"

"Is Owen home from school yet?"

He shook his head. "Not for another hour. What's up?"

"Luna's missing. I wondered if she might have said something to him."

"I doubt it. They only spoke at the wedding and then a couple minutes the other day when she came to help him with math, but they didn't get very far."

Because of Jolene. Right. He had to admit, he hadn't thought of Luna and the promise he'd made to her all that much the last couple of days. Now, with Luna gone, it was only right to tell Hannah the truth.

"Do you want to sit down? I could make you a sandwich." He gestured to his simple dining room table where his plate and glass lay.

She shook her head. "I don't think so."

He squinted at her. "Hannah, what's wrong? She'll come back. Or maybe she went to her hometown. She could have been homesick."

Hannah crossed her arms in front of her. He'd seen her use that stance before, but when? With one of her children, maybe? Was he in *trouble*?

She flung her arms downward. "You knew Luna's mother was alive and you didn't tell me."

There it was. Of course, she'd be upset. Could he blame her? If she'd known something important about Owen, wouldn't he expect her to inform him?

He swallowed, choosing his words with care. "Hannah, I'm sorry. Luna asked me to give her some time. I wasn't sure what to do, that's why I urged you to talk to her the other night. With everything happening with Deidra, I admit it slipped my mind."

She opened her mouth, then stopped, concern etching her pretty features. "What's happening with Deidra?"

He shook his head. "I can fill you in later. Right now, it's important you understand that I never meant to hurt you. I was giving Luna some time to tell you on her own. I take it she did?"

"She didn't. Jolene showed up on my doorstep this morning after Luna left."

He pinched the bridge of his nose. "Oh, boy. That woman is not the most tactful. I'm sorry you had to go through that."

"There's a lot I'm dealing with right now, not the least being a social media catastrophe involving the bed and breakfast and an unexpected visit from Luna's mother."

"Hannah—"

"It just would have been nice if I knew the facts before today. It would have been nice if you'd told me right away."

"I was trying to do the right thing. Me tattling on Luna to you wouldn't have done anything good for the girl. I encouraged her to talk to you."

"Two days ago! Don't you think you could have spoken to me by now?"

Kevin closed his eyes, attempting to get a handle on his emotions. "I was kind of busy wrestling my drugged-up sister away from a parental visit and trying to run an intervention with my parents for Deidra. But yes, I should have told you, and for that, I'm sorry."

Hannah rubbed her temples. "Deidra showed up high for her visit yesterday?"

"High as a kite. I ended up bringing her to my parents. Still not sure that was the way to go."

"It didn't go well?"

"She didn't agree to get help, no. Painful things were said, mostly on Deidra's part. She went through a lot as a teenager—more than any of us realized. But I think my parents could apologize until the cows came home and it wouldn't make a difference. She asked me to adopt Owen."

"Oh, Kevin."

"Of course, I will. I don't see her leaving the slimeball that beat on the poor kid. I don't see her getting clean. But I can't help wondering if I agree to adopt him, if that's giving her an out, you know? Like releasing her from her job as a mom and giving her freedom to ruin herself more?"

Hannah pressed her lips together before speaking. "Using Owen as a pawn in trying to help Deidra is not going to help anything."

He nodded. "You're right." Maybe he needed to hear that. To give himself the freedom to take the boy in, no strings attached. To give himself the freedom to let Deidra go.

"It might be too late for Deidra. It's not too late for Owen."

Silence hung heavy between them. "Hannah, I'm sorry about Luna. I thought I was showing her I was on her side, trusting her to do the right thing after being found out."

She bit the inside of her cheek. "I think I can understand that, but it hurt, Kevin. Hurt to know you were keeping something that important from me." She turned toward the screen door, looking through the black weaving to the neat backyard of Orchard House. "It's been a long time since I trusted a man . . ."

She let her words hang in the air between them. She didn't have to finish the sentence for him to understand her thoughts.

She'd trusted Amos. Maybe he'd even regained her trust after his infidelity. That had been more than twenty years, after all. Surely, he'd proven himself trustworthy again. Unless . . .

Oh, man. He hadn't thought through the full implications of keeping Luna's secret. But it wasn't as if he'd been unfaithful to Hannah. This one error would not be the downfall of his budding relationship with her.

He couldn't let that happen.

Slowly, he went to her, placing his hands gently on her arms as she continued to stare outside, away from him.

"Hannah, honey, I'm so sorry. In my mind, you were talking it out with Luna that very night."

"Don't you think I would have told you about it all?"

"Yes. I suppose you would have. I hoped you would. But I was —" He stopped the words coming out of his mouth, for what could he say that would make this all go away? He was caught up with his sister? That simply sounded as if Hannah were less important, not one of his top priorities. And was that true? For he hadn't sought her advice and help in the last day as he waded through the muck with Deidra. He hadn't texted her or called her, preferring to leave her out of his mess. But loving someone meant sharing it all—even the hard.

"I'm sorry, Hannah. Please forgive me."

She nodded. "I understand. You had a lot going on. Poor Owen."

His heart grew light. "But I should have known there was a lot of pain when it came to you and Luna. I should have been more sensitive. Told you the truth and let you handle it how you wanted."

"I—I don't know." She stepped away. His hands fell to his sides. "We both have a lot going on right now, don't we?" She turned to him, gave him a half-smile.

His pulse ratcheted up, every cell in his body on high alert. "No. Don't do this." He spoke slow, as if any rapid words might startle her away.

"Maybe it was silly to get involved so fast. Maybe we both need some time—"

Forget startling her. He needed to startle some sense into her, after all. He took a step closer, raising his hand to her cheek. "We don't need time. I don't need time. I love you. This was one misunderstanding. Do you not have faith enough in us to see us through it? Come on, Hannah. Don't jump ship now."

A small, sad smile pulled at her pretty mouth. "I'm not jumping ship. I'm climbing the crow's nest. Everything's happened so fast. I don't think it's unwise to step back while you figure things out with Owen. While I work through some of my own history."

He grabbed for her hands. "Let's do the work together. Isn't that what love does?"

She glanced at the floor, not pulling away. "Yes. Yes, it does. But you didn't reach out to me in your hard with Deidra, did you? And as much as I wanted to confide in you all my trouble with Luna this morning, I couldn't because I was too hurt that you kept it from me."

"Hannah—"

She squeezed his hands. "I'm not mad and I do forgive you. But I need this time in the crow's nest. Please, allow me to climb it alone."

Heat climbed his chest. She was actually going to throw their relationship away over this? Couldn't she understand all he juggled? He didn't think Hannah Martin gave up so easily. Or maybe, he simply wasn't something she wanted to fight for.

His jaw tightened. "Fine, then."

She blinked. "Thank you."

He opened his mouth to tell her he wasn't going anywhere. That however long she needed, he'd be waiting. But his heart couldn't handle the likely rejection. Neither, apparently, could his pride.

She sniffed. "Will you ask Owen about Luna when he gets home?"

"Of course. I'll text you."

"Thank you." She pushed open the screen.

He watched her retreating back, fighting the urge to run after her. But what would he say? Accuse her of being selfish? Tell her he loved her even though she couldn't see past her own problems to his?

All he could do now was pray. Pray that she would see whatever she needed to see up in that lonely crow's nest.

30

I slipped into Orchard House and swallowed down my emotions. Despite my efforts, my eyes stung and I breathed deep as I closed the door.

"Oh, boy." Charlotte stood at my kitchen counter, frosting her famous chocolate cake. "Looks like I finished this just in time."

I threw back my shoulders and walked toward the bar. "I'm fine."

"Did Owen know anything about Luna?"

"Not that Kevin knew. But Owen won't be home for another hour. He's going to ask him then."

"And that's what has you so upset?"

I flopped onto a barstool. "No, that's not what has me so upset," I nearly snapped. "Sorry, Charlotte." I ran my hands over my face. "You've come all this way, made me a chocolate cake, cleaned my kitchen, and I'm jumping down your throat."

"Honey, it's going to take way more than that to offend me. You're worried about Luna. I know you're upset."

I folded my arms on the counter and slumped, something I had always harped on the kids not to do. "I *am* worried about Luna. But I'm afraid my heart isn't nearly that pure. Because I'm still angry at her. And I'm angry at Kevin. And . . ." My bottom lip trembled at my next thought. But I needed to get it out. Here and now, with my best friend. "I'm angry at Amos. Charlotte, if he *were* here, I'm afraid I'd kick him out the door. I'm so angry at him. For breaking our marriage vows all those years ago, for not being there for Luna, for not being here for me now when I'm trying to wade through all of this."

"Oh, honey." Charlotte came around the bar and folded me in her arms. "There's no right way to feel right now. This has all been a blow, and you threw yourself into it, like you do most everything. You tried to bring Luna into your family, and that's a beautiful thing."

"I don't know. Maybe it was a mistake to welcome her in. Maybe it only caused her and the kids more pain. Me more pain."

"Hannah Grace, are you telling me hospitality is a mistake? Because I'm pretty sure that's one of your great gifts."

I forced a small smile. "Our social page might state otherwise."

She patted my arm. "Having Luna here has stirred up a lot for you. Even if you fully forgave Amos, the consequences of his actions have a lasting effect. I don't know if you'll ever get over it fully. Keep giving it over to God. Let Him capture it for you."

That sounded beautiful. Like my problems were nothing but timid butterflies that the mighty hand of God could reach out and scoop up with a net to take away.

"Hannah, Kevin may have made a mistake, but don't inflate it. It's surely not on par with Amos's past sins."

The door behind me burst open and Bronson's voice filled the room. "I came over as soon as I could."

I looked up at my handsome son, looking so like his father in khaki pants and a button-down shirt, his normal teaching attire.

I groaned. "I take it the breakfast news hit the middle school?"

Bronson did a double take at Charlotte standing beside me.

He flung an arm around her. "Hey, Charlotte. Didn't know you were visiting."

"This was an emergency visit."

Realization dawned over my son's features. "Oh." He raised an eyebrow at the chocolate cake sitting on the counter. "Is that part of emergency protocol?"

"Absolutely, kiddo. We were just about to have some. Care to join us?"

"Do I ever."

Charlotte grabbed plates from the cabinet and pulled them down.

Bronson slid onto a stool next to me. "One of the other teachers pointed me to the clip this afternoon. What a wreck. I'm sorry, Mom."

"Maggie did online damage control as best she could. I guess that's all we can do right now."

His mouth turned downward. "One of the parents that signed her daughter up for camp called me concerned about it."

My chest deflated. "Really?" I mean, what did they think, that Luna was going to seek out the campers and throw their cell phones across the room? But no, that wasn't fair. Parents absolutely had a right to be assured their kids were safe while at Orchard House. Luna may not be a threat in my mind, but . . . "The video must have been worse than I thought."

Bronson shoved his hands in his pockets. "It was pretty bad." He accepted a cake plate from Charlotte. "Thanks, Charlotte."

Charlotte dished out a plate for me. "You know these online disasters. They're all anyone can talk about for a twenty-four-hour period, and then they're forgotten. Hang tight, Hannah."

Bronson forked in a bite of cake. "Oh, man. This is good." He jerked his head toward the stairs. "She here?"

I shook my head. "Listen, Bronson. It turns out Luna has some mental health issues we weren't aware of. I'm not trying to make excuses for her, but I'm hoping that, with time, the community will indeed forget this incident."

"Not before they decide who receives the money for the hospitality grant."

I exhaled slowly. "Is it horrible that a tiny part of me feels that Jolene is absolutely enjoying this?"

"Oh, she totally is." Bronson shoveled another bite into his mouth.

"That's not helpful." Charlotte shoved Bronson's shoulder then scooped my hands into her own. "But that is not for us to worry over. You have built a beautiful, thriving business. One incident is not going to ruin that. If you don't get the grant, you will move forward as you always do."

I squeezed her hands. "I don't know what I'd do without you."

"We're all grateful for Charlotte," Bronson interrupted, talking with his mouth half-full. "Especially when she drives two hours to make us her famous cake. But Mom, don't forget you have us. We're here for you even if we don't live at Orchard House anymore."

My eyes grew watery. What was with me today? "Thanks, honey. You couldn't have said anything better to lift my spirits."

Bronson smiled. "And you've got Kevin, too. What does he think about all this?"

I forked up the triangle edge of my cake, but couldn't bring it to my mouth, my appetite again suddenly soured. "Kevin and I have decided to take a step back from things."

Bronson froze midbite. "What?"

"We both have a lot going on right now, and—"

"Mom, the guy's crazy about you. I thought you liked him. What happened?"

Strange. Since when had Bronson become such a huge proponent of me and Kevin? "Like I said, there's too much—"

Bronson lowered his fork to his plate. "Wait. He asked you to marry him, didn't he?"

"What? Bronson, no."

"Are you sure, Mom, because when I talked to him the other —" He stopped, seeming to catch himself.

My brow furrowed. When had Bronson and Kevin spoken? And what in the world did it have to do with marriage? Luna's remark the other night floated back to me. I hadn't thought about it much, but . . . "Bronson." I dug out my I'm-your-mother-so-you-better-tell-me-the-whole-truth voice. "What did you two talk about the other night?"

Bronson slid out of his seat, cake still on his plate. "You know what? I just remembered Morgan needs help with dinner. She's making shrimp and the entire deveining process grosses her out. I told her—"

"Honey, finish your cake first." The way Charlotte spoke, it wasn't a suggestion, it was a command.

Bronson didn't sit back down, but he slid his cake plate to the edge of the bar so he could better reach it. "It was nothing, Mom. Really. We were just having a man-to-man talk. I gave him the okay to date you."

Charlotte's mouth twitched. "You did, did you? That was mighty sweet of you, Bronson."

He shrugged. "Yeah, I can see he makes her happy. Happier than I've seen her in maybe ever."

Charlotte drummed her fingers on the counter. "And what's this about marriage?"

I shook my head. "Never mind, I don't want to know."

Even though I very surely *did* want to know.

The edges of Bronson's ears turned pink as he met Charlotte's probing gaze. "Nothing, exactly. He just said he planned to ask my permission before he proposed to Mom, that's all. That's why I was surprised when—" He shook his head. "Never mind. I opened my mouth when I shouldn't have. Now the guy will never trust me."

Propose to me? Kevin was thinking about marrying me? Of

course, I'd be lying if I said the thought hadn't crossed my mind—in the way hazy, future possibilities sometimes do cross one's mind—but hearing the words from my son's mouth, that Kevin had actually spoken to Bronson about the matter, caused a pleasant, dizzying sensation to wash over me.

And then I saw Bronson's face. My heart went out to my son. We shouldn't have wheedled the information out of him. He'd spoken to Kevin in confidence, much like Kevin had spoken with . . . Luna.

The realization came tumbling down upon me. No, the situation wasn't exactly the same, but perhaps I'd been a bit unreasonable to think that Kevin should have come running to me with news about Luna. Luna wasn't my charge. Yes, she stayed with me, and I wanted to help. But she was an adult who'd asked Kevin for time. And I had handled it oh so badly.

"Can I go now?" Bronson practically squeaked after shoveling in the last bite of his cake.

"Yes, honey. I'm sorry we pushed you."

Charlotte threw down a dishcloth with a *humph*. "Speak for yourself. It's only right you have all the information."

I cast a disapproving look in my friend's direction.

"Okay," she muttered. "It's only right *I* have all the information."

I laughed and gave my son a hug. "Thanks, Bronson."

"Listen, Mom. I wasn't exactly supposed to go blabbing about the proposal thing. He just said it in passing. Maybe he meant years from now, I don't know. But I do know he cares about you. That's the only reason I spoke up."

I squeezed his arm. "I know. Thanks for stopping by. Now, go be a good husband and devein that shrimp."

That earned me a wry smile. "I can hardly wait." He waved to Charlotte. "Thanks for the cake and the interrogation, Charlotte!"

"Anytime, darlin'!"

When the door closed behind him, I sank back down at the bar.

"Well?" Charlotte leaned on the counter.

"Well, what?"

"Does that piece of information change anything for you?"

I sighed. "It was wrong to wheedle that out of him."

She raised an eyebrow. "Was it?"

I ignored her, still caught up in my musings. "I haven't forgiven Amos," I whispered. "I thought I had, but that was before I knew all the implications of his unfaithfulness. Does that mean I never really forgave him in the first place?"

Charlotte slid onto the chair beside me, cup of tea in hand. "You never do ask the easy questions, do you?"

I released a humorless laugh. "I suppose not."

She patted my arm. "I think that's why we've gotten on so well over the years. You think deeply, Hannah. And you never settle. But I can't help but wonder if you're thinking too deeply when it comes to Kevin. You love him. Was him not telling you about Luna a malicious act that deserves to obliterate every last shred of trust he's earned from you?"

I didn't answer, allowing her words to swirl around my conscience, to poke and prod at the loose strings of my harried thoughts.

She shifted in her seat. "Amos hurt you, honey. That pain requires forgiveness. God asks it of you, and your soul yearns for it. I have no doubt that you did forgive Amos all those years ago. There was a lot of pain, and though it must have been tender over the years, you chose the path forward, the path of forgiveness." She sipped her tea. "Now that same sin has dredged up more pain for you. Perhaps more pain requires more forgiveness. Maybe it's a one-and-done deal. Maybe it's a conscious, everyday choice."

I swallowed, her words sifting through my mind like powdered sugar through a sieve on pound cake. Finally, after a good long while of silence, I leaned my head on her shoulder and sighed. "I suppose you're right."

"Of course, I am."

I laughed. Who knew what the future would bring for me and Kevin, but before I could dwell on it, I needed to address something of ultimate importance: unfinished business with my late husband.

3 1

Kevin let the axe fall onto a piece of wood, barely pausing to take up another one and send the axe through the air once more.

What else could he do?

In between praying for Deidra, Owen, and Hannah, he tried to ignore the emotion he hated above all else—feeling completely and utterly helpless.

He'd been helpless when Katherine was diagnosed with cancer. When he watched her shrivel away to a shell of the woman he'd once known. He'd been helpless when his little sister had left home, refusing to contact them or give a clue to her whereabouts. Helpless when she'd shown up the other day, high for her visit with her son. And helpless again when she refused to get the support she desperately needed, when she all but handed her only son over to Kevin.

And now, he was helpless remembering how Hannah walked away from him, claiming she needed time. Space. A crow's nest.

But how he wanted to climb that crow's nest with her! Instead, he was here, sweat dripping down his forehead as the physical exertion of his body served to numb a small part of him to the pain of losing Deidra, the pain of losing Hannah.

All he could do was give it over to God. Place Hannah and Deidra in the arms of a loving Creator who cared for them with His perfect and abounding grace. And if God opened doors for Kevin to push his way through, then all the better.

His cell phone rang from where he'd left it on the edge of the porch. He scooped it up, a cold sweat breaking over him at the sight of Rita Bridges' name. He should have called her already. Updated her on the status of their visit, the status of his drugged-up sister. But he hadn't the heart.

Now, it appeared, there was no getting out of it.

"Hello?"

"Hello, Mr. Williams. It's Rita Bridges."

He cleared his throat. "Hello, Ms. Bridges."

"I'm calling because I just received a phone call from Deidra."

He blinked. Deidra had actually gone through with calling the social worker?

"Is that so?"

"It sounds like your visit yesterday was less than successful."

"That's one way of putting it."

"I'm sorry to hear that."

He rubbed his damp brow and lowered himself to the porch steps. "I really saw all of this going differently. I thought this might be a new beginning for our family."

Rita sighed, long and deep over the line. "I know this didn't go how you'd pictured it, but it *can* be a new beginning. Most importantly, for Owen."

"So, she actually told you she was ready to give him up?"

"She said she's willing to sign over her rights. She admitted to struggling with her life, said that she didn't see herself getting things together before Owen's eighteenth birthday. She said she was done with the visits and she thought Owen should stay with you."

A lead weight filled his chest. "I wish she'd get help. We tried. I told her I wanted to do whatever I could to get her healthy."

"It's not your fault, Kevin." It was the first time she'd used his first name, and the weight of her words settled over him. He didn't know why this absolution from a near-stranger affected him so, but it did.

"Thank you. I'd hoped for different things. Truth be told, I'll never stop hoping that she'll turn things around. And I'm not writing her out of my life, either." There was always hope. He glanced at Orchard House, imagined Hannah inside cleaning rooms or doing dishes or baking her heavenly coffee cake.

"I admire you for that." He heard shuffling of papers. "Now, how you want to proceed is completely up to you. There's no reason why Owen can't stay under kinship care with you for the foreseeable future. If you ever want to take this further, just let me know."

The weight in his chest lightened as the knowing of what he would do came upon him. Of course, he still needed to talk to Hannah. After he carried her down from that lonely crow's nest, of course. "I want to explore the idea of adoption, Ms. Bridges."

Sudden stillness over the line. "Well, then. Okay. Of course, we have some additional paperwork and interviews to go through, but yes. Certainly. As soon as Deidra signs over her parental rights and as soon as you've had some time to think on this, we could set the ball moving."

Kevin's head swirled. He was doing this. Of course, he was. It was what was best for Owen. Sure, he didn't picture himself a father for the first time at the ripe age of fifty-six, but why not? He loved the boy, would do anything for him. There would be struggles, but love in the hard was where love counted the most. "Okay," he managed.

"In the meantime, it would be a good idea for you to talk this over with Owen. There'll be a lot of emotions, as you can imagine."

He nodded. "Of course." This would be tough on Owen. But the boy had seen his mother the day before. Surely, he knew the likelihood of their situation improving. Wouldn't he be happy Kevin wanted to adopt him?

He'd talk to Hannah, too. Whether she wanted him in her life or not, he valued her take on the matter.

After the social worker rattled off a few more logistics, he hung up the phone, his mind reeling. He barely had time to let the last fifteen minutes sink in when the sound of Owen's bus stopping at the end of the driveway caused him to utter a prayer and straighten with resolve.

Owen walked up the drive slowly, his backpack slung on one shoulder. When he reached Kevin, he nodded in acknowledgement.

"How was your day?" Kevin asked, as he always did.

"Fine." The usual answer, although sometimes of late, he'd get an inkling more. An "Uneventful" or "Stunk." This time, though, Owen raised hopeful eyes to Kevin. "How'd it go with Mom?"

When Kevin had seen Owen this morning, he'd simply told him that Deidra was sleeping at their parents', that he planned to return and talk to her while Owen was at school.

Kevin gestured to the porch. "You want to sit?"

Owen slumped over, lowering himself to one of the rockers and letting his bag fall to the wooden planks of the porch. "Not good, I guess."

"I'm sorry, Owen. We tried to talk your mom into getting help. She seems to realize the problem she has, but she's not ready yet." Better to continue this frame of mind. That Deidra *would* one day be in a place where she would voluntarily get help. Perhaps, in Owen's case though, it was better to cling to reality. Kevin could only guess. He had a sneaking suspicion that a whole lot of his parenting would be based on guesses, so he better get comfortable with that fact, starting now.

Owen kicked his bag with light, consistent movements. He shrugged. "Shouldn't have expected anything different, I guess."

He started to stand, but Kevin placed a gentle hand on his shoulder. "Owen, I'd like to talk to you about something."

Owen slumped back in his chair, shrugged again. Kevin's heart went out to him. The kid had learned to build a calloused, hard shell around himself in order to stop more pain from entering. God help him, he wanted to support his nephew. Maybe this was simply the next step in doing so.

Kevin lowered himself to the chair opposite Owen. No sense mincing words. "What would you think if I adopted you?"

The kid's face twisted. "What?"

"I was talking to Ms. Bridges today, and the possibility came up."

Owen shot to his feet. "You told her what happened with Mom, you mean. Now, they'll never let me go back."

Kevin shook his head, taken aback by Owen's vehement response. "I didn't breathe a word. Your mom's the one—" But he stopped, already wanting to whip himself for not catching his tongue. He should have thought this through better. Much better. Owen didn't need to know his mother had called Rita Bridges, willing to give up her parental rights. And yet, the boy was sixteen. He'd find out eventually, wouldn't he? While the facts would be painful, maybe they were the only way forward.

Owen stood above him, seething, as if daring Kevin to finish his sentence. Kevin scratched his brow, finding a respite from the boy's searing gaze with the gesture. He'd evaluate his cowardice later. Now . . .

He met his nephew's dark eyes, so like Deidra's. "I wish things were different. But your mom's ready to sign over her parental rights. I think she realizes living with her is not the best thing for you. She loves you, Owen. She's doing this because she loves you."

"That's bull and you know it. You all think I'm stupid, don't you? Mom doesn't love me. She loves her drugs. She loves Sam.

And you . . ." Kevin waited for the words, hoping for the boy to put him out of his misery. "You don't want me, either. You're going to marry Miss Hannah. Then, where will that leave me?"

"Hannah loves you. Listen, we have a lot of thinking and praying to do over this, but I thought—"

But the teenager was gone, screen door slamming, footsteps stomping up the stairs, leaving Kevin with a silence that was both incredibly needed and incredibly haunting all at once.

He'd talk to the boy. But maybe after a little space. Maybe after some time to wrap his head around what Owen said, search out if there was any truth in it.

And if there was, what, in the name of all that was good, was he going to do about it?

❧ 32 ❧

I approached the bench at Curtis Lighthouse Overlook with something like reverence. The last time I'd come here was the day before Amos died. Though still technically within walking distance, the Overlook was closer to our old home—the one Amos and I had built together. The one I'd sold after his death to make a way for my new life.

Some of my children came here often, especially Josie. This place held special memories for Amie as well. And, although I never shared this fact with them, the Overlook held a spot in my own heart. It was here that Amos first told me he loved me. Here, he'd asked me to marry him.

Right before he died, we'd been having some problems. No one knew this, but the last time we spoke had been an argument. Amos had been ready to sink the last of our savings into a food truck for the homeless—an extension of his mission—and while his vision was admirable, I'd been scrupulously saving my meager income as a part-time librarian for a trip to Italy. I'd always wanted to see the ancient churches of Rome, to see Saint Peter's Basilica, the Colosseum, the Duomo di Milano, Venice, Tuscany, Pompeii, to backpack through the mountains and inhale the breathtaking coast. With Amie graduating high school, I'd come to think of it as a second honeymoon.

And Amos couldn't understand how I could want something so *temporal*. I'd begged him to find a way to fundraise the money for the food truck, but he never liked asking people for money. Had never been good at fundraising, either.

But I'd put my foot down. Wanting a trip to Italy didn't make me selfish. It made me human, wanting to experience the beauty and history of the world as a way of celebrating our last child's journey to adulthood.

It was the first time I'd denied my husband's dreams, and he'd been shocked. Then, angry. He'd even accused me of being hormonal, which I probably was, thank you very much. But you know the thing about being a perimenopausal woman? The hormones sometimes tell you the truth about what's *actually* lying just beneath the surface. The truth that we as women learn to stuff away and hide. So, in that moment, I'd been thankful for my crazy hormones and the gumption they gave me to finally speak my mind.

We were taking the trip to Italy. And if he didn't like it, I'd take the trip alone.

Amos's heart attack occurred later that night. I never spoke to him again. I never took the trip to Italy.

And neither did I ever visit this place, this symbol of our love, again. As a way of moving forward, I'd shoved it into things of the past.

Now, though, after speaking with Charlotte, an overwhelming urge to find this long-ago symbol, to sit on this worn bench of my history, flooded me.

I lowered myself to the bench and savored the breathtaking view of the Curtis Island lighthouse, picture-perfect and white-washed with its red-roofed lighthouse keeper's cottage. I inhaled the scent of briny sea and earth, allowing it to cleanse my lungs, to cleanse my soul.

I prayed.

For Luna, and then for my children. For my beautiful grand-children, those I'd had the pleasure of wrapping my arms around and those yet to be born. I prayed for Charlotte and our businesses, that Orchard House would survive the social media catastrophe. And then I prayed for Kevin and Owen.

When I could think of no more prayers, I simply sat in the silence, breathing. Finally, I allowed my mind to rest on Amos.

I dragged in a deep breath, unsure if my next words were addressed to an Amos in the afterlife or an Amos of my history. "Amos, I don't know why you went into Lila's arms that night. I know I wasn't the perfect wife, but you could have saved us a whole lot of heartache if you'd fled temptation." My words drifted toward the sea, the wind picking them up and sweeping them away. "But then Luna wouldn't be here. And I know God has a plan for her. Maybe one day He'll even show me if I'm supposed to be a part of it. But right now . . ." My voice wobbled and I sniffed back tears.

"I'm angry at you still. Angry that you created this situation and left me alone to deal with it. Angry that you broke the promises you made to me. Angry that we argued that last day, that I never seemed like enough for you. Angry that your memory is making it difficult for me to trust again."

I soaked in the silence for a good long while, the road before me obvious. Like walking in the woods and coming along two paths. I would have to choose.

Two paths.

I meditated on the image, the long-ago memorized words of the apostle Paul entering my mind.

One thing I do: Forgetting what is behind and straining toward what is ahead, I press on toward the goal to win the prize for which God has called me heavenward in Christ Jesus.

Forgetting what is behind. Straining toward what is ahead. Living every aspect of life beneath God's dominion and grace.

"Amos," I whispered, allowing my dead husband's name to wind around me, bringing with it every joy, hardship, elation, and sorrow our relationship ever held. "Charlotte's right. Pain makes it harder to forgive. And I think I'll always feel pain when it comes to some of our struggles. But I'm ready. I can't keep carrying this with me. So, Amos, I forgive you. I'm really and finally letting you go."

Stepping into forgiveness, straining toward the new, was almost like stepping out on the street without clothes. At first, I felt vulnerable, as if I was releasing my protection against the world. And then, without warning, a beautiful, gorgeous freedom filled me. As if leaving that part of myself behind had given me a divine liberty I hadn't dwelled in for a long time.

"Thank you, God."

The breeze played with my hair, whisking it from my face and I closed my eyes, living in the tender caress of it, sensing that no matter what happened with the bed and breakfast, this was my way forward.

After many more minutes sitting in the silence, I finally stood. "Goodbye, my love," I whispered.

As I walked up the path toward Bay View Street, a sense of peace and quiet washed over me. And I realized that while I walked down this path of forgiveness, God led me by the hand.

And with His leading, I no longer needed to be afraid. About Luna, about my children, about Orchard House, or about my relationship with Kevin. It might not always go smoothly. Things may sometimes be downright bumpy. But the One who created and loved my soul would always be there, gently leading me home.

33

Kevin shot up in his bed, eyes wide, searching the darkness of his bedroom. What had jolted him out of his sleep? An intruder? A storm?

He glanced at his bedside alarm clock. Eleven-thirty. He'd only just gotten to sleep. When Owen had claimed he wasn't hungry for dinner, Kevin had left the boy alone, promising himself he'd get up the gumption to talk to him in the morning. Surely, the pain would ride over him and yes, leave him raw. But in that rawness, perhaps there could be a new beginning. A healing.

The sound of a car motor met Kevin's ears through the open window. Though High Street could be busy, something about the sound of the idling engine made him peer out his window into the moonlight. Through the thick trees, he just made out an old Honda at the end of his drive. He blinked, forcing the remnants of sleep away. He was a tree guy, not a car guy—that much should have been clear with how he'd completely overlooked Owen getting his permit—but something about that car was very familiar.

And then the pieces of a puzzle he couldn't quite grasp until that moment came together, sharply in focus. That was *Luna's* car.

He placed his hands on the sill, leaning toward the screen as if getting an inch closer could help him better understand what Luna was doing at the end of his driveway. He'd thought she was long gone. Why would she stay in this town if she didn't want to be found?

And then he saw the dark figure running lightly toward the car, backpack on and bouncing with his steps. Kevin pressed his forehead against the screen, ready to call out to his nephew.

Owen was going with Luna. And Kevin had a terrible feeling that it wasn't just a sneaking out for the night affair. Not that that would be ideal, either. But the backpack, the way the girl parked at the end of his drive, how no one knew where Luna was . . . did Owen intend to leave home altogether? To run away?

A strangled cry left his throat, but Owen didn't turn back. Probably didn't even hear him.

Kevin pushed back from the sill, searching his drawers for a pair of jeans. He yanked them on, nearly tripping over his legs as fear pulsed adrenaline through his limbs.

Deidra.

Deidra had left home and never come back. She'd disappeared, left their parents' safe haven for a life of men and addiction. What if Kevin never saw Owen again? What if now was his only chance to set things right?

He flew down the stairs, scooping his phone and keys off the kitchen table and slamming out the door. Luna's Honda pulled away just as Kevin slid into his truck.

Two minutes later, he followed the car at a safe distance, not wanting to scare the girl or his nephew. What was he doing? Would he follow them all night? And to where? Surely, there wasn't a romantic relationship between them with the age difference? If so, he'd have an altogether different problem on his hands.

He groaned. Would Hannah want to know about Luna's middle-of-the-night escapades? Did she have a right to know?

After all, she wasn't Luna's guardian. Luna was an adult. But what in the world was he supposed to do? If he called the police, he could get Luna in a lot of trouble. And if he didn't? What did those two have in their heads?

Without thinking further, he told Siri to "Call Hannah."

The phone rang for what must have been thirty seconds. Then, finally, a groggy voice. "Kevin? Are you okay?"

"Hannah. I'm sorry to wake you. I—I didn't know what to do."

"What's the matter? Where are you?" More awake now, he could almost picture her sitting up in bed, hair mussed.

"I think I'm on a car chase."

"A what?"

"Luna just picked Owen up at the end of my driveway. I'm following them." He shook his head. "Should I be following them? Am I some crazy overprotective parent?" How quickly things had changed.

"Luna's with him? You—you're sure?"

"Yes. I recognized her car. I don't know what to do. She shouldn't be taking him away in the night. He went willingly, but he's only sixteen. And he was upset when I spoke to him this afternoon." He was rambling. But suddenly he doubted running out of bed to follow his teenaged nephew down Route 1 in the middle of the night. Owen's actions weren't out of the realm of normal teenaged behavior, right? Was Kevin the one being downright neurotic? He should just call Owen and order him home, shouldn't he?

"Kevin, yes. Yes, you should stay with them. Luna is sick. Her mother told me this afternoon she has bipolar disorder and hasn't been taking her medicine. I'm not even sure she should be driving."

He swallowed down the information. "Oh, man. Okay, I don't know where they're going, but I'll follow them."

"I'm getting in my car now."

"Hannah, no. I'm with them. There's no sense in both of us chasing them around town. Besides, for you to catch up with us would be—"

"I need to talk to Luna. She's not answering my texts or calls. I —I need her to know something."

He sighed. "Okay. We're heading south on Route 1. No telling if they intend to drive through the night. I don't even know what I'm going to do once they stop. I might not be able to make Owen get in the car with me."

"Don't call the police. Please." Hannah whispered the words. "I know maybe we should. I don't know, maybe there's no reasoning with Luna right now. But I don't want to break her anymore."

His thoughts before he knew about Luna's circumstances. But now, was Owen in danger? "As long as I don't see anything that raises warning flags, no police." Luna drove the speed limit, inside the white and yellow lines of the road. As far as he could tell, she was in her right mind.

"Thank you," Hannah breathed. "I'm turning out of the drive now."

They stayed on the phone for twenty minutes, Kevin grateful for a full tank of gas and a phone charger in his truck. When they finally pulled into a run-down neighborhood not far from the bay, he found himself both relieved and terrified all at once.

"She's bringing him to his old home. To Deidra's apartment."

A pinch of betrayal wound through his gut, but he brushed it off. Maybe this was how things were supposed to be. Maybe Owen needed to hear from Deidra's own mouth about the adoption.

As Luna parked on the street, he did the same a few car lengths away, unrolling his window to hear anything he could. "I'm not going to interfere. He wants to see his mother. It's not proto-col, but I think I'll do more harm than good dragging him away now."

"I'm almost there. I understand. Maybe just keep an eye on things?"

He nodded. "I intend to. There's a parking spot behind me."

He watched as Owen left the car and let himself into the apartment building. Luna stayed in the car, letting it idle. The wind swept a fast-food burger wrapper down the street and a moment later, Hannah pulled up behind him, shutting off her headlights.

"How's it going?"

"I feel like I'm either an undercover cop or a neurotic parent."

"You might be both."

He snorted. "Lights just came on in the second floor."

Another couple minutes more and he groaned. "I can't believe I'm spying on my nephew. I hate this."

"I know." Hannah's voice smoothed out the rough edges sawing at his conscience. "Let's just see how this plays out. I don't think we should let him get back in the car with Luna. Not with what her mother told me—"

But her words were cut off by a bloodcurdling scream. Kevin dropped his phone, pushing out of the truck faster than he'd moved since he was on the football team in high school. He ran toward the apartment, taking the stairs two at a time. But the door to the building opened and he smacked into it, stumbling back down the stairs.

"Your mother don't want you, boy. What don't you get about that?"

The tall man—Kevin could only guess him to be Sam—shoved Owen down the stairs, pushing him into Kevin. Owen looked up, surprise etched on his features at the sight of Kevin. But the surprise only lasted a minute.

"I just want to talk to her, Sam. Let me talk to her for one minute. Please."

"Don't make me get my metal, boy."

Kevin pushed Owen behind him. "Get in my truck, Owen."

"No. I want to see my mom."

Sam turned around. "You asked for it, kid."

While a fierce part of him wanted to chase after the man who was actively ruining both his sister and nephew's life, the rational part knew he simply needed to get Owen out of here. He dragged him toward the truck, but Owen was having none of it.

"Let me go! Mom!" The boy's cry pierced the air, sounding so much younger than his sixteen years. "Mom!"

With a strength he didn't know he possessed, Kevin lifted his nephew off the ground and started for his truck, waving for a distraught Luna, still in her car, to leave the premises.

"Wait." Deidra's voice from behind caused Kevin to stumble and Owen to fight all the harder for Kevin to release him.

Owen twisted from Kevin's grip. "Mom."

"I'm here, baby."

Owen ran up the steps to his mother, clad in a slinky piece of lingerie, the strap falling off her shoulder. He stopped short of hugging her.

Kevin stepped forward, but a gentle hand stopped him. Hannah behind him.

"You—you don't want to be my mom anymore?" Owen stood, slumped on the bottom step and Kevin held his breath.

Deidra ran a hand over Owen's hair. "Baby, it ain't that simple. You know it ain't."

Behind her, Sam reappeared. He slung an arm over Deidra's shoulder, wrapping it around her neck. He propped a handgun on her shoulder and aimed it at Owen.

Kevin stepped forward with slow movements, hands up, his heartbeat skyrocketing, his knees as brittle as a dead tree branch. The hand he reached out to Owen trembled. "Owen, come with me."

"First, I need to hear it from her. I need to hear that she doesn't want to be my mother."

Had the boy not noticed the gun?

Deidra cursed and flung her boyfriend's arm away. "Sam, get that out of here."

Owen didn't even flinch. Kevin's breathing stuttered. Perhaps gun waving was a normal everyday occurrence for the boy? His chest twisted at the thought.

The tall man tightened his arm around his sister's neck. "Don't tell me what to do, Deidra." He brought the gun up again, pressing the barrel into her skin.

In the distance, sirens sounded. Sam cursed and pushed Deidra away, hard.

And then he was gone, back in the house.

Kevin didn't realize how tightly every ligament in his body was wound until Sam left. He swallowed, took a step toward his sister. "Deidra, it doesn't have to be this way. Come with us."

"Yeah, Mom. Come on." Owen held out a wobbly hand to his mother.

His sister looked back into the dark house, and then at her son's outstretched hand. She twisted to gaze into the apartment. "I can't," she whispered, her tone strangled. "Go with your uncle, baby. Go."

"Mom."

"Go!" She nearly yelled the words.

Owen stumbled back and Kevin guided him away from the stairs into Hannah's waiting arms. Kevin turned to Deidra. "The invitation never expires. I will always be waiting for you, little sister."

Deidra raised a hand to her trembling mouth, but the sirens drew closer. And then flashing lights came up the street. His sister disappeared inside the house.

34

Luna didn't look at me until the police officers finished their questioning and slid Sam into the back of the police car. By then, I had already shot off a text to Lila.

"I was just trying to help." Luna crossed her arms in front of herself.

I rubbed my temples. "I think we should all get home."

Kevin nodded. "I second that idea." He squeezed Owen's shoulder. The boy hadn't spoken much during the questioning, not while the police demanded Sam open the apartment door, and not while they took him away in the police car. His mother stayed inside.

Owen was shaken, no doubt. I had a feeling it wasn't about the confrontation with his mother and her boyfriend so much as his mother's refusal to be a part of his life.

Luna opened the door to her car, and I placed my hand on the hood of her Honda, as if that could stop her from leaving.

"Where are you staying, Luna?"

She shrugged. "Nowhere."

"Would you come back to Orchard House with me? I—I really want to talk to you."

She sighed. "Look, I know I messed things up for you and I really am sorry. I don't think me coming back now is going to help anything."

"Luna, please? I—your mother came to speak with me."

Her eyes widened. "She did?"

I nodded. "Can you stay one more night at Orchard House? I could make some tea for us when we get home."

She bit her lip. "Why would you want me to come back after what happened?"

"Because, Luna, you're family. And family doesn't abandon one another, ever."

Her bottom lip trembled. "I'll come."

A balloon of air deflated in my chest. "I'll follow you back?"

She nodded, her gaze moving to Owen's. "I'll talk to you tomorrow, Owen?"

"Sure."

I turned to Kevin, who squeezed my hand before guiding me back to my car after Luna had sat in the driver's seat of hers.

When he released my hand, it felt cold. "Could we talk tomorrow, too?" I whispered after Owen had settled himself in the passenger's seat.

"There's nothing I'd like more, Hannah." He kissed me on the cheek, and I slid into my car, pulling out after Luna, praying for the conversation I would have with her, as well as the one Kevin was sure to have with Owen.

❦

A HALF HOUR LATER, LUNA SAT AT THE BREAKFAST NOOK WHILE I warmed up tea and cut two pieces of Charlotte's chocolate cake. I carried the plates over to the table before sliding across from Luna. "My two favorite comfort foods."

One side of Luna's mouth lifted. "I've never had chocolate cake at two o'clock in the morning."

"Me neither. I guess it's a first we can share together." My gaze met hers. Beating around the bush wouldn't help. "Luna, I want us to share more firsts. No, you are not my daughter and yes, you hurt me by being dishonest about your mother. But you *are* Amos's daughter. A part of him. And for that reason alone, I love you."

I hadn't realized the truth of that statement until I saw Luna on that darkened street in her car. Trying to help a troubled teenaged boy connect with his family. Trying to help him fix his own life even when she'd muddled up hers.

When I looked at her, I didn't feel the weight of Amos's unfaithfulness, I felt a window of grace that God had orchestrated. He *had* brought Luna here. And though it hadn't and wouldn't always be easy, I refused to ignore that fact.

Luna tapped her fork on her cake plate. "I'm sorry, Hannah," she whispered. "My mother told you? About me being . . . bipolar?"

I nodded.

"As soon as I left this morning, I transferred my prescriptions to the local pharmacy. I—I feel terrible about what happened."

"Why did you lie to me about your mother?" I asked gently.

"I thought there'd be a better chance you'd let me meet my half-brother and sisters. More of a chance you wouldn't push me away."

And maybe there would have been. Wasn't it easier to take in Amos's orphan child than a young woman who had a loving and stable home apart from Orchard House? While I didn't think I would have sent Luna packing, I suppose I'd never know.

"At the time, I was mad at my mother. She kept the truth from me all these years—" She stopped talking, her words seeming to hit her. "I did the same, I guess, while I stayed with you."

I reached out a hand, just shy of touching her. "God's teaching me an awful lot about forgiveness lately. And I won't hold a grudge, Luna. I forgive you. Let's move forward, however that looks."

Thirty years ago, I made a promise to love and cherish my husband always. In the last couple of months, I'd wondered if that promise held beyond the grave. I had seen it as an obligation. Now, though, I saw it as an opportunity. An opportunity to show grace and love even when it was hard. Even when there were no guarantees. And when were there guarantees in love? The only fact I knew for sure was that I wasn't made to harbor ill will and fear and guilt. I was made to love.

Luna squeezed my hand. "I wish I could make things right with the bed and breakfast."

"It'll straighten itself out."

She sniffed. "I need to go home and talk to my mom. Sort things out with her, you know? But, do you think it'd be okay if I still visited once in a while? Helped out every now and then?"

I smiled, feeling the gesture down to my toes. "It would be more than okay."

The young woman's eyes watered and she nodded, sipping tea to hide her emotion.

"Miss Hannah, I'm glad my mother is alive so I can try to make things right. But if she wasn't—if I really did have no one—you would be the person I'd want on my side."

I got up from the table and hugged her, squeezing. Amos would never get to meet his fifth daughter. But in that moment, I was certain that God had orchestrated the events of the last several weeks to draw me closer to grace, closer to Himself, and closer to a picture of divine love.

And for that, I was thankful.

KEVIN KNOCKED LIGHTLY ON OWEN'S BEDROOM DOOR.

No texting tonight.

"Come in."

He pushed open the door and took in the room, surprisingly neat for a sixteen-year-old boy. Owen lay sprawled on his bed, face up, staring at the ceiling. A dim glow came from his desk lamp. His phone lay beneath it, well out of reach.

Kevin grabbed his nephew's desk chair and straddled it. He took in the sight of the teenager, one arm slung over his forehead, hair falling in front of one eye, the holes in his ears still loose but beginning to close. "Owen, I'm sorry, son."

"I shouldn't have went," he said softly.

"No, you shouldn't have left without telling me, but I understand why you did. Doesn't make it right, but I get it."

"She really doesn't want me. She's picking Sam and his drugs and sleeping with guys she doesn't know over me."

Kevin's throat threatened to close. What was he supposed to say to that? He couldn't deny it.

"Your mom is in a sort of jail right now. She's chained to a lot of stuff that's not good for her, or you. But I'm not giving up hope that someday, things will change. We can keep hoping and praying together."

The boy inhaled a big breath.

Kevin continued. "In the meantime, I think we need to move forward. Owen, I don't have to adopt you. We don't need all the formal papers for you to know that I'm not leaving or kicking you out. I guess adopting you was my way of showing you that. But maybe it's too much. You're sixteen, after all. Just as long as you know you have a place here as long as you need. Got that?"

Owen nodded, mouth tight.

"Guess we should get some shuteye, huh? I'll take you to school tomorrow if you want so you can get a little extra sleep."

The boy didn't move, so Kevin stood. "Goodnight."

"Uncle Kevin?" The bed creaked and Kevin turned but was met with a fierce hug from his lanky nephew. He stood for a second, shocked, before putting his arms around the boy in a bear hug that rivaled a grizzly.

"Thank you," Owen croaked.

And Kevin thought it the best present the kid could have ever given.

35

"**C**an you please never leave?" I asked Charlotte the next morning as I loaded the dishwasher after breakfast. "That was the most flawless breakfast service I've ever had."

Charlotte sprayed down the counters before wiping them clean. "I'm going to stay a couple more days, but the Beacon is my home. You know I'd miss it too much."

"I know. If I can get a chance to get away this summer, I'll come return the favor."

Charlotte smiled. "Although I'd love a visit, there's really no need, Hannah. My place isn't near as busy as Orchard House."

"Guests haven't run out over our little social video, but getting new bookings might be another story." And the grant was down the tubes for sure. But if I could simply hold onto what I had, that would be enough. More than enough.

A knock on the back door caught our attention. I glimpsed Kevin through the window.

Charlotte elbowed me. "That doesn't happen to be Prince Lumberjack, does it?"

I rolled my eyes. "Prince Lumberjack? Goodness, Charlotte, *you* might need to get out more."

We giggled like schoolgirls before I went to answer the door, my heart ratcheting up at the sight of Kevin in jeans and a t-shirt that defined his broad shoulders. I opened the door. "Hey."

"Hey, yourself."

My stomach fluttered. "Would you like to come in?"

He glanced at Charlotte, wiping down the counters and humming as if she didn't have any interest at all in our conversation. Which she most certainly did.

"Actually, I was wondering if you might want to take a ride?"

I turned to Charlotte. "Charlotte, do you think—"

She waved a dishcloth at me. "Oh, go on now."

I grabbed my phone before closing the door behind me. We walked across the grass toward Kevin's home. "How'd it go with Owen last night?"

Kevin shoved his hands in his pockets. "Good, actually. He was broken over Deidra, of course. But he seemed more willing to accept it after what happened. I hate that he ran away, but maybe it all worked out. Deidra would have never approached him herself to tell him she was giving up her parental rights."

"I'm so sorry."

"He said if he couldn't have his mother, then I was the next best thing. I chose to take that as a compliment."

I smiled. "It is. You're doing a spectacular job, Kevin."

He opened the passenger door of his truck, and I climbed in. "That means a lot coming from a mother of five."

He shut the door, went around to the driver's side, and started the truck. "How did it go with Luna?"

"Better than I could have imagined, actually. I forgave her. She's going back home to her mom, but we're going to keep in touch."

"That's great, Hannah."

"I guess it all worked out after all." My sentence seemed to hang suspended between us. Because *we* hadn't yet worked everything out.

We drove in silence. Through downtown and onto Bay View Street. When Kevin parked alongside the road at the Overlook, my blood froze and then thawed like an ice cream cone on a hot July day, rushing to my limbs. "W—what are we doing here?"

"Hannah, I know you said you wanted to be in the crow's nest alone, but I'm not ready to let you climb up there by yourself. Could we talk this all out? Please?"

"But—why are we here?" The place I had thought of as mine and Amos's. The place where I had released my late husband from my future just the day before.

Kevin glanced at the path leading to the Overlook. "I don't know. I thought it was a nice place for a small breakfast picnic."

I swallowed.

"Listen, if you're sure about what you said yesterday . . . if you want me to drive you back home . . . I'll do it. But after last night, when I was on Deidra's steps and I saw that gun on Owen, I'd never been more scared in all my life. Not when they diagnosed Katherine, even. And while I would never in a million years want to put you in harm's way, having you with me meant more to me than I could have known. Hannah, there is no one else I want beside me more than you. No one else I want to stand beside."

I smiled. "We do make a pretty good pair of undercover neurotic cop parents."

He laughed. "Does that mean you'll have this picnic with me?"

I nodded, pushing open my door.

Kevin grabbed a basket from the back of his truck, and we walked up the path to the empty bench, lowering ourselves to take in the view. I breathed it all in, surprised at how different this place felt alongside this man.

"Kevin." I swallowed down the lump in my throat. "I realized yesterday I was still carrying around a lot of pain and unforgiveness when it came to Amos. I see now that you didn't mean to deliberately hurt me, that you were trying to be everything to me, to Luna, to Owen, to Deidra. I haven't been great at leaving the past behind, but I think I'm ready. I'm sorry I pushed you away when I needed you most. If you're willing, I'd love to have some company in that crow's nest."

His smile was the most beautiful thing I'd ever seen on a man. Oh, he was breathtaking. He wrapped his arms around me, drawing me close, and kissed me. Gently at first. Slow, as if savoring the moment. And then more urgent, every ounce of desire of the last few months seeming to erupt in this ground-breaking kiss.

When we finally parted, I nudged his nose with mine. "So, I guess that's a 'yes'?"

He settled back on the bench, crushing me to him with his left arm. "Hannah Martin, I think I could be content the rest of my life sitting on this bench with you."

I leaned my head on his shoulder, gazing at the puff of cotton clouds floating over a backdrop of blue sky. In that moment, my past, present, and future seemed to converge in one beautiful story that only God could have written. For while I'd made a promise to the husband of my past and may very well make a promise in the future to Kevin, God was the one who'd made the ultimate promise to never leave my side. Through the struggles and the joy, through the tears and the laughter.

His promises were the ones that always remained.

36

In the middle of breakfast cleanup three days later, I stilled at the sink, taking in the sound of the windchimes on the back patio through the screen, the birds chirping, the distant sound of children in the orchard as Bronson and Morgan opened the camp for the summer.

I breathed deep, glancing out the window at Kevin working on his shed. We had a date later in the day. He called me to confirm the details that morning. And to tell me that Deidra had gone to rehab. Apparently, Sam getting arrested had changed a few things.

Whether or not that changed things for Deidra and Owen, we'd have to wait and see.

I allowed my eyes to linger over Kevin's frame. I already felt myself falling headlong for this man all over again. And it was the most exhilarating, breathtaking ride of my life.

Charlotte and Luna had left two days ago, both promising to come visit soon. Luna planned to attend Lizzie's birthday party in a week and she and Lila were looking for a family therapist that would work with them together.

It seemed my days were settling back into themselves. Though no children slept in my home, I'd never been more full of joy. Yes, Maggie had reported below-average bookings over the last couple days, but I hoped business would remain steady enough through the summer that by fall, perhaps our little social media scandal would be forgotten.

I could only hope.

The back door burst open and Amie and August appeared, nearly looking like Barbie and Ken dolls with their sun-bleached hair and Caribbean tans. "You're back!" I left my dishes and threw my arms around my youngest daughter. "How was it?"

"Beautiful. Gorgeous. Incredible. And yet for some reason I'm beyond grateful to be back in boring old Camden, ready to start my new life with my husband." She smiled up at August. That boy had adored my daughter since they were five years old. I was so happy they'd found their way to one another.

"Don't help an old lady out of the car or anything." Aunt Pris shuffled in behind them, a mischievous smile on her face.

Amie put an arm around the older woman. "Sorry, Aunt Pris. Guess I was more excited than I thought to see Mom."

My heart bloomed. Behind Aunt Pris, Ed Colton trudged in.

"Wow, the whole gang's here. To what do I owe this pleasure?"

"I invited them, Mom." Maggie called as she pushed her way through the butler's pantry doors, laptop in hand.

"Okay . . ."

Ten minutes later, my house was just the way I liked it—bursting at the seams with all the people I loved most. Josie and Tripp pulled up in Tripp's truck with Amos and little Eddie tucked in the backseats, Lizzie and Asher came a moment later. Even Bronson somehow sneaked away from the orchards. And then Kevin was leaning up against my living room wall.

"What on earth is going on?" I asked.

Maggie fiddled with her laptop and a cable near the television in the living room. "We wanted to show you something."

I looked at Kevin, but he just shrugged.

The television flickered on and I recognized Maggie's Facebook feed. She typed in the business page of the bed and breakfast and clicked on a video, making it full screen.

When a clip of the Orchard House Bed and Breakfast sign appeared along with some beautiful classical music, I shook my head. What in the world was this?

And then a clip of Luna, speaking to the camera. "I came to Orchard House at a confusing time in my life. Hannah not only welcomed me, she let me help her with the bed and breakfast, teaching me skills I never thought I'd learn. Even when I messed up, she never gave up on me."

I blinked back the sting in my eyelids as the video moved to a couple that came to stay with us several times a year. The Pelletiers. "We think of Orchard House as our second home. We've never felt more welcome, more at peace, more well-fed, than when we're staying at the orchards."

I covered my hand with my mouth as the shot zoomed to another repeat customer, and then another, then another. Then Martha from the mission, singing my undeserved praises, then Missy and even Calvin telling the camera how I'd helped them find jobs. I couldn't hold my tears back when Charlotte came on, testifying to my thoroughness as a fellow innkeeper. And then, my children. Each of them speaking honestly into the camera about how much I poured into the bed and breakfast, how I treated each of our guests as if they were a long-lost friend.

When the video came to Luna again, tears streamed in swift rivers down my cheeks. "I suppose when you try to help people, you stand a chance of opening yourself up to hurt. I'm sorry to say I hurt Hannah and the Orchard House with my actions last week. You see, my mental health was suffering, and I shouldn't have been serving guests that day. Hannah didn't realize my whole story. She was only trying to help me. But I'm here now to say I'm sorry. To beg you to put aside my blunder and embrace what all these wonderful people have said about Orchard House. And, if you struggle with mental health, please know you are not alone. There is help."

Another cut to Maggie. "Hello, I'm Maggie, administrative director of The Orchard House Bed and Breakfast. The Martin family is proud to serve Camden and we would love to host you for your special getaway soon. To thank you for keeping our business alive, we're awarding a free night's stay to the first fifteen guests who book a three-night stay with us. Vacation in the beautiful foothills of Camden, the jewel of the Maine coast. Enjoy a five-course breakfast and your private en suite room inspired by your choice of a classical New England author. Hike, bike, walk, shop, eat, and explore all Camden has to offer in the midst of five-star hospitality. We hope to see you soon!"

A few credits rolled, thanking the customers who'd given their testimonies.

By then, my throat had closed with emotion. "Maggie, all of you . . . I can't believe that. It's the most perfect thing imaginable. I don't know what to say."

"It was Luna's idea," Maggie said. "She and Charlotte were the brains behind it. I simply reached out to some of our customers explaining the trouble we were in and asking them to help. It went live last night and we've been booking like crazy online ever since. Even past the fifteen free nights."

"Luna . . ." I dug out my phone, searching for her number.

"No need, Mom," Josie called. "I've had her on Facetime the entire time. She wanted to see your reaction."

I laughed, taking Josie's phone from her and scooching into the kitchen. On the screen, Luna sat in a tank top and ballcap, cuddled with a gray and black cat. "Luna, I don't know how to thank you. What a beautiful gift."

"It's the least I could do. I hope it helps."

"From what Maggie says, it has. Thank you, honey. How are you doing?"

We chatted for a few more minutes before Josie ushered me back into the living room, taking the phone from me as I bid goodbye to Luna's deep, soulful eyes.

"What's up? I'm not sure I can take any more surprises."

Maggie grinned and my children tittered. What had gotten into all of them? "Well, you'll have to take one more because I received a call from the Chamber of Commerce this morning."

My breath caught.

"Congratulations, Mom. They awarded you the grant."

No . . . I had written the grant off in my head. It was gone. Probably awarded to Jolene and the Red Velvet Inn or some other more deserving bed and breakfast.

My mouth fell open. "You're not serious?"

Maggie nodded. "I guess they'd been undecided, but the video pushed them over the edge. They made their decision early this morning. There'll be a small ceremony to award you the check this weekend."

I gave a small, excited shriek, throwing myself into Maggie's arms and jumping up and down, then searching for my Josie, who had started it all. My sweet Lizzie who inspired me with her gentleness. My headstrong Bronson who would always see himself as my protector. My bold Amie who knew how to keep me on my toes. And then Aunt Pris, my gracious benefactor.

When I made my way around the circle, only Kevin was left. I threw my arms around his neck. "I'm glad you were here for this."

"I wouldn't have missed it for the world. Congratulations, Hannah." He whispered the words in my hair.

When I finally pulled back, I threw my hands up in the air. "Well, I think you all know what this calls for."

"I don't know, but I'm hoping it involves food," Bronson said.

I grinned at him. "A dinner party, of course. If you're all available tonight, that is. I'll run to the grocery store and make sure I have everything, especially for the littles, and you better believe there's going to be cake and lots of it."

Cheers erupted and everyone broke off to return to their day, agreeing to meet back later. When it was just me and Kevin remaining on the back patio, waving to Aunt Pris and Ed in the backseat of Amie's car, I leaned into him.

"You guys sure know how to do family," he said.

I snuggled into his arms. "We mess up a lot, that's for sure. But we know how to love." I craned my neck so I could better see his handsome face. "You know, you love pretty well yourself. You might fit in pretty good around here."

"Is that a hint that you might be ready to move this relationship to the next level?"

I bit my lip, trying to hide a smile. "How do you think the kids will feel about that?"

He cleared his throat. "Well, I know how one feels, because I already talked to him."

"Owen?" I guessed.

He shook his head, sliding a ring from his pocket. "Bronson."

And then he was down on one knee. And I was saying yes and throwing my arms around him before he could even get the words out.

I was fifty-two years old, after all. And I knew what I wanted.

And while I was most confident in the promises God made, I wasn't quite ready to be done with the promises I could make in this life, with this man.

When we finally came up for air, Kevin pointed toward the horizon. "Look." A rainbow cast itself above the green orchards, bold and full against sherbet streaks of pink and orange brightening the sky.

"But it hasn't even rained." I shook my head.

"Oh, it has." Kevin kissed me soundly on the lips. "But I think it's time for the sun to shine down on us once again."

I snuggled back into his arms and sighed. My family would continue to grow—not just in grandbabies, but with a husband who would love me and my offspring with the same tenacity I did. Though there was sure to be hard times again, right now, all I could do was soak in the gratitude and love swirling around me as we gazed at the bow of hope above us.

THE END

Read on for a glimpse of my standalone novel,
The Edge of Mercy!

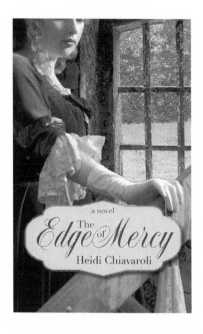

CHAPTER ONE

Swansea, Massachusetts

I slipped the two rings off my finger to cradle them in my palm. Warm and bright beneath sunlight, no one would guess they taunted echoes of a failed marriage.

I stretched out my left hand and glared at my naked fingers. I couldn't imagine never wearing the rings again, couldn't imagine who I was without Matt to define me.

Sudden anger made me tremble. I'd been faithful. I'd held up my end of the wedding vows. This was not how things were supposed to be. Fumbling with the rings, I gripped them tight with my right hand, prepared to shove them back on my ring finger with force, but they slipped from my quaking fingers.

Time slowed as I watched my wedding rings tumble downward, bouncing a couple times off the side of the large rock I stood upon. I fell to my knees and a pathetic whimper escaped my mouth as I heard the first *clink* against the stone.

My blood ran like ice. I caught a glimpse of platinum, then nothing. I'd have to search on my knees for hours if I expected to find them.

I remembered what Dad taught me to do when I dropped something.

Don't lunge after it. Stop, think. Let your eyes follow what you've lost. You'll see where it's gone. Then, Sarah, you'll be able to get it back.

Strange how when I told my parents Matt was leaving me, Dad hadn't encouraged me to stop and think. He'd told me to fight for my husband. He wanted to know if I planned to live on alimony for the rest of my life.

I sighed heavily and stood to take in the scene I'd come for in the first place. The scent of pine and warm earth wafted through the air. Bright sunshine pooled around me, and the massive boulder stood solid beneath my feet. Like an ancient warrior, it offered majestic security, and I gleaned comfort from it. This rock wouldn't betray me. It wouldn't crumble beneath me as my marriage had.

Maybe that's why I came here whenever problems encroached upon my life, pressing in, squeezing tight. Eleven years ago, my neighbor, Barb, introduced me to these hiking paths, and to Abram's Rock. She told me stories of this boulder—legends, really—and though I wrote them off as fictional, I found myself returning here in times of need over the past eleven years, bonding with the sensation that another had indeed suffered in this place too.

Much older now, Barb hadn't been able to make the trip here in years. But that didn't change my attachment to this place.

I looked down to where jagged rocks and hard earth met, swaying before me until I grew dizzy—though likely more from my circumstances than the incredible height of the rock.

I hadn't seen it coming. My husband of seventeen years wanted a separation and I couldn't fathom why.

At least that's what I told myself. Sure, Matt and I had been distant of late, but I chalked it up to busyness—a mere ebb in the many up-and-down waves of any normal marriage.

Yet even Kyle had noticed, commenting just last night on the fact that his father hadn't been home for dinner more than twice in the last month. Not one to bare his feelings, I could tell our sixteen-year-old son was bothered by his absence. I wondered how such a separation would affect him.

As I started down the gentle slope of the opposite side of the boulder, my cell phone vibrated in my pocket. Its upbeat tone rattled the peaceful quiet of the forest.

My heart ricocheted inside my chest at the thought of hearing Matt's voice on the other end of the line. Maybe he'd realized his mistake. Maybe—

I fumbled to see the screen and gulped down the bubble lodged in my throat. My sister, Essie.

"Hey."

"I thought you'd be at the hospital. Where are you?"

I groaned. Calling out of my shift two days in a row wouldn't put me on the director's good list, that was for sure.

I picked my way toward the base of the rock, to where I thought the rings had fallen. "I'm in the woods, trying to find the lost symbols of my marriage."

"I take it you won't be done in another hour or so, then?"

"Ha. Ha." My sarcasm fell flat when I told my sister what I'd done with my wedding rings.

"Your marriage can't be hopeless, Sarah."

I leaned over a hollow area between two rocks. Dead leaves cradled the middle. No rings.

"What's Matt's deal anyway? Did you two talk anymore last night?" Essie's assertive voice knocked against my eardrum.

I knew what she was thinking. Another woman. I'd already entertained the thought. It was one of the many reasons I found myself seeking the solitude of the woods.

"No, and he left before I got up this morning." I'd made sure of it.

"Well, maybe you two can work through this. Lots of couples go through slumps."

Was "taking a break," as Matt put it, a slump? I grabbed hold of a tree branch and pulled myself up the first part of the steep slope, on top of another rock that created a small cave. "Working through a marriage requires two people. Matt doesn't want to work. He wants out."

"Come out with me and the girls tonight. Get your mind off things."

I scrambled for an excuse. "Kyle has a track meet."

"Come after."

"I planned on taking Kyle out. You know, talk things over."

Essie snorted. "The person you need to talk to is Matt."

"I—I'm not ready." This could be worse than a simple "break." There could be another woman. Matt could insist on divorce. My chest began to quake. "I have to go."

"Call if you change your mind."

I hung up the phone, shoved it in the pocket of my jeans, and resumed searching for my wedding rings with newfound exuberance. For what must have been an hour I pushed aside leaves, scraped crevices with my fingernails, stepped back to search for a glint of platinum beneath the sun's rays. Nothing. I sat at the base of the rock and let the tears come.

In the aftermath of my quaking sobs, a numbing quiet overtook my soul.

This place seemed ageless, as though the channels of time sometimes overflowed their banks. It reminded me that many other women had walked these very trails, and I felt certain some of them must have known a pain similar to mine.

❧

I wasn't supposed to fall in love with Matthew James Rodrigues. Not according to my parents, anyway.

The first time Matt showed up on my doorstep, Dad took one look at his rumpled hair, his Elvis tattoo, and his idling jalopy and told him he could take a long hike off a short pier if he thought he'd get anywhere near his daughter.

Back then, Matt had been nothing more than a teenager with a lawnmower, a shovel, and a good tan. But he had something else —business smarts. He knew how to work people.

He knew how to work me.

He used to visit me at the high school lunch table while all my friends tittered not-so-conspicuously. I still didn't know why he approached me that first time to introduce himself. I wasn't anything to look at. Matt smelled like fresh wood shavings from the vocational shop. His rugged dark looks and persistence caught me off guard.

Before long, I was begging Daddy to change his mind about Matt. He didn't budge.

"Do you think I worked hard all these years to have my oldest daughter marry some trailer trash? And a Catholic at that?"

He said *Catholic* as if the devil himself had spawned the religion. As if half the boys I went to school with weren't Catholic.

"I don't want to marry him, Daddy. I just want to get to know him."

"No. End of conversation." He went away mumbling about how he should have never taken the pastorate position in New England all those years ago.

I snuck off to meet Matt that night. It was the first time I'd disobeyed my parents.

Matt had a Volkswagen with a tape deck. That first night we drove to Newport, listening to Elvis tapes. Matt wasn't like other boys I knew, listening to Pearl Jam or Billy Joel. He liked what he liked, whether it was popular or not.

He liked me.

I'd never known such attention before and I fell. Hard. Every night I snuck out my bedroom window to the end of the long drive where Matt's car waited. We went everywhere the water was, but that summer our favorite place was Newport. We shared our dreams beneath a vast sky. Matt told me about his fatherless childhood, how he avoided his trailer park home—and his mother—whenever he could. He hated being poor and vowed that someday he'd be successful.

My dreams seemed less important beside his. More than anything, I wanted him to succeed. And I wanted to be by his side when he did.

I lost my virginity in a fold of earth alongside the flat rocks of Newport one warm August night. I still remember the crash of the waves, the spray of the surf, Matt's arms around me, his heart beating heavy against mine.

The night I told my parents I was pregnant was the worst night of my seventeen years.

Mom cried. Daddy got so red in the face I thought he'd split open and burst like one of the overripe tomatoes in Mom's garden. He said God would curse me for my sin and if I didn't repent I was on the road to hell. Then he left the house—Mom, in tears, calling out after him.

I felt sure my father went to find Matt and kill him. Instead, he dragged him back to our house, and inside for the first time. I could scarcely look at him from my petrified spot on the bottom of the red-carpet steps.

"You will marry my daughter."

"Yes, sir."

"And you will provide for her if it takes every ounce of your strength. Is that understood?"

I felt Matt's gaze on me and I looked at him, telling him with my eyes I was sorry. I knew he wished it wasn't this way.

"Yes, sir."

And that was as close to a proposal as I'd ever gotten.

Matt quit school to mow lawns and landscape yards full time. Three months later we'd both turned eighteen. I graduated and Matt saved up enough money to rent us a room at the Holiday

Inn on the night of our wedding. It was a simple affair, with only my parents and Essie and Lorna, Matt's mother, at the ceremony.

When I lay with him that night, Kyle already grew strong within my womb. I nestled my head in the crook of Matt's shoulder, felt a tear on his cheek.

"Are you sorry you married me, Matthew Rodrigues?" I asked, scared to death of the answer.

He grabbed my wrists and pulled me on top of him. Shook me slightly. "I never want to hear you say that again, you understand me Sarah *Rodrigues*? I love you. I will always love you." He crushed me to his chest. "You saved me, Sarah. You saved me."

I never asked what exactly it was I saved him from. Now I wonder—if I'd saved him so good back then, why was he so eager to get rid of me now?

CHAPTER TWO

I stared at the pristine quartz countertop of my kitchen. Atop the perfect marbled specks of black and green sat a loaf of bread. I'd taken it from the breadbox without thinking.

I shoved the loaf back into the box with a bit more force than necessary. Matt could make his own stupid lunch. I yanked on the handle of the refrigerator, searching for comfort food.

The front door opened and I straightened so fast I slammed my head on the inside of the fridge. Stifling a yelp, I rubbed the sore spot and closed the refrigerator door too hard.

Kyle walked into the kitchen, dumped his backpack on the floor, then sat at the breakfast bar. "Hey, Mom. You okay?"

Oh, how to answer that question.

I released a frustrated sigh and shook off the hurt. "I'm fine. I thought you had a meet this afternoon. I was going to head out in a few minutes."

"Dad called, said he'd take me. He wants to ask me something."

Ask him? More like tell him his decision to leave his wife and son.

I looked at Kyle, nearly an adult. Lucky for him, he'd inherited both his father's height and looks. More and more lately, I noticed a younger version of Matt in our son. Those brown eyes, so like his father's until . . . until when? Until he'd married me? Until the combination of stress and success had rubbed the shine from them? When had my husband stopped being happy?

I blew a strand of hair from my face. "I guess I'll meet you two there."

Kyle grinned, a shadow of guilt playing on his dark features. "Dad said something about us catching up. Mine is one of the first races, so even though Coach'll kill me, I'm going to skip the rest. Dad has a meeting tonight so it's the only time we can talk."

Behind Kyle, the grandfather clock my great-aunt handed down to us called out the hour with four simple chimes. I loved that clock. Always steady, always consistent, even through the night while we slept and didn't pay it any attention.

"I thought this was a big meet."

Kyle shrugged. "Aren't you the one always telling me family's more important?"

"Okay . . . I'll see you there, then."

"Don't even bother, Mom. D-R has the top sprinter in the state. Enjoy the rest of your day off. I can hang with Dad."

Did he not want me there?

"I don't care if you come in last. I love watching you run."

He shrugged. "Whatever makes you happy."

But I had a terrible sense he really didn't want me to go. Had Matt said something to him? We should all talk together, shouldn't we, as a family?

I brushed off the feeling, tried to convince myself it was only my imagination.

A warm arm came around me and I gave my son a hug, grateful he still let me. When we parted, I tapped him on the top of his chest, and when he looked down I chucked him on the chin. "No worries, kiddo. Go out there and whip those Falcons, okay?"

He gave me a lopsided smile and ran upstairs to change. Ten minutes later he was out the door, his father's shiny Rodrigues Landscaping truck waiting in the drive.

I headed upstairs to the master bathroom, peeled off my clothes, and pulled on some jeans. Who was Matt to dictate me missing my son's race?

⚜

I checked my makeup in the rearview mirror and grabbed my purse from the passenger seat. Just before my fingers pulled the handle of the door, I thought of my husband, certainly in the bleachers, ballcap on, watching our son complete warm-ups.

Something like a soggy tennis ball settled in my stomach. I remembered the last time I'd seen him—night before last. The way he'd stood at the mantel, one hand on it, facing the window. Telling me he needed a break. He didn't want to be with me.

Bitter bile gathered in the back of my throat. I thought of Kyle's not-so-subtle suggestion that I not come to his race, and quite suddenly my hand felt too heavy to pull open the door.

I grabbed my keys back up and started the Mercedes. Half an hour later I walked into Chardonnay's, and glanced around the posh room. A squeal from a corner booth caught my attention. Essie—dark blond hair primped and large silver hoops dangling at her ears—waved from the center of the group of women.

I greeted the ladies and squeezed in next to Jen, Essie's friend from college and now my coworker at the hospital. She gave me a sideways hug, a thousand unspoken words in the action.

My sister always did have a big mouth.

"So she told you guys, huh?" I ordered a chardonnay from the waitress.

Across from me, Mariah reached out a perfectly-manicured hand. "I've been there, honey. I know it hurts like the dickens now, but when he's dishing out those alimony checks, he's the one who's gonna be groaning."

Essie slapped Mariah's arm. "I didn't say they were getting a divorce, stupid."

Mariah stared blankly between Essie and me. "I thought you said—"

"A break. I said he wanted a break."

Mariah raised her eyebrows and grimaced, as if to say, *What's the difference?*

Indeed. Besides a few signatures, what was the difference?

"My friend and her husband split apart for a time and it did wonders for their marriage," Katie said from where she sat on the other side of my sister. "Maybe good will come of this yet, Sarah."

I closed my eyes and shook my head. "Listen, I appreciate you all trying to make me feel better, but I didn't come here for sympathy. I just want to get my mind off things."

They nodded. An awkward silence filled the table as the waitress brought my wine.

"How are the boys?" I asked Jen.

She folded her napkin on her lap. "Let's just say the promise of this night out was the only thing that kept me sane today. Would you believe I left those boys alone for ten minutes outside and next thing I know they're making our shed into their own personal bathroom? Complete with a beach pail urinal." She stuck her tongue out. "I'm lucky I got to it before they decided to do more than pee in it because believe me, that was coming next."

Katie laughed. "At least your kids are old enough to be alone for a few minutes. I got in an argument with my trash man today. He refused to take my trash because it was too heavy. I told him three infants in diapers don't make light trash. He told me I should try cloth diapers."

Mariah wrinkled her nose. "You all are sure making me want to pop out a few. Rick's been hounding me. I can't imagine. I told him no ring, no babies. And truth is, I'm not even sure I want a ring that badly after all I went through with mistake number one."

Essie breathed in deeply, then out. Then again, with dramatic flair. I stifled a laugh. "What's she doing?" I mouthed to Mariah.

"It's some yoga-Buddha technique she's learning."

Essie, with much show, continued her breathing. "T'ai chi. I'm learning a calming technique. When I'm tempted to contribute to the complaints and negative thoughts of those around me, I try to center myself into a state of peace. You guys should try it. It works."

While I embraced—or rather, never contended—my parents' faith, Essie had done all she could to avoid it. Whether through self-help books, t'ai chi classes, a study on transcendentalism, or many hours on a shrink's couch, she tried everything, drinking in each new venture with wholehearted enthusiasm.

"Well I don't know about the rest of you, but I didn't come out tonight to center myself. I came to get a buzz and complain about life." Mariah tipped back her gin and tonic.

Jen flagged down the waitress and ordered nachos for the group. "I'm just happy to go back to work tomorrow and get a break from their shenanigans. We're still short on CNAs though, so chances are I'll be bleaching out bedpans anyway. Beach pails, bedpans . . . I suppose I'm destined to clean urine."

"'The only person you're destined to become is the person you decide to be.' Ralph Waldo Emerson." Essie tossed her honey-colored hair over her shoulder.

"Will someone shut her up?" Mariah rolled her eyes.

Undeterred, my sister put a hand on my arm. "Speaking of making your own destiny . . . maybe now's your chance to do something more than bleaching out bedpans yourself. You've always talked about going back to school, becoming a nurse prac- titioner. This is an ideal time, sis."

I'd learned long ago not to be offended by Essie's offhand comments. Still, I loved my part-time job as an RN. I didn't even mind cleaning out the occasional bedpan. Besides, now was not the time to find my wings. Now was the time to stay grounded, to fight for my marriage, fight for my family. "I'm still processing the fact that my husband's leaving me. I don't think I'm ready to hurl myself into school just yet."

"Why not? Maybe now's the perfect time. What else are you going to do when you're not at the hospital your twenty hours a week?"

"Remind me why I came tonight?" I said. Yes, I knew I had no life outside of work and my family, but it never mattered to me. Even now, I didn't need anything else. Didn't want anything else. What I needed was Matt, Kyle, and my part-time job.

Essie crossed her arms and rested them on the table. "Sorry. Didn't mean it like that. It's just . . . you've been living for Matt and Kyle all these years, even for your patients. Maybe it's time you did something for yourself."

Maybe she was right. I thought of the other night, of Matt standing at the mantel of our spacious living room, his hand rubbing the back of his neck, his soft yet piercing words.

"I need some time, Sarah. Some time away to think. We need a break."

Suddenly all I'd worked for, all I put my hope in, unraveled before my eyes. Essie was right. What did I have to show for my thirty-five years? An outgoing, handsome son, yes. But what else? A broken marriage? A boxy, three-story colonial? A part-time job I'd originally taken as a step toward my true dream?

I wanted to go back home, climb into bed, pull the covers over my head, and not come out again until God realized I did nothing to deserve this disorderly bump in my otherwise smooth life.

Mariah's face blurred before me. The room swayed. I fumbled for my purse and keys, throwing a twenty-dollar bill on the table. "I need some air."

I stumbled toward the door, my chest tight and my stomach queasy. My life was not supposed to fall apart like this.

I pushed open the heavy black doors. The cool night air washed over me in swift waves. I sat on a bench and breathed deep. In and out. In and out.

"Hey, that's some good t'ai chi."

I looked at Essie, rubbing her sleeveless arms against the chill. She slapped my leg to signal me to move over before she sat. "I'm sorry, Sarah. I didn't mean anything by it. I get it, and you're right —it's too soon to start rearranging your life. You haven't even talked things through with Matt."

I nodded. Ground my teeth.

"Are you mad at me?"

"No. I think I am going to head home, though. I shouldn't be out tonight. I should be home, trying to fix things."

Essie gave me a hug and walked me to my car. I slid into the silver Mercedes Matt bought me on my thirtieth birthday and lowered the window.

"Sometimes things need to break," Essie said. "That way they're stronger when they're put back together."

I forced a smile. "Who's that, Henry David Thoreau?"

"No, that's an Essie Special."

I gave her a wave and pulled onto Route 44.

I didn't want a broken marriage, a broken anything. After I married Matt, I'd worked hard to have my life—our lives—neat and orderly. Essie was wrong. Broken things never became stronger. They weakened, were more susceptible to damage. That's why I kept Grandma Martha's teacup on the top of my hutch where no one could see. If I ever dropped it again, it wouldn't be a single crack.

It'd be an unfixable mess.

ACKNOWLEDGMENTS

Thank you to the team that helped with so much of this series—Melissa Jagears, Sandra Ardoin, Donna Anuszczyk, Erin Laramore and Priscilla Nix. Each of you added your unique insight and value to these books. Thank you!

Thank you to Doug and Louise Goettsche, who own our favorite inn, the exquisite and charming Cornerstone Victorian Bed and Breakfast in Warrensburg, NY. Not only are Doug and Louise fabulous hosts, they were beyond generous in answering my many questions and sharing their experiences and stories with us. The Orchard House Bed and Breakfast (including Hannah's five-course breakfast) is modeled after the Cornerstone Victorian. I highly recommend a stay!

Thank you to my ever-supportive family—my husband, Daniel, and my sons, James and Noah, who always cheer me on. Lastly, to the Author of Life. You write the best stories. Thank you for allowing me the privilege to join in for a scene or two.

ABOUT THE AUTHOR

 Heidi Chiavaroli (pronounced shev-uh-roli...sort of like *Chevrolet* and *ravioli* mushed together!) wrote her first story in third grade, titled *I'd Cross the Desert for Milk*. Years later, she revisited writing, using her two small boys' nap times to pursue what she thought at the time was a foolish dream.

Heidi's debut novel, *Freedom's Ring*, was a Carol Award winner and a Christy Award finalist, a *Romantic Times* Top Pick and a *Booklist* Top Ten Romance Debut. Her latest Carol Award-winning dual timeline novel, *The Orchard House*, is inspired by the lesser-known events in Louisa May Alcott's life and compelled her to create The Orchard House Bed and Breakfast series. Heidi makes her home in Massachusetts with her husband and two sons. Visit her online at heidichiavaroli.com